AF304749

# WISDOM
# CORNER

# WISDOM CORNER

DAVID HESKA WANBLI WEIDEN

**SIMON &**
**SCHUSTER**

London · New York · Amsterdam/Antwerp · Sydney/Melbourne · Toronto · New Delhi

First published in the United States by Ecco, an imprint of HarperCollins Publishers, 2026

First published in Great Britain by Simon & Schuster UK Ltd, 2026



1 3 5 7 9 10 8 6 4 2

Simon & Schuster UK Ltd, 7th Floor,
199 Bishopsgate, London EC2M 3TY



Simon & Schuster Australia, Sydney
Simon & Schuster India, New Delhi

www.simonandschuster.co.uk
www.simonandschuster.com.au
www.simonandschuster.co.in

The authorised representative in the EEA is Simon & Schuster Netherlands BV, Herculesplein 96, 3584 AA Utrecht, Netherlands. info@simonandschuster.nl

Simon & Schuster strongly believes in freedom of expression and stands against censorship in all its forms. For more information, visit BooksBelong.com

A CIP catalogue record for this book is available from the British Library

Hardback ISBN: 978-1-3985-0934-4
eBook ISBN: 978-1-3985-0935-1
Audio ISBN: 978-1-3985-0936-8



Printed and Bound in the UK using 100% Renewable Electricity
at CPI Group (UK) Ltd

*Dedicated to James Aubrey Cordry, who faithfully
served the citizens of the Rosebud Reservation.*

Old cars and new scars.
—X, *"Big Black X"*

I surveyed the wreckage around Wisdom Corner. Dozens of empty cans of Joose malt liquor, crumpled cigarette packs, old containers of butane and fuel injector cleaner, an exhausted bottle of Purell and water. No one was sitting in the battered gazebo, just outside an abandoned storage building and a parking lot. Three dirty benches under a corroded aluminum canopy, graffiti sprayed on every surface: HALF PINT; STAY HARD; KILL EVERYONE. Off to the side, someone had scrawled OMAKIYA YO. Help me.

In the old days, Wisdom Corner was the place on the Rosebud Reservation where elders would gather to tell stories and provide counsel to those in need. They'd be there nearly every day, speaking to each other in Lakota, offering advice if asked, and entertaining little kids with traditional tales and stories. Now the panhandlers, drunks, and addicts had taken over the space, using it as their own area to mingle and ingest their substance of choice. Most afternoons there were a handful of people there, drinking and drugging, many more joining as the day gave way to darkness. For now the place was deserted, only the waste and ruins of yesterday's wayward souls remaining.

"You see anyone, Virgil?"

I shook my head. I'd been asked to accompany Pudge Iron Shell to a meeting with some gang members from the neighboring Pine Ridge Reservation who wanted a piece of his business.

Pudge was a bootlegger, someone who bought liquor across the state line and sold it for a profit here on the rez. There were about ten bootleggers on the Rosebud Reservation, but Pudge was the most successful by far. He was known as the ethical boot—he wouldn't sell to kids, didn't mark up prices too much, never took advantage of a drunk woman, and refused to sell bottles of hand sanitizer mixed with water, the cocktail of the truly desperate. Because of all this, he sold far more hooch than anyone else on the rez, and now he had a target on his back.

I met Pudge back when I was drinking too much. He helped me out a few times when I was short on cash, and I hadn't forgotten that, even though I'd given up alcohol. I guess I owed him, and now I was paying my debt. The gangsters from the Pine Ridge Reservation—just a hundred miles from our rez—had told him they wanted to expand and start selling bootleg liquor to our people. Pudge worked solo, but he'd agreed to talk with them. I'd been asked by our local medicine man, Jerome Iron Shell, to go along with Pudge and keep an eye on him. A big, gentle guy, Pudge was no brawler or fighter. Pudge was Jerome's nephew, and there was no way I could say no. I owed Jerome as well, more than I could ever repay.

"What time are they supposed to be here?" I asked Pudge.

"Half an hour ago." He shook his head. "I don't know, maybe they're not coming. You want to take off? I got a delivery to make over at the apartments." He carried a paper sack with a big glass bottle of Tvarscki vodka, called T-Var by the locals.

Just then I heard the sound of a busted muffler roaring, and an old sky-blue Chevy pickup pulled up. Two guys were in front and two in the back.

I looked over at Pudge.

He nodded, then stuck his hands in his pockets. "That's them."

The guys climbed out of the truck. They looked to be in their late twenties, maybe younger. Supposedly they just wanted to talk to Pudge, but I was here to make sure things didn't get out of hand. I was the reservation's vigilante—the guy you hired when you couldn't get justice from the courts or the tribal council. Some called me a thug, but I didn't see it that way. The US government had sole authority to prosecute felony crimes on the rez, but they declined about half of those cases, even after the criminals had been caught. This meant that child abusers and worse were released, free to commit more crimes. That's where I came in. Victims and their families hired me to lay down a beating on the assholes who'd hurt them. One hundred dollars for each broken bone, knocked-out tooth, and black eye—that was my price, and I had no shortage of customers.

Except that I wasn't doing it anymore.

Last year, heroin started appearing on the reservation, and I'd been hired to find out who was bringing that crap to our lands. It got personal when my nephew Nathan overdosed on black tar heroin and nearly died. It took some time, but I eventually discovered how the drugs—both heroin and pills—were getting here, and I put a stop to it. I nearly died in the battle against the dealers, and I made a promise to the Creator that I'd quit hurting people, even if they deserved it. I'd try to help people in other ways—get on the Good Red Road and find another job. Change my profession and my life.

The people kept coming, asking me to avenge the wrongs that had been done to them. But I turned them all away, keeping my promise to stay away from violence. Some got angry, telling me I was an asshole for abandoning them. Others said I had a duty to uphold justice on the rez, since the US government wouldn't do it. I'd been tempted, especially when I heard stories of kids being hurt or abused. But I hadn't raised my fists since I'd made my vow.

The Pine Ridge guys came over to the gazebo. One guy walked

ahead of the others. He was a little older than the other three; stocky, with short hair and a tattoo on his arm that read OGLALA PRIDE. He was carrying a can of Monster energy drink. The logo on the can—three jagged green lines—reminded me of Unktehila, the Lakota water serpent.

"You're Pudge, right?" the guy said, then looked over at me. "But who the fuck is this?"

"Virgil," I said. "Virgil Wounded Horse."

He smirked. "I heard about you. You the OG who lays people out. You jumpin' bad today?"

Pudge raised his hand. "No, Virgil's just here to help me out. It's all good. My uncle asked him to come along. Jerome Iron Shell? He's a healer, our medicine man."

The guy stared at me for a few seconds, then looked over at Pudge. "Jerome your uncle, huh? That's cool. He come over to Pine Ridge sometimes. Run some ceremonies." He took a drink from his can. "We all here to talk, yeah? Dang, I been rude. I know who y'all are, but you don't know us. I'm Bear—some call me Mato, right? Keepin' it real in Lakota. And that's Jay Jay, Stacks, and Shorty."

I glanced over at them. Young guys, all trying to look hard. They were here to scare Pudge into giving up his business. But I wasn't going to let that happen. I'd vowed not to fight, but I was confident I could handle this without having to use my knuckles.

Bear motioned with his head, and the other guys moved behind us. "Anyway, we been wantin' to yap with you. We hear you the top boot around; people say Pudge the man. That right?"

"I sell a little," Pudge said. "Plenty of other bootleggers here."

"Yeah, but you the boss, right? Been slinging hooch the longest."

"I guess. Doing this about ten years, I think. Just getting by."

"Well, damn!" he said. "Today's your lucky day! Because we gonna up your sales like a mofo. What you think of that?"

I figured it was time for me to step in. "Pudge don't need no help. He's doing fine."

Bear shifted his attention to me. "I hear that. He selling a lot of hooch. But we gonna help you sell more to the skins here, a lot more. See, we from Pine Ridge."

"I figured that." I pointed with my lips to his OGLALA tattoo.

He smiled. "Good eye. You see this one?" He pulled the sleeve on his other arm back. An image was inked on his skin in an ornate style: 705.

I knew what it meant. That was one of the dozens of Native gangs that existed on Pine Ridge and Rosebud. He was trying to scare us.

He smirked. "We like you Rosebudders. Y'all are nice, like little puppies. We like you so much, we decide to come over here and show y'all how it's done." He took a long swig from the energy drink. "Deal is, you gonna start working with us on the hooch sales. We gonna be your muscle, and Shorty over there help you with deliveries."

"Hey," Pudge said, "that's cool, but—"

"I ain't finished!" Another swig of the Monster. "Thing is, we gonna take care of the competition for you. We find the other boots and they gonna stop slingin'. Unless they wanna partner with us. You feelin' me? In six months, we gonna control *all* the hooch round here—be like damn Amazon. You know, doing business like the wasicus."

This triggered considerable laughter from the Pine Ridge boys.

"We gonna be the kings. Split the dollars fifty-fifty. That's fair, yeah? Doin' it Lakota style. So what you say?"

I glanced over at Pudge, who was staring down at the ground.

He cleared his throat and looked up. "Well, uh, it's like this. I'm kind of a lone wolf. Been selling a long time with no one helping.

You know, I got my own way of doing things. So, thanks, but I'm gonna pass."

Bear smiled. "Lone wolf, I respect that. Goin' solo." Another drink. "But maybe I didn't say shit the right way. We ain't asking you. You gonna partner with us, or we bring some Pine Ridge thunder down on your ass. Hear me?"

I looked at Pudge. This was the scenario he'd been dreading. Pudge had been a football player back in high school, but he was a hundred pounds and twenty years away from any physical confrontations. It was on me to send these guys back to Pine Ridge.

"Hey," I said. "This ain't gonna happen. You want to sell some booze, go ahead. Free country. But don't go threatening us, not on our patch. Why don't you guys head back home, and we call it even."

"Uh-huh," Bear said. "Maybe you don't know about the 705. We run shit at Pine Ridge. And now we gonna run shit here. You don't like it, you can fuck off. You hear me, Chief?"

The other three guys moved behind Bear, waiting for me to make a move.

This was the moment I'd been trying to avoid for the last year. I'd worked hard to change my ways and become a better person. My girlfriend Marie had convinced me to quit smoking, and I'd done that. I'd gone to sweat lodges and spoken with my spiritual adviser Jerome regularly. I'd even started trying to learn to speak Lakota better. But most importantly, I hadn't beaten anyone up since I got out of the hospital a year ago. The calluses on my knuckles had even started to soften and heal.

Did I miss it? Yeah, I did, much as I wanted to believe otherwise. I missed the feeling of kicking the shit out of someone who deserved it, and the gratitude I got from the person who'd hired me. And I couldn't deny that I was bored most of the time. I earned some cash by serving legal papers for my attorney, Charley

Leader Charge. Subpoenas, summons, complaints. I rarely encountered any problems in that job, beyond a few rude comments from pissed-off litigants. But I'd stayed with it, because I didn't want to let my family down, and I knew people would judge me if I went back to my old ways.

But here I was, facing a group of dipshit gang members that wanted to muscle my friend Pudge out of business. If they knew my reputation, they'd leave without trying anything. That was one good thing about my former job as an enforcer.

I stepped away from Pudge. "Here's the thing. Pudge already told you that he don't want to work with you. You fuck with him, you're gonna answer to me. And that's it. We're taking off now."

I motioned to Pudge to follow, but the one called Bear stepped in front of me, blocking my way.

"Like I said, we ain't asking," he said. "We taking over the bootlegging. Gonna happen with you or without you."

Bear signaled to the guys standing behind me. I turned around and one of them punched me in the stomach. Hard. I dropped to the ground, doubled over in pain. I hadn't had time to brace myself, and it felt like my intestines had ruptured. I couldn't breathe and started gasping.

"See," I heard Bear say. "Damn weak-ass Rosebudder."

I was still wheezing and feared I was going to throw up. I'd been hit hard in the solar plexus, and it felt like something was trying to crawl out of my midsection. It had been a long time since I'd had the wind knocked out of me. I focused on the trash on the ground to deal with the pain. I stared at an empty can of Bud and concentrated on the words KING OF BEERS while I struggled to clear my head.

After a minute, I was able to look up and survey the situation. Pudge was off to the side, away from the gang members. He looked confused, and I couldn't blame him. I'd been asked to keep the peace, and I'd ended up on the dirt almost immediately.

"Now we straight," Bear said, looking down at me. "We the new boots in town. So, y'all ready to join the 705?"

I was starting to get my wind back. I moved to a sitting position and slowly lifted myself while the four of them watched me. Pudge, still holding his vodka bottle, looked away.

"Okay," I said. "You got a point. Change is good, right?"

Bear smiled. "Knew you'd see it the right way."

"I get it now," I said. "You guys just want to make some cash. Pudge, you cool with that?"

He nodded slightly. He was trying to stay calm, but I could see the tension in his face.

"How about we have a drink?" I said. "Pudge, you share that vodka?"

He handed the bottle to me without saying anything.

"Now you talkin'!" Bear said. "Share a little hooch, celebrate this shit."

"I don't usually drink, but today's a special day," I said. "Maybe make a little toast. You speak Lakota?"

Bear shook his head. "Naw, not really. Only the old people speak Indian at Pine Ridge."

"That's cool," I said. "I can't really speak it well, but I remember a few words."

I held the vodka bottle in front of me in order to make a toast.

"So here it is," I said, and raised the bottle up. "Ayustan yo!"

"Hold on," Bear said. "What does that mean?"

"It's not an exact translation," I said, and looked over at him and the other gang members. "But it's close enough."

I gripped the vodka bottle tightly. They stared at me, waiting.

"Basically, it means FUCK YOU!"

I smashed the full bottle on Bear's head, glass and vodka flying everywhere. He stumbled and fell, his hands going to his head. The bottle had shattered, but the neck stayed intact, with several jagged pieces of glass sticking out like a double-edged knife. The space reeked of vodka, and I realized I was drenched.

Two of the guys bent down to help Bear, and the other one started moving toward me. I backed up a few steps.

"Don't move!" I said, while holding the bottle in front of me. Pudge was frozen, standing over to the side.

All of a sudden, the one called Shorty rushed at me. I faked like I was moving left but went to the right. I tried to get past him, but he came at me with his fist raised.

I took the vodka bottle and swiped the jagged edges across his face. The sharp glass went straight to the bone of his cheek, just under his eye. I could see the bloody flesh and subcutaneous fat gleaming in the wound I'd opened. He screamed and raised both hands to the left side of his face.

The other guys looked stunned, and I saw our opening.

"Come on!" I shouted at Pudge.

I dropped the broken bottle, and we took off running for my truck. My hands shaking, I fumbled for the keys. After a few seconds, I was able to fish them out of my pocket and unlocked the doors. Pudge jumped inside, and I started the engine.

I glanced back and saw that both Bear and Shorty were kneeling on the ground. The third guy was calling someone on his phone, and the last guy was standing still, watching us. I put the truck in drive and hit the accelerator. Within minutes we were on the road, driving past the St. Francis school. I opened the window to let some fresh air in.

It was a beautiful day, and I watched the road and the trees and the bushes glide by me as if I were in a dream. I realized I felt better than I had in months. I knew the gang would come for revenge, but that didn't bother me. After a long time, I was in motion again.

After dropping Pudge off at his house, I headed for home, reeking of vodka and regret. The exhilaration of the fight had worn off, and I was left with the reality of what had happened at Wisdom Corner. For the past year, I'd worked hard to avoid violence and brutality, but all of that effort had been waylaid in twenty minutes. Despite my good intentions, I was no better than the drunks and druggies who inhabited the space. I'd yielded to my base instincts and cut open a gangster's face rather than find a way to defuse the situation. Yes, they'd started the fight, but I'd reacted too quickly. Now the Pine Ridge gang might try to come after me—or Pudge—and I'd have to deal with them again.

I realized that I needed to speak to Jerome as soon as I could and alert him about the gang. Jerome had helped with my nephew Nathan's problems last year, and I'd repaid him by making a bad situation worse. And I'd have to own up to Marie, who'd never liked my work as an enforcer and believed I could leave all of that behind.

I'd always heard that people never changed, no matter how hard they worked at it, that it was impossible to alter one's fundamental nature. And folks around here liked to complain that the rez never changed because the white man made sure that Indians could never succeed.

But I didn't want to accept that—it seemed too cynical and

negative, and not at all in the Native tradition. After all, in the old days Indian kids earned new names as their lives progressed and they gained glory and honors. Crazy Horse was first called Among the Trees, then became known as Curly before earning his final name later in life. My mother used to tell me that people are like rivers—they start small but change and evolve as they travel through the land.

And some things had changed on the reservation over the last year. There were new businesses, new people, and a new tribal council. And most of the people nearest to me had grown, in ways major and minor. Marie had become active in reservation politics. Nathan had switched high schools and now attended St. Francis. To my surprise, my friend Tommy Good Shield had gotten a job, his first in many years. He was working as the kitchen manager at Rations, the new restaurant at the casino, and taking classes at our tribal college. And even our casino had made a major change—smoking was no longer allowed inside, a regulation that was despised by local gamblers.

I'd stopped smoking myself upon the recommendation of Marie and found it to be way more difficult than I'd anticipated. But not as hard as giving up the beatings and the fights, which I'd apparently become dependent on, not only for my livelihood but also my mental health. Serving legal papers on an occasional basis barely paid the bills and provided no job satisfaction. Truth be told, it was hard to avoid punching some of these jerks when I handed them their summonses and subpoenas. Most kept their mouths shut, but a handful had tried to start some shit with me, as if I was to blame for their lawsuit or custody hearing. I'd kept my cool and simply walked away from these encounters, but my year-long record of practicing nonviolence was over.

I pulled up in front of the house and saw Marie's Subaru there. She and I essentially lived together, since she tried to avoid spending time at her own place. Marie was now the sole resident of her parents' fancy house on the reservation, which she'd acquired after she'd shot and killed her father, Ben Short Bear, during a standoff. He'd confessed to being the major drug dealer on the rez and was threatening to kill me to keep me quiet, but Marie had prevented that. After the news came out, Marie's mother, Ann, had left the reservation in shame and gone back to Oklahoma. Marie's sister was in California and wanted no part of small-town life. That left only Marie in the house, where she had to confront her memories of her father and her own role in his death. I'd suggested selling or renting out the place, but she wasn't ready for that. Instead, she went there once or twice a week to do laundry or grab something she needed. Marie's sister Julie also wanted to sell—and apparently so did their mother—but Marie was holding out for now.

I paused for a moment, then went inside. Ava, the little white bichon frise we'd inherited from Marie's mother, greeted me with a tail wag and a lick on the hand.

Marie was in the kitchen tending to a large stockpot on the stove. She was wearing blue denim shorts and a pink T-shirt featuring an image of a bison from her favorite Indigenous designer, Lauren Good Day. Her long black hair hung down the back of the shirt.

"Hey, I'm making—" She stopped speaking and gaped at me. "Oh my god, what happened to you?"

I looked down at my shirt. It was covered in dirt and blood spatters.

"And what's that smell? Is it—have you been drinking?"

I shook my head. "Long story. Let me take a shower, and I'll explain." I wanted to rinse off as soon as possible and get rid of my sodden clothes.

"No, tell me now! Did you serve papers on someone?"

I brushed some dirt off my pants and sat down at the kitchen table. No sense in putting this off. "You know Pudge Iron Shell? Jerome's nephew?"

"Yes, of course. The bootlegger." She shook her head.

"Well, Jerome asked me to go with Pudge to Wisdom Corner. Keep him safe. Some dudes from Pine Ridge are trying to take over his business. Gangsters. They wanted to meet and, you know, try to scare him."

She stood up. "Did you fight with them?"

I didn't say anything.

"Virgil, what happened?"

I thought for a moment. "I didn't start it. One of the Pine Ridge guys hit me when I wasn't ready. And we were outnumbered, four to two. Could have gotten real bad. I smashed a bottle of Pudge's vodka over one dude's head, and we got the hell out of there." I didn't mention that I'd cut another one's face open.

"Sounds like it was pretty bad, if you had to break a bottle on somebody." She walked over to the stove and stirred a large pot. It looked like wohanpi, my favorite bison and potato soup. "Why did you go along? You had to know this wouldn't end well."

Now was the time I really craved a cigarette. "It was a favor to Jerome. You know how much I owe him."

She put a bowl of soup in front of me, but no silverware. "Yes, you owe Jerome, but you also owe me, and Nathan. Not to mention yourself. I don't understand why Pudge would even go to some meeting with gang members. That's really stupid. And now you're involved in it."

I got up, fetched a spoon from the drawer, and poured myself a glass of water. "I'm pretty sure it's over. They thought they could come in here from Pine Ridge and bully Pudge. They were talking shit about Rosebud people—you know how they are."

The Pine Ridge Reservation was home to the Oglala Lakotas,

a separate branch of the Oceti Sakowin Oyate. There were numerous branches of Lakota, Dakota, and Nakota people. We Sicangus and Oglalas had always been close, given that our lands were right next to each other, but there was often a rivalry between the two bands, like cousins or brothers. We felt that the Oglalas tended to get more national publicity, due to the fact that some of the greatest Native leaders—Crazy Horse, Red Cloud—were from there. Our own great chief, Spotted Tail, had a more complicated history, given that he was one of the first Indian leaders to advocate working with the white people rather than fight until the end. This earned him some hatred from other Native leaders back in the day, but his emphasis on diplomacy had been justified, historically. Hostiles versus friendlies, fighters versus diplomats—these distinctions between the Pine Ridge and Rosebud peoples had continued for generations, and resentments sometimes boiled over. And now I had to worry about some Pine Ridge gangster idiots coming over here and starting more trouble.

"Yes, I know how they are!" she said, frowning. "That's why you should have stayed away from that mess. Let Pudge fight his own battles. And it wouldn't be a bad thing if we had one less bootlegger around here."

"Hey, that's not fair," I said. "Pudge is a decent guy—he won't sell that hand sanitizer shit, and he don't rip people off."

"Oh, okay. Just because he occasionally does the right thing, you have to step in and protect him. You know it's going to get around that you helped Pudge. How much you want to bet Mitch Gagnon will use this against me in the election?"

I hadn't thought about that. Marie was running for tribal council as the representative for the Two Strike district against the incumbent Mitch Gagnon, who I knew from school. Everybody seemed to like Mitch except me. He'd been elected before as the treasurer and now as a member of the tribal council, so he had some support from the local community, but Marie had decided to challenge him in our tribal election, which was coming up soon.

"No one from Rosebud was there besides Pudge and me. Nobody saw what happened."

She rolled her eyes. "Come on, Virgil. There are houses right across the way from Wisdom Corner. And you know it's impossible to keep a secret around here."

This was true. The moccasin telegraph, as it used to be called. Now it was the moccasin internet, since every little beef or piece of gossip was instantly broadcast on social media.

"Look, I'm sorry if Mitch says something. But this is on me, not you. Let him talk whatever bullshit he wants."

She shook her head. "It's not that simple. Everyone knows who you are, and some people still hold a grudge. He'll find a way to make me look bad, and—"

"He's too much of a chickenshit."

"No, he's not," she said. "But this isn't about the election. It's about you. You told me—*promised me*—that you were going to stop kicking the crap out of people. You said it was time to get on the Red Road. What about your promise?"

I didn't say anything, just stared out the window.

AFTER A SHOWER AND a change of clothes, I decided to go and see Jerome Iron Shell before he heard about the incident from anyone else. That would give Marie time to cool off, and I'd be able to stop by the convenience store and pick up some energy drinks for Nathan, who was hanging out with his girlfriend. Marie refused to buy those for Nathan, claiming that they were full of corn syrup and chemicals. But he loved his Red Bulls and declared that he couldn't stay awake in class without them.

Nathan had been through a rough time, to say the least. Last year, he'd been framed for drug dealing, and then kidnapped and tortured by the people bringing heroin to the reservation. After it was over, he was too depressed to go back to school, afraid of what people would say. He transferred to another high school twenty miles away to make a fresh start. He'd also started dating Shawna Little Moon, a young woman with pink hair he'd met the previous year. When Shawna found out what bad shape Nathan was in, she'd shown up at my house with chocolate bars, potato chips, and her backpack, and sat with him in his bedroom for hours, doing her homework and playing music, until he eventually started to come out of his funk. After a while they began to leave the house, usually going to the Starlite Snack Shop for hamburgers and slushies. Now they were inseparable.

I climbed into my Ford F-150 and started it. The truck still reeked of cheap vodka, now reminiscent of dollar-store rubbing alcohol. I drove past the Gus Stop market and the new Taco John's drive-through, which was the hit of the reservation. Tommy was addicted to their fried chicken tacos and potato olés. For Mexican food, I preferred the little food truck located out by Soldier Creek—Rapper's Delight Tacos, all their items named after hip-hop artists. Snoop Dogg Nachos, 2Pac Carnitas, the Biggie Burrito. I thought their food was better, but they weren't always open, despite their posted hours. It was always a gamble as to whether you'd get some grub there.

As I drove, I thought about what I'd say to Jerome. In many ways he was like a father to me, and I was afraid I'd let him down by not protecting Pudge. It wasn't enough to say that I owed him. When Nathan was kidnapped, Jerome had conducted a spiritual ceremony called a yuwipi that enabled me to find out where Nathan had been taken. But Jerome had collapsed during the yuwipi and nearly died. We'd each had a vision during the ceremony, but I believed that he'd taken all of the negative energy into himself so

I could go out and rescue Nathan. Jerome had never revealed what he saw that night. Since then, I'd been spending more time with him at his camp, helping him run the sweat lodge or just cooking for him over the fire. Sometimes we spoke, sometimes we didn't.

When I arrived at his house, Jerome was on the porch, a mug in his hand. He was wearing an oversize denim chore coat with a corduroy collar, his long gray hair pulled back.

"You want some coffee? It's pretty fresh."

Fresh coffee to Jerome meant that it had been brewed sometime in the last twelve hours.

"Little late for me." It was dark outside, a full moon in the sky. I pulled up a chair, sat down next to him, and reached for my cigarettes, then realized I didn't have any. We sat for a while without saying anything.

"You hear about the bison?" Jerome asked. "Think I saw them yesterday."

"Yeah, I heard. Crazy." The tribe owned a herd of bison on the reservation, but they'd somehow escaped and had been roaming the streets and alleys for a week now. Tribal officials had been trying to round them up but hadn't managed to catch even one. People had been posting pictures of the animals on social media, demanding that they be captured and returned to their enclosure. I couldn't deny that I was secretly cheering them on.

"How's Nathan doing?" Jerome asked. "He still dating that young lady?"

"Shawna? Yeah, they're still together. But she's been talking about going off to college out East after she graduates. She wants to live in a big city; I guess it's too slow around here for her."

"Sounds like a lot of our young people," he said. "Can't wait for anything. Fast food, cell phones, video games. No patience, no stillness—got to get a quick thrill." He shook his head slightly. "But that's not the Indian way. We know it takes time to build something that matters. You make something that lasts, that's more important than a fast buck. Teaching a child to read, making a star quilt, things like that—those stay with you."

I nodded.

He took a drink of his coffee. "I saw some story on the TV news last week. It said that Pine Ridge and Rosebud are the two poorest places in America. I guess they mean people here don't have giant bank accounts or fancy cars. But the thing is, we've always judged a person's wealth by how much they give away, not how much they keep."

I thought about the Pine Ridge gang and their plan to take over Pudge's business. "Maybe the old ways are gone now. Maybe it's too late for kids like Nate and Shawna."

"They'll be fine," he said. "They're at the beginning of their journey. Wherever they end up, they'll remember their Lakota values. It may not seem that way now, but it's true."

I was quiet again as I considered how to tell Jerome about the incident earlier in the day. After a few minutes, I spoke. "So, I went out with Pudge to Wisdom Corner."

"Yes, I know. Sounds like those Pine Ridge boys got more than they expected."

I should have known that Jerome would have heard already. He seemed to know everything that happened on the rez.

"They want to take over Pudge's business. And they were talking shit about Rosebud. Pissed me off."

He took another drink. "Yeah, always been some scraps between Oglalas and Sicangus. You know, their name means 'Scatter Their Own,' but we used to call them Dust Scatterers in the old days. I worked with Pete Amiotte over there, a long time ago. He told me that Oglala really means 'Take Me Back Home.'"

"I never heard that."

Another swig of the coffee. "I hope those Oglala boys stay on their own land, leave Pudge alone. You know I don't like Pudge selling booze, but he has to make his own choices. I did tell him not to sell to no kids."

"He doesn't. And he treats people right, not like some of the boots around here. I'll keep an eye on him, make sure those Pine Ridge guys don't start no more trouble."

He nodded.

"You running a sweat tomorrow?" I asked. "You want me to help out?"

"No, I got to go to Rapid City. Another damn thing for the Land Project."

Jerome hated to travel off the reservation, but he'd become part of an Indigenous group that was working to reclaim some land on which he had a personal connection. As a young boy, Jerome had been a student at the Rapid City Indian School. The state forced many Indian families to send their children to Native boarding schools, where they were forbidden to speak their language or practice their culture, and sometimes physically and sexually abused. The Rapid City boarding school was just one of hundreds, the first and most notorious being the Carlisle Indian Industrial School in Pennsylvania. Luckily, Jerome hadn't been taken out of the state, and his family was able to get him back.

Decades after that, the Rapid City boarding school was turned into a tuberculosis clinic for Natives, and later a hospital. But a huge amount of land remained: three thousand acres, nearly five square miles. The US Congress passed a law allowing the property to be given for free to the city, so long as it was used for municipal or educational purposes. If the land wasn't used in those ways, it would revert back to the Department of the Interior or be given to "needy Indians," according to the statute. But the city sold the land to private developers rather than use it for any charitable purpose. Over time the illegal sale was forgotten, and businesses continued to operate on the land.

A group of savvy Natives called the South Dakota School Land Project had discovered the illegal transfer a few years before and filed an action in court for the return of the land—all of it—to the Lakota people. Naturally, the city leaders and business owners were outraged, and they were staging a full-court press to derail the lawsuit. One real estate developer was building an upscale apartment complex on the site, another group was planning an outdoor shopping mall, and yet another developer had earmarked land for a luxury hotel. These businesses were leading the effort to fight the lawsuit, and they'd hired the top law firms in the city. The mall and apartments were the largest building projects in the state, and construction had already started on them. When finished, the apartment complex would contain hundreds of units, several outdoor pools, basketball and volleyball courts, fire pits, rooftop patios, feng shui serenity gardens, a dog park and pet spa, and a putting green. I was pretty sure that Natives were not its target demographic.

Jerome had been asked by the Indigenous group to take part in the effort to reclaim the land, given his status as a former student at the school and his standing in the Lakota community. He'd agreed, but it had taken up a lot of his time and energy. He'd done dozens of interviews with journalists and writers and even appeared on television a few times. Jerome had become the face of the effort to regain the land, and the issue was starting to get national attention. He was getting interview requests from some of the better-known magazines and newspapers, who'd begun to sense that this might be a story with larger implications.

I'd been happy to drive him to events and strategy sessions in Rapid City and wait in my truck while he spoke about his time as a student at the old school and the significance of the land to the Native community.

"You need a ride there?" I asked.

"No, Rocky's going to take me." Rocky was Jerome's grandson and protégé, who'd been learning the ceremonies and traditions from him. "Figured we'd stop at the Indian Walmart in Rapid, and I'd pick up some groceries."

"What's the latest with all that legal stuff?"

"We're going to hold a Ghost Dance around the entire development—shame them into shutting the whole thing down. It'll be the largest Spirit Dance in a hundred years."

"Count me in," I said. "Anything else?"

"Yeah, and it's not good." He poured the remains of his coffee into the grass. "They found out that a bunch of kids died at the school, more than they thought. There's already an old cemetery there, but they're starting to find unmarked graves on the site. Terrible."

I felt sick. Little children who'd died at the boarding school, buried there with no family present to grieve for them. The same thing had happened at the former Carlisle Indian School out in Pennsylvania, now an army base. There was a cemetery there with hundreds of graves of deceased kids. Our tribe had fought with the US government for four years to have Sicangu children exhumed and repatriated back to our homeland. We'd won, finally; eleven were returned to where they belonged. But now it seemed that even more Lakota children had been discovered at the Rapid City site.

I heard a phone ringing from inside the house. Jerome had a cell phone but rarely used it.

"Be right back," he said.

I stared off into the distance, thinking about my own mother, father, and sister, buried in the little cemetery near the tribal college. I periodically went there and picked up branches, leaves, and debris. I thought about what it would be like to have a family member buried in an unmarked grave, far away. Even the basic decency of a gravestone had been denied to these children.

Jerome came back out and sat down.

"What's up?" I said.

He tilted his head. "That was the director of the Land Project. Somebody started a fire at the construction site in Rapid City. The apartments. One of the buildings under construction burned down. Gonna be a real shitstorm now."

The significance of this washed over me. The dispute over the school land had been heated, but now it would be a war.

The next morning I woke up early, brewed some coffee, and started making breakfast. I'd surprise Marie and Nathan with some blue corn pancakes topped with chokecherry wojapi. It was Sunday, so they'd both likely sleep in.

I mixed some blue cornmeal with a little salt and sugar, then folded in an egg and some butter. I stirred the whole thing, tossed in two teaspoons of baking powder and a half-cup of flour, and let the mixture stand while I heated up our battered cast-iron skillet. When it was hot, I poured some of the batter onto the pan. I made ten pancakes and put eight of them aside, saving the last two for myself. Marie had made the wojapi earlier in the week, and I spooned some of it on top of the cakes. Delicious. The chokecherries weren't too sweet and blended well with the pancakes. Ava smelled the food and came into the kitchen. I handed her a bite, which she sniffed suspiciously before reluctantly eating it. No doubt she'd been hoping for some bacon, but Marie had declared a moratorium on all processed meats.

I poured myself another cup of coffee and was debating having one more pancake when I heard some noise coming from Nathan's bedroom. After a few minutes he came out into the kitchen and sat down. He was wearing his gym shorts and a St. Francis Indian School T-shirt. His black hair hung down to his shoulders. He'd made the decision to grow it out last year, which he'd proudly announced to me one evening at dinner. He'd also gained about twenty pounds and two inches in height, almost overnight.

"You want some pancakes?" I said. "They're still warm."

"Uh, yeah. Is it okay if Shawna has some, too? Like, if there's enough for her."

For the last few months, Shawna had been occasionally staying over at our house. The first time was a surprise; I'd discovered her in our little bathroom, wearing only a T-shirt and a pair of Nathan's boxer shorts. But what could I say? They were old enough to make their own decisions, and I couldn't stop them from being together, even if I wanted to. I was a little worried about Shawna's mom, but apparently it was cool with her if she stayed overnight. Or so I'd been told. Not long after, I'd asked Nathan if he and Shawna were boyfriend and girlfriend now, but he'd just shook his head like I'd said the most ridiculously old-fashioned thing possible. Then I tried to ask him about birth control, but he ran away from me as fast as he could.

I put some silverware down, along with two plates of pancakes and glasses of orange juice. Nathan went back to his bedroom and came out with Shawna. She was wearing one of his ball caps, embossed with the logo of the Denver Broncos, his favorite team. Her hair, now a mixture of bright green and brown, peeked out from under the cap's crown.

"Hi, Virgil!" If she felt any embarrassment for showing up at breakfast, it wasn't apparent from her cheery greeting.

"Hey, Shawna, you hungry? Got pancakes."

"Yes, please!" She and Nathan sat down and started eating.

"You guys ready for the end of the school year?" I asked. Nathan rarely shared any information with me, but I could sometimes get Shawna to talk.

"Uh, kind of," Shawna said. "I've only got two exams. And, oh right, that stupid paper in English." She looked over at Nathan, who didn't say anything.

"Is this the class you both have? With that one teacher?"

Nathan nodded. I'd gotten two calls from the school in the last six months, informing me that Nathan had violated the dress code by wearing a bandanna, and—in the second call—wearing the hood of his sweatshirt up on his head and refusing to take it off. He'd told me that other kids wore bandannas and hoodies, but his English teacher had been singling him out.

"Just try and keep it cool until the end of the semester, okay?"

"That guy's an asshole," Nathan said. "He just hates me. Wants to make my life miserable."

I looked over at Shawna to see if she had anything to say.

"You know, Mr. Choate isn't so bad," she said. "Nathan just got off on the wrong foot by calling him by his nickname. Not your smartest move, N!"

"Nickname?" I said. "What is it?"

Nathan looked at Shawna and shook his head. She started giggling and said, "Mr. Choad. But some kids just call him the Chodis." Now they were both laughing.

I had started cleaning up the dishes when Marie stormed into the kitchen, her hair askew and wearing an old sweatshirt.

"Did you see this?" She held her phone out.

I took it and enlarged the text on the screen. It was a post from one of the Facebook groups on the reservation.


MARIE SHORT BEAR helping out boot leggers!!! Her man Virgil spreading booze on our lands! And supporting Pine Ridge gangbangers. I feel kuja over this. Share if you love the oyate.


I didn't recognize the name of the person who'd posted it, someone called Akicita. "You know who this is?" I asked.

"It's obviously Mitch! Using a fake account. I told you that jerk would spread some lies. What am I supposed to do now?"

I felt like an ass for contributing—whether my fault or not—to the situation. Running for a tribal council position was massively important to Marie. She'd quit her job and been living on her savings in order to focus solely on the election, which was just a few months away. She wanted to sponsor new laws and regulations that made sense for the Lakota people—policies that made a difference. But there was a deeper reason, of course. After her father—also a tribal councilman—was exposed as a criminal and drug dealer, she'd felt the need to atone for his sins. Before the revelation of his duplicity, she'd been proud of him and his work. Although she'd never said it out loud, I knew she wanted to restore some honor to the family's reputation.

But Marie had the bad luck to be running against Mitch Gagnon, one of the most experienced politicians in the area and also one of the most feared, as he had a reputation for playing dirty. Grazing permits, tribal jobs, business loans—he had a hand in all of those. It was rumored that he got a kickback for these deals, which would explain why he was so fixated on remaining in tribal government.

Marie knew what she was up against. For the last several months she'd been busy putting up yard signs all over the rez, taking out ads in the local newspaper, and plastering the area with flyers. The first public candidate forum was only several weeks away, and I'd just handed an advantage to her opponent.

"No one takes that social media crap seriously," I said. "Most people just ignore it."

"You're probably right," she said, sitting down. "But there's no point in giving Mitch any more talking points. He already called me out for associating with you."

This hurt. I liked to think that most people around here appreciated my work as an enforcer for those seeking justice. But the ones who'd been on the receiving end of my fists had a different take.

"What an asshole." I put a plate of pancakes in front of her. "It's not like he's some saint."

She sighed. "Look, can you just stay away from Pudge and that whole situation for the next few months? Until the election is over."

This put me in a tough spot. The Pine Ridge gang might come back for Pudge, and I had a duty to protect him. But I didn't want to stir up any more shit for Marie.

"Maybe there's another way," I said. "Do you want me to talk to Mitch—tell him to back off?" I didn't know him well, but maybe I could persuade him to play fair in the election.

Marie held her hand up. "Please don't. He'd just twist whatever you said and use it against me. He's already trying to tie me to my father."

Another low blow. Smearing Marie was a nasty piece of business—she hadn't known anything about her father's drug dealing, and no one had ever stated otherwise. Only I knew the tremendous guilt she felt about shooting her father, which had happened during our final confrontation. That guilt, combined with the shock of learning about his opioid business, made the grieving process even more difficult for her. Some might have found it strange that she had mourned her father, but I knew how much she missed him. How could she not? He had helped raise her and been, by all accounts, a good father, devoted to both of his daughters. It seemed to me that Marie was grieving not only his death but also the loss of the way she used to view him. She'd seen him as a good man, devoted to the Sicangu oyate, but he'd shown otherwise. She was trying to reconcile the father she'd loved with the person who was now universally hated on the reservation.

No one knew this, but Marie had consulted with our medicine man about the Wanagi Yuhapi, the keeping of the soul ceremony. Given the circumstances of her father's death, she'd completed the ceremony privately, under Jerome's guidance. She'd prayed daily for her father for a year and then released the spirit. There'd been no feast or giveaway, just a simple meal where Marie said a few words about her father and then met with Jerome to complete the ceremony. Given my role in exposing her father, I'd stayed quiet and just listened to her.

I poured myself another cup of coffee and saw that I'd gotten a text message. I hated communicating by texts, but on the urging of Marie and Nathan, I'd reluctantly upgraded my cell phone and learned how to send them. Nathan mocked me when I initially signed my texts with my name. He laughingly told me that everyone knew who sent them by the sender ID on the screen.

I clicked on the Messages button and discovered that Charley Leader Charge had some papers for me to serve. He wanted to meet me later in the day at the casino. I was happy to get the message, as I could use the money. Charley paid me a hundred bucks for each service of process, twenty-five more if the target lived in a remote area. He used me exclusively for all papers served on our rez and sometimes hired me for a job in Rapid City if he needed extra muscle. It was a good arrangement all around: Charley needed a dependable process server who knew the reservation, and I was happy to pick up some cash every few weeks.

I decided to leave early for the casino. I said goodbye to Marie, Nathan, and Shawna and headed out. As I drove, I thought about Mitch Gagnon. He'd been a few years ahead of me in school, but I remembered him well enough. The teachers and administrators loved him because he volunteered for every club and activity—student body vice president, National Honor Society, pep club. He was viewed as one of the good kids who wanted to make something of his life. A role model.

But I had a different view of him. He was nice to teachers and popular kids, but nasty to the people he viewed as being beneath him. The metalheads, the smokers, the kids who didn't say anything in class. People like me and my friends. He pretty much left me alone, but others weren't so lucky. One afternoon I'd been skulking around the back hallway of the school, ditching algebra class. Mitch was there, too, but didn't see me. He passed a first-year student, some little kid I didn't know. The boy's back was turned, and he was putting his backpack in his locker. Mitch looked left and right, then grabbed the kid's hand and locker-slammed it. The kid screamed, and Mitch walked away like nothing had happened. No warning, no provocation. Just sheer malice. The boy's finger was broken, but Mitch never got in trouble for it. Just another day for a budding politician.

I never had a reason to interact with Mitch, in high school or after, but never forgot the locker incident. Now my girlfriend had a chance to keep him off the tribal council—if I could avoid fucking it up for her.

I pulled into the casino's parking lot and parked my truck at the back, near the marker for the South Dakota–Nebraska state line. There were a fair number of cars in the parking lot—the early slot-machine crowd. I went through the main doors, past the security guard, and into the gaming room. A large sign proclaimed SENIOR WEEK! DRAWINGS FOR $50! FREE PLAY EVERY HOUR! The air—shockingly—was devoid of stale cigarette smoke, due to the smoking ban. About twenty-five seniors were already playing the slots, but none of the gaming tables were open yet. The casino's customer base consisted of both Natives from the rez and white folks from the neighboring Nebraska town of Valentine.

People around here loved to repeat the old joke about Indian casinos, slot machines, and white gamblers: getting our money back, a quarter at a time.

I didn't gamble myself, but I spent a fair amount of time at the casino restaurant visiting my friend Tommy. He'd started as a prep cook at Rations and worked his way up to kitchen manager, which surprised everyone. Tommy usually hung out at the casino after his shift ended and would often slip me the leftovers from the previous night's specials. I appreciated that, as I didn't get to dine there very often. A famous Indigenous chef, Lack Strongbow, had visited Rosebud the year before and completely revamped the restaurant. Now customers could eat locally sourced bison, greens, and grains, rather than the sodden fried chicken and instant mashed potatoes once served at the buffet. Of course the prices had sharply increased, which sparked considerable outrage from the locals. Many had complained that the restaurant was too fancy for the rez, but I disagreed. On those rare occasions when I had an extra hundred bucks, I'd take Nathan and Marie out for a nice meal there.

I wandered back to the restaurant, where Tommy would likely be in the kitchen, prepping for the lunch rush. But I discovered him in the dining room, sitting with someone I didn't recognize.

"Hey, Virgil! What you doin' here?" Tommy was dressed in his cook's uniform—gray-checked pants and a white chef's coat, not his usual garb of T-shirts and ancient jeans.

"Meeting Charley Leader Charge in an hour. Thought I'd see what you were up to."

"Pop a squat, man." He pulled out a chair for me. "You know Professor Cortings? He's my teacher over at Sinte."

Tommy was taking classes at our tribal college, Sinte Gleska University, even though he was working full-time at the restaurant. I'd been skeptical that Tommy—not exactly known for his scholarly ambition—would continue at the college, but he'd hung in there.

Tommy's teacher stood up and shook my hand. "Call me Rich."

"Virgil." I sat down and gave the guy the once-over. He was dressed in black jeans and an old blue chambray shirt. Tall, light-skinned, salt-and-pepper hair parted in the middle and hanging down to his shoulders. It took me a moment, but then I remembered who he was. I'd read a story in the *Lakota Times* about him a few months before. He'd been some big-shot professor of Native American studies out East but had left his university and moved out here. Apparently it had been a real coup for our little college to hire him.

"Nice to meet you," he said. "You from around here?"

"Oh, yeah. Born and bred. You?"

"Originally from Wisconsin. My folks were from Oklahoma, though. Cherokee, Choctaw, Pawnee. Typical Okie mutt."

I cleared my throat. "Pawnee, huh? Might want to keep that quiet around here." The Pawnee had assisted the US Army during the Plains Indian Wars, a fact the Lakota people had never forgotten.

"Good point. Old wounds, right?"

"Virg, you hungry?" Tommy asked. "If you can wait, there's some food coming. I got behind today because of the damn rainwater thing."

He'd complained about this before to me. Chef Lack had installed a rainwater collection system for the bathrooms in the restaurant. All water for the sinks and toilets would supposedly be supplied in this environmentally sound manner. However, because of the irregular rainfall in South Dakota, the toilets and sinks frequently didn't work, which meant that Tommy had to go in and unclog stuck pipes.

"Got some bangin' bison stew going," he said. "Threw in some hominy, mint, and maple syrup. Be ready in about half an hour."

"That your recipe or Lack's?"

Tommy gave a half smile. "It's from Lack. He won't let me cook my own stuff yet. He said I could fly out to his main restaurant in LA and try some new dishes out. But I ain't gonna do that."

"Why not?" I asked.

"You know I don't like no airplanes! They freak me out, the turbines and all."

"Turbines? You mean the engines?"

He looked at me like I was stupid. "When the dang plane shakes around, up in the air? Like you gonna crash? Last time I flew, I was shittin' crickets."

Rich raised his hand. "That's turbulence, son. Not turbines."

"Whatever," Tommy said. "And I don't like no airports, either! I went to that big one in Denver once—man, I was buggin'. Hundreds of people walkin' around, right? It hit me that I'd see each one of 'em once and never again. They'd live their whole lives and I'd never know a thing about them. How they lived, when they bit it. Made me feel like a clog in a machine. Rather stay on the rez where I know everyone."

I didn't bother to correct him on *clog*. "Yeah, but that can happen anywhere, right? People you don't know? Even in Rapid City or Sioux Falls."

"I stay away from them places, too! Especially Rapid. Rode out there with Velma last week and tried to order some pizza. But the damn counter girl was a slice-ist."

This one I couldn't let go. "You mean racist?"

"No, a slice-ist, dude! I went up to buy a slice of 'za and she said they just ran out. Uh-huh! Person right in front of me got one. Dang slice-ist."

Rich looked amused. "Tommy, where are your manners? Get

our friend Virgil here some coffee while that stew's cooking. Get a pot going. And use the good beans, not that pre-ground crap. You drink coffee, right?"

"Don't expect you could be Indian if you didn't," I said. "Take a cup if you got some."

Tommy looked at me apologetically and went back to the kitchen.

"So, you teach out at Sinte now?" I asked Rich.

He nodded. "First semester there. Really enjoying it. The students are great, not like the privileged little pieces of shit I was teaching before. Christ, am I glad to be out of there."

"Where were you at?"

"Maine. Hadfield University. Home of the wealthy and inbred. Little fuckers loved me, though. They could tell their rich parents they were being taught by a real American Indian. White guilt, you know. Administration was happy until they caught wind of my research. I discovered the university was on treaty land. Founders of the college had stolen it from the Natives. I published an article arguing for reparations to be paid by the school. They didn't like that. Started making noises to get rid of me, even though I was tenured. So much for academic freedom, right?"

I nodded, even though I wasn't completely following his story.

"I figured it was time to get out while the getting was good. I visited Pine Ridge way back when, so when I saw Sinte Gleska was hiring, I jumped at it."

"How are you liking Rosebud?"

He nodded. "Love it. The slower pace suits me. Plenty of time to read and think. Ponder the meaning of life and all that. Not to mention, it's cheap as hell to live here."

Tommy came back with three cups of coffee. "Man, it's good to see you, Virg! Can't talk too long, though—gotta get back to it. Get some salad goin'. You staying for lunch?"

"No, just meeting with Charley. He's got some papers for me to serve."

Tommy glanced over at Rich. "You know that Virgil here is the baddest mofo around! He just hand out legal papers now, but he used to be the rez punisher! Somebody fuck with you, you hire my man. Lay down some Native justice."

Rich rubbed his chin. "What is it that you do, exactly?"

"Ah, Tommy's just exaggerating. That's not what—"

"Hell no, this here the Creator's truth! Virgil a badass gunslinger, only he use his fists. People hire him to lay down a beating when the dang FBIs don't do nothin'. People be callin' him the rez avenger."

"That so?" Rich said.

"Not really," I said. "I used to help out a few people, but I'm just working for a lawyer now. Living a peaceful life."

Tommy raised his cup. "Cheers, homeboy. You talked to the Creator and got on the Red Road. Now you got to figure out how to stay there."

AFTER FINISHING MY COFFEE and saying my goodbyes to Tommy and Rich, I wandered around the casino while I waited for Charley. In addition to the smoking ban, the casino had changed its interior decor, adding new carpet and inviting local artists to display their work on the walls. There was some ledger art, some abstract work, and a painting of a giant bear. Farther down were photos of some of the great Lakota leaders: Spotted Tail, Red Cloud, Sitting Bull, Touch the Clouds, Hollow Horn Bear. I stopped at the last one and studied it. Hollow Horn Bear, one of the bravest Sicangu warriors ever, who'd fought in thirty-one battles, including the Battle of the Greasy Grass against Custer. He later traveled for the inauguration of Woodrow Wilson to Washington, DC, where he caught pneumonia and died. He'd triumphed over hundreds of enemies—both Native and white—only to fall victim to a bacterium brought to North America by the colonizers hundreds of years ago.

After a few minutes I wandered over to the slot machine room and the silver urns, where tired gamblers could enjoy a complimentary cup of bitter coffee and powdered creamer. I poured myself some and went back to the lobby to wait for Charley.

He showed up forty-five minutes later, wearing tan walking shorts and a bright-red polo shirt. I was used to seeing him in his three-piece suit and tie, and it took me a split second to process the casual Charley.

"Virgil, good to see you. How are you today?" He stuck out his hand for a firm shake, not the gentle clutch usually practiced on the rez.

"Not bad, not bad," I said. "Yourself?"

"Busy, as usual. Driving out to Parmelee in a bit to meet with a client. Then I think I'll take the afternoon off and do some hunting."

I knew the kind of hunting he meant. Mushrooms, not deer. Charley once regaled me with copious details of his hobby as a mycologist—a word he'd had to define for me. He was obsessed with finding morels, which he'd told me is the king of all edible fungi. He wouldn't reveal exactly where he searched, but he explained how to look under rotted leaves and broken branches for these prizes. Which trees to search under, the right slopes on which to forage. Then he explained the numerous ways to dry and cook the mushrooms. He favored dipping them in egg batter and frying them in butter, claiming that this removed the sourness and greatly improved the flavor.

"You find any, let me know. Marie would be out of her mind."

He gave me a nod. "You got it. How's she doing, by the way? The election heating up?"

"Yeah. But not in a good way. Mitch Gagnon is going after her father, which ain't cool. And now he's trying to make me look bad, because I helped out Pudge Iron Shell."

Charley furrowed his brow. "You mean Sam? Jerome's nephew?"

It took me a second. "Is that his real name? Been calling him Pudge so long, I forgot."

"That's it. I represented him on a tribal misdemeanor back in the day. Pro bono. He's a good guy. Pretty decent left tackle, too, as I recall."

"Those were the days," I said. I didn't want to get Charley going on high school football, one of his other passions.

"What's happening with Sam? You said you helped him out."

I paused for a moment while I decided how much to reveal. But there was no point in holding anything back from Charley. "Nothing too bad. Some dudes from Pine Ridge are trying to muscle into Pudge's business. I went along to keep the peace."

Charley shook his head. "I've been saying for a long time we need more off-sale here. If people could buy booze more easily, there'd be no need for independent contractors."

"You may be right." I took the last drink of my lukewarm coffee. "So, what do you have for me today?"

He reached into his impossibly slim leather briefcase and pulled out a folder, then gave me some documents.

"Jesse Legrand. Skipped out on his wife and kid four years ago, so she's filed for divorce and child support. Need you to serve him with the complaint and summons. He's from Pine Ridge but might be in Rapid City now."

"No current address?" I asked.

Charley shook his head. "Unfortunately not. You need to stop by the wife's place in Rapid first, and she can tell you what she knows. His job, places he frequents. I know this is a pain in the posterior, so I'll give you an extra hundred."

He handed me another piece of paper. "Her name's Norma Legrand; there's her address. But one more thing: I ran Jesse, and he came up with about ten priors. All for disorderly, DUI, or assault. Norma tells me he's a bad one. You want to keep your wits about you up there."

I didn't know Jesse Legrand, but I knew his type. The kind who liked to talk big, but dodged confrontations with anyone tougher or meaner.

"I'll be fine. What's the timeline?"

"Soon as possible. Next week, at the latest."

"No problem. I could head up there tomorrow. Need to get some gas, though. Can you maybe spot me half of the fee?"

"Absolutely—I'll just pay you the whole thing now. You know I trust you."

He handed me the cash, which I'd use to buy a tank of gas and some windshield wiper fluid before I drove up north. Then I remembered. The Land Project and the fire. Maybe Charley knew something about it.

"Hey, you hear anything about that mess up in Rapid? The old boarding school? Saw there was a fire."

Charley grimaced. "It was all over the news. Looks like arson. Big surprise."

"Cops have any leads?"

"Haven't heard anything. You know, the Land Project people hired me a while back. I did some legal research in the early stages. Terrible, what they did to those kids at the school. Wouldn't let them speak Lakota, no ceremonies. Beatings, abuse, diseases. Lots of them tried to escape. They all wanted to go home."

I shook my head. "Jerome Iron Shell was at the school for a bit. He got out, though. One of the lucky ones."

"Did you hear the latest? The Land Project folks found out that more children died at the school than had been accounted for. It looks like the school administrators were covering up some of the kids' deaths and not reporting them. Apparently, they'd bury the kids without headstones so no one would find out."

"Yeah, Jerome said something about that," I said. "But I don't get it. Wouldn't the parents know their children had died and go there for the burial?"

"You'd think, but remember, this was before modern communications. The boarding schools discouraged any contact with families because they were trying to get the little ones to assimilate. By which I mean, stop being Indian. But even if parents finally learned about a child passing, the schools would just send a form letter expressing their regrets. What could the parents do? They didn't have the resources to have a child's body repatriated to their home."

This was worse than I'd thought. It was bad enough that these parents had their children taken from them, but to be denied even the basic dignity of a funeral was horrifying. "That's really awful. I hope they find all of those kids."

"That reminds me," he said. "They just released a list of the dead children that the school tried to cover up—the ones who weren't reported to the state. They think there are more, but this is the first batch. I was looking at it earlier and saw a Wounded Horse. That one of your people?"

"Really?" I said. "Who is it?"

"Let me pull up the list." Charley messed around with his cell phone for a minute. "Here it is. Take a look, down at the bottom." He handed the phone to me.

I had to squint to read the tiny letters. Then I saw it near the end of the list.

Josephine Wounded Horse (16, Rosebud)

For a moment, I was confused. Then I remembered.

"Oh my god," I said. "That's my auntie Josephine. My mom's older sister. Mom used to talk about her, but I never heard what happened."

A flood of memories from my youth washed over me. My mother, talking about her parents and her sister. Stories from when my mother was a child. She always became sad when she mentioned Josephine, but I never knew why. Until now.

"So this means that my auntie might be buried out there?"

"It looks that way," he said. "I'm sorry."

I was dazed by the news. Disoriented. It seemed impossible that I'd never known about my aunt Josephine and what happened to her. I'd just assumed that she lived her life on the rez and then passed on to the spirit world. I'd never asked my mother about Josephine's life story. The arrogance of youth. For decades she had lain out there, forgotten.

It was time to visit the Rapid City school and see for myself.

At the crack of dawn on Monday morning, I left for Rapid City. I was still thinking about my aunt Josephine and the boarding school, but I had to put that aside and get ready to serve some papers. My plan was to visit Legrand's estranged wife and find out what she knew about him—his address, his job if he had one, places where he used to hang out. Anything she could tell me.

Norma lived in the North Side neighborhood of Rapid City, which was no surprise; that had been the traditional area for Lakota people to live for over a hundred years, going back to the founding of the Rapid City Indian School in the late 1800s. When Native children were snatched by the state and sent to the school, many families set up tents along Rapid Creek to be closer to them. The area became known as Indian Camp, and families continued to live there until the 1950s, when the city cracked down. Government agents forced the Native families to relocate to a housing development north of town, the Lakota Community Homes. That neighborhood went without water or sewer services for fifteen years, and it still had a rep as a tough place to live. The police were a constant presence there, and most Indians believed they had a shoot-first mentality. It made sense to get there in the morning while everyone was still asleep.

While I drove, I thought about my strategy for serving the

papers. The best case would be if I could find out where Jesse lived and hand them to him, if he was home. If not, I could just leave the documents with somebody at his residence, but the person would have to verify that Legrand still lived there, and people seldom gave out that information. If that didn't work, I'd have to find him and hand over the papers or, more likely, just drop them if he refused to take them. Nearly everyone believed they could avoid being served by not actually touching or holding the documents, but that didn't matter to me. I'd just leave the papers at their feet and wish them a good day. Sometimes the person got angry and tried to start something. I'd say I was only the messenger, but they didn't want to hear that. They just wanted to lash out at someone. To defuse the situation, I'd explain how the process worked and tell them to call the lawyer listed on the papers. But if they became physically aggressive with me, I had the right to defend myself.

My gut told me this might be one of those services. If Legrand got angry and wanted to start something, I needed to find a way to peacefully shut him down. What had happened at Wisdom Corner still bothered me, as well as the fact that everyone on the rez apparently knew about it. No doubt most of them had already judged me without knowing the facts.

I'd once been the guy who brought justice to the wronged. Now I was criticized for helping a bootlegger, not to mention being a process server. This job meant bringing bad news to people when they didn't expect it. No one was ever happy to see a process server, and no one thanked me for delivering the papers. Well, Charley Leader Charge was grateful, but he was the only one. People on the rez didn't trust the American judicial system, and who could blame them? It had taken me less than a year to go from rez avenger to courthouse flunky.

I drove for an hour, taking the back roads until I merged onto

I-90. My stomach grumbled, and I realized I'd skipped breakfast in my hurry to get out the door. Spotting one of the many roadside signs for Wall Drug, I decided to stop for some food. Wall Drug was one of South Dakota's most famous roadside attractions; not really a drugstore anymore, but a block-long complex with an arcade, museums, numerous shops, and even an animatronic T-Rex sculpture. I was most interested in their five-cent coffee and fresh doughnuts.

Even in the early morning, the parking lot was packed. I made my way down the block, past the jewelry store, clothing mart, endless rows of souvenir racks, and a pressed-penny machine. I turned in to a hallway that contained a bookstore, a sign reading HANDMADE INDIAN JEWELRY, and sculptures of gunfighters, cowboys, and Annie Oakley. Right next to Annie was a large wooden booth with glass windows and a life-size mechanical figure inside, the word PAPPY stenciled on the front in an ornate font. I stepped in front of the machine, and the robot opened its eyes and said, "For a fair price, I'll tell ye your fortune. Come set a spell and listen to old Pappy."

I examined the machine more closely. Pappy was an unlikely fortune teller—he appeared to be an old-fashioned Western miner who'd been unlucky with his prospecting. His hand rested on a murky crystal ball, and his face bore an agitated expression. The price to learn my destiny was only a dollar.

I fed an uncrumpled bill into the machine and waited for something to happen. After a few seconds, Western music began to play and Pappy came to life, his hand moving back and forth over the crystal ball.

"Hey there," he said, "this here's Pappy, and it must be your lucky day, 'cause I have some words of wisdom just for you. Listen up now, y' hear." Pappy's hand stopped moving, and the automaton looked straight at me. "As you ride off to the future, remember that it's a whole heap better to do the things you ought to do than to spend the rest of your life wishin' you had. Don't you be leavin' this life with regrets, no sirree! So get on out there on the trail you were meant to ride. Start livin' the right life and give old Pappy some more coins for words like this 'un."

The robot stopped moving, and a printed card emerged from a slot at the bottom of the machine. I pulled it free and looked at it. "You are riding the seas of change, and things may seem to be out of your control, but soon you will find your way. Remember that events fall apart but rise and converge again. To make sense of your life, you will find the answer is to be found in how well you can foresee affairs and act accordingly. The power is yours and the answer is within you. Your lucky numbers are 16, 11, 30, 21, 3, 13. PLAY AGAIN!"

Even a broken-down penny-arcade machine was telling me to take control of my life. I stuck the card in my pocket and headed to the restaurant, passing two jackalope sculptures, several carved Indians, and the Traveler's Chapel. I glanced inside the chapel and saw three men wearing trucker hats seated inside, their hands joined and heads bowed deeply in prayer. I considered taking a brief detour to the art gallery, where hundreds of rare photos of Lakota people—including some of my ancestors—were displayed. But my hunger overwhelmed my desire to commune with my forebears, and I kept going to the restaurant.

Inside the large dining hall, dozens of stuffed animals were mounted on the walls, along with Old West photographs and prints. I walked over first to the coffee station, where fresh cups of java were available on the honor system. A small wooden box was carved with the inscription COFFEE 5¢. I dropped in a quarter and poured myself a mug, then made my way to the hot food section, where I grabbed a tray and got in line behind a family of four, the two children gazing at the desserts and breakfast foods. Although

I was tempted to order hotcakes, I grabbed three chocolate dough-nuts and waited in line for the cashier.

I looked down and saw that the two little kids were staring at me with their mouths open. They looked to be around three or four years old and were dressed far more nicely than anyone else in the joint. The older boy pointed at me and said, "Hey mister, are you an Indian?"

The mother heard the boy and quickly turned around and looked at me. "I'm so sorry," she said, and hurried the children off to a table in the dining room before I could say anything.

I didn't understand why the mother had rushed the kids away—it was as if she feared I'd kidnap the kids and take them to the reservation. But then I realized she probably thought the word *Indian* was offensive and that her child had insulted me. Some-how, the word had entered the realm of taboo terms that couldn't be spoken aloud in general society. I didn't know about Natives in other parts of the country, but the word *Indian* had long been used on our rez. The teenagers even liked to use the acronym *NDN*. I wondered if I should go over to the table and explain but decided against it. More trouble than it was worth. I took my doughnuts to another room to spare the family any anxiety and ate in silence, the sweetness of the fried pastries boosting my mood.

In a few minutes I was back on the road, dodging the begin-ning of the rush hour on the outskirts of town. Rapid City was hardly a giant metropolis, but the number of people and cars compared to the reservation always unsettled me. Thirty min-utes later I found myself at the Lakota Homes. After a few wrong turns, I located the house on Crazy Horse Street; it was a small beige wooden home surrounded by dozens of identical structures. A white van with peeling paint was parked in front.

I looked around, then grabbed my folder, walked up to the door, and rang the bell. After a minute I rang it again. It slowly opened, and I saw a little Native girl, about seven years old. She was cute, dressed in a pink SpongeBob SquarePants T-shirt.

"Hello there," I said.

"Hi," she said haltingly.

"Is your mother here?"

An Indian woman, dressed in a Black Hills State University T-shirt and blue sweatpants, appeared at the doorway. "Who are you?" she said.

"Are you Norma? Norma Legrand? I'm here to—"

"I said, who are you?" She crossed her arms and frowned at me.

"Virgil Wounded Horse. I work for Charley Leader Charge. Didn't he tell you I'd stop by?"

She shook her head. "No, he didn't say nothing. Last I heard from him was two weeks ago."

"I'm serving the papers on Jesse. For your case. Hoping you could tell me where I could find him."

She stared at me. "I'm gonna call Charley," she said finally. "Wait here."

The front door closed. I stepped back and looked up and down the street. The houses looked alike at first glance—they had the same dimensions and features and were painted either beige or light gray. But, looking more closely, I noticed subtle differences. One house had a small garden to the side; next door, the window frames had been repainted bright red. Another flew the AIM flag in front, the American Indian Movement logo prominent on the four stripes of black, yellow, white, and red. Yet another had children's drawings—a dog, a buffalo, and what looked like Godzilla wearing a headdress—taped to the inside of the windows.

The door opened. "Okay," Norma said. "I couldn't get Charley, but the person answering the phone vouched for you. Come on in. Hold on while I put Kayla in her room."

The little girl smiled at me as Norma took her hand and walked away. I stepped into the small living room. An old couch, a battered coffee table, and a big-screen TV tilted precariously against a wall. Children's toys were everywhere—I spied a decrepit My Little Pony and an old Mr. Potato Head, missing an ear and arm. I hadn't seen that one in decades.

Norma came back and motioned for me to sit down. "So, you got legal papers for Jesse?"

"Yeah," I said. "The complaint and summons."

"What's a summons?"

"Orders him to show up in court. Thing is, I got to hand him these papers for the case to get started."

She nodded a little.

"How long ago did he live here?" I asked.

"I tossed his ass out four years ago. Asshole started doing meth, then lost his job. Got hooked on that shit real quick. Took all the money we had and smoked it up. Last straw was when he slammed Kayla's head into the wall when she wouldn't stop crying. Gave her a concussion. He was real sorry, said he was super high, but I told him to get the hell out."

I had a sense this guy was a fuckup, and now it was confirmed. Any guy that hurt a kid deserved to get his ass beat, but I had to put those thoughts aside.

"You have any contact with him since?"

"Not really. He came by and got his stuff after I threw him out. That was the last time I saw him. I called him a few months later and told him he owed me money for Kayla, but he said to fuck off. I told him to eat his own dick."

"Any idea where he lives now?"

"No clue. I tried calling a couple of years ago, but the number was disconnected."

This wasn't good. "What about his family? Sisters, brothers?"

"One brother. Terry. Last I heard, he took off with a woman from Crow Creek."

"You know any of his friends or where he used to hang out?"

She smirked. "Only friends I ever saw him with were those damn meth heads. Probably all dead by now."

"You know their names?"

She looked at me like I was stupid. "Uh, no. But here's the thing. Few months ago, friend of mine tells me that he's back in Rapid. Supposedly clean. Drinks but no drugs. Says she ran into him at a bar, and he was trying to hit on her. Said he'd changed his ways. Whatever. Asshole told her he was working at some big warehouse on the west side. She called me right away and told me she'd seen him."

"She tell you anything else?"

"No. But, you know, she did me a solid, letting me know he was back. That's when I called Charley. Figured I might as well finally divorce his ass, get him to pay for his kid."

I nodded. "Right. This warehouse, she say what it was called?"

"No. Something to do with roofing."

"A roofing supply warehouse?"

"Maybe. I think so. That's all I know. Well, I know Jesse's a jackass. Nothing new about that."

IN MY TRUCK, I did a search for roofing supply companies in Rapid City. It didn't take long to find the place. There were only about ten of those in the city, and only one on the west side of town, Matco Building and Roofing Products. I'd give it a shot and see if Jesse Legrand still worked there. Given his record, I gave it a fifty-fifty chance at best.

As I drove, I thought about Jesse slamming his daughter's head into a wall. In the Lakota tradition, children were wakan—sacred. The word for kids was wakanheja, or sacred beings. Our people believed that kids were closest to the Creator, and needed to be protected and cared for, not treated like punching bags. Jesse was another sleazeball who'd put his desire to get high above every-thing else.

Half an hour later, I found the place. It was a medium-sized warehouse with roofing pallets stacked outside, and a large sign that read SIDING. I walked over to the main entrance and went in-side. An older woman with an old-fashioned beehive hairdo and a tan blouse sat at a desk, staring at her cell phone.

"Hello," I said, smiling. "I'm looking for Jesse Legrand. He here today?"

The woman looked at me closely. "Yes, he is. What is the na-ture of your visitation?"

"I have some papers for him. Legal papers."

"What category of legal documents?"

This was a question I hadn't been asked before. "Uh, documents regarding a matter with his . . . family."

She set her phone down. "Nothing concerning Matco Prod-ucts?"

"No, absolutely not."

"Then you'll have to administer those disconnected from busi-ness hours."

"Um, sure," I said. "What time does he get off work?"

"I'm not at liberty to pronounce that. It's a personal matter."

How was it a personal matter? "Do you mean *personnel*?"

She looked confused. "I'm sorry, I can't divulge any factual evidence about our employees' personal data." She picked up her phone again. "Is there anything else I can assist you with?"

I wondered whether to try again but decided against it. "No, thank you."

I walked back to the parking lot until I was out of her sight and then circled around to the side of the building. I saw two men standing outside. One of them had a cigarette, which triggered a craving in me. For a fleeting moment I considered bumming a smoke from him.

"Hey, Jesse here?" I asked. "Got a delivery for him."

"Yeah, he's over in loading."

I strode over to the back of the building, trying to look like I belonged. At the rear of the structure, there were four large loading bays, with a delivery truck parked in one of them. Three men were working there, moving bundles of shingles labeled GAF ROYAL SOVEREIGN to the vehicle. Two white guys and one Indian.

I went inside the bay and stayed about ten feet away from the men. They were working steadily and didn't notice me.

"Jesse?" I said.

One of the men—the Native guy—looked up. He was about six feet tall, had short black hair, and wore a white work shirt that was bathed in sweat. Youngish dude, looked to be around thirty.

"Yeah?"

"Jesse Legrand?"

"What do you want?"

"Got some papers for you." I held the folder up so he could see it.

"What papers?"

I moved closer and took out the documents. He gazed down at the papers but didn't take them. The other two men watched us.

"Who the fuck are you?" he asked.

"I'm just the messenger, man. Here to give you these legal papers. Name and phone number of the attorney is in there."

He looked incredulous. "This is, what? Are you, like, suing me?"

"Like I said, I ain't doing nothin' to you. My job is to hand you these papers and get out of here." I saw from the corner of my eye that the other two men had moved behind me. "Here you go," I said, and held out the papers again.

"I ain't taking those," he said.

"No problem." I dropped them at his feet. The papers scattered as they fell, creating a scramble of documents on the dirty floor. "You been served. Have a good one."

I turned around to leave, but one of the guys blocked me. The white dude. He had big shoulders, big arms, and a tattoo that read *100%* on his neck. I knew what that meant. He was one of the white power assholes who liked to proclaim that they were one hundred percent pure Aryan. I wondered if Legrand knew about this.

"Hold up," he said. "Jesse told you he didn't want no papers, so why don't you take those back to the shitbag lawyer you work for."

I glanced over at Jesse and the third guy. They were puffing up and giving me some hard looks. I turned and considered my exit options. I could rush my way along the side of the delivery truck if I could get past the men, or I could make my way to the other side of the bay and get out there. Or I could punch my way out. But I remembered what Pappy the robot had said—that I should live without regrets. Would I regret it if I stomped the bastard that hurt his kid?

"You do what you want with those," I said, pointing to the documents. "Throw them away, burn 'em, I don't care."

"Pick 'em up," the white guy said.

I stared at him. "Not gonna happen."

"Pick 'em up, or I'm gonna bust your head open, Tonto."

I looked over at Jesse, who was Oglala. He appeared to be unbothered by the slur. "Look, I don't want no trouble," I said. "How about I just take off and you guys go back to work?"

Jesse took a step toward me. "You heard Buck. Pick up them papers!"

"Uh-huh," I said. "You gonna hit me in the head like you did to your kid?"

He looked away. The other guys stopped moving.

"That's right, I just talked to his wife. She said this bastard gave his daughter a concussion. Slammed her head into a wall."

"You married, Jess?" said the one called Buck.

"Well, kind of. I mean, not really," he said. "This guy's lying."

"Yeah, he's married, and his wife wants to divorce his ass." I glared at Buck. "So back off, dude."

Buck looked over at Jesse, then focused his attention on me.

"I don't give a shit about no bitch," he said. "You don't come to our work and start mouthing off. I told you, grab them papers right now. Otherwise, I'll cram 'em up your asshole."

"You heard him," Jesse said, realizing that he had backup. "Do it!"

I flashed back to Jesse's daughter. She must have been three or four when this prick decided to get high and hurt her. The little girl with her big smile.

Fuck this guy.

"Okay, big man," I said. "We know you can take on kids, but how about someone your own size? You and me, no one else. Cool?" I looked over at Buck and the other guy.

Buck stared at me for a moment, then nodded. He stepped back, giving me a clear shot at Jesse.

Jesse looked over at his co-workers, surprised. "Guys, this motherfucker can't come in here and talk shit. Am I right?"

They didn't say anything. Jesse was on his own.

"Last chance," I said. "You gonna take them papers?"

Jesse glanced once again at the other guys, then turned to me. "Fuck you."

Okay, this was how it was going to be. This dimwit couldn't

risk looking weak in front of his friends, so he was willing to start something. Well, it was his funeral.

He put up his fists and moved to my left. Taking a step forward, he threw a looping right-hand punch, which I blocked with my left arm and shoulder.

He tried again, this time landing a punch to my neck. I brushed it off and moved a few feet to the side to give myself some room. He tried a clumsy left hook, leaving his right side wide open, his face and head completely unprotected. I wondered in a flash if I should take it easy on this guy, this scumbag who'd hurt his kid.

The hell with that.

I landed a hard left to the jaw with everything I had, right on the button. His head snapped to the side, and he made a sound like a dying animal as he went down. His head bounced on the concrete when he landed. I could practically hear his brain bouncing around inside his skull. Not just a glass jaw, this guy had a crystal jaw. He was out cold, his mouth wide open.

The other two guys in the garage stared at me, not saying anything, just watching. I kept my eye on them and stepped over to the pile of legal papers on the floor. I bent over and grabbed the first page of the complaint, which had some dirt and a little grease on it. I crumpled it up into a ball, then stuck it in Jesse's mouth, making sure it was all the way inside.

I wiped my hand clean of his saliva and walked out.

My mind raced in twenty different directions as I drove away from the warehouse. My hand hurt like a son of a gun after hitting Legrand, but I felt great. I hadn't landed a haymaker like that in a long time. I'd forgotten what it was like to be in a real fight, one where I squared off against some asshole who wanted to crack my skull open. The intensity of the battle, the exhilaration when I saw an opening. The split second before the punch landed was what I'd missed most of all. In that tiny fraction of a second, time would slow down, almost like one of those cheesy movies with slow-motion fight scenes. I'd notice the other guy's face in deep focus, and sometimes I could even sense what he was thinking right before he got hit. And for a moment, just a moment, all of the voices in my head—the doubts, the fears, the worries—would be silenced.

The pain in my hand and wrist began to get worse. I thought I'd hit Legrand cleanly, but the throbbing told me otherwise. It was surprisingly easy to break the knuckles of the ring and pinkie fingers if you used enough force and hit someone at an angle. And I'd really nailed him. That punch had been like a twenty-pound sledgehammer landing on a concrete slab.

I gripped the steering wheel with one hand and drove around aimlessly, trying to ignore the guilt I was starting to feel. I'd made good on my vow to avoid violence for the last year, but somehow

I'd gotten in two fights in a week. Yes, I'd tried to handle both situations calmly, but each had turned violent. And I had to be honest with myself—that's what I'd wanted. What I'd hoped for. A break from the routine existence I'd been living. I couldn't avoid the suspicion that I might have arranged the situation so Jesse had no choice but to fight me. Maybe I'd gotten what I truly wanted, and maybe what my enemies were saying was right: that I was just a thug, someone who lived for the battles and confrontations. Just one step above the gangbangers on our rez who sought out never-ending beefs with other gangs, or the addicted souls who turned to their substances daily. Maybe I was an addict too, drawn to the adrenaline and the rage and the buzz of a battle. I'd worked hard to change and stop the fighting, but I'd had to do it on my own—no twelve-step programs, no interventions, no making amends. Just sitting and talking with Jerome for hours on his porch, soaking up his wisdom and his understanding. I decided to head over there as soon as I got back to the rez. I needed to hear his words and see his face.

The throbbing in my hand was getting much worse, and it was becoming difficult to move my fingers. I wondered if I should stop by a clinic for some meds, but I remembered that I might have some strong painkillers stashed in the truck. My doctor had prescribed them after I was shot last year, and they'd gotten me through the worst of the recovery. I was wary of taking them, given how much misery on the rez was due to pill abuse, so as soon as I could, I'd switched to plain aspirin. I'd kept a few for a rainy day, which had come sooner than I'd thought.

I seemed to recall sticking the nearly empty bottle in my glove compartment, but maybe I was just imagining that. The pills might be in the old grocery sack in my bathroom back at home, where I kept half-used prescriptions, soap remnants, and cleaning supplies. If they weren't in the truck, I'd be in trouble; I'd have to hightail it back home or to the closest Indian Health Services clinic.

I pulled over to the side of the road and started digging in the glove box. It was hard to do with just one hand, and I tossed all of the registration and insurance papers on the floor, along with the assorted junk in there: fast food napkins, a greasy map, straws in paper wrappers, and the set of heavy wheel locks for my tires. I dug around for a few minutes without any success, feeling more and more frustrated. I found an empty bottle of hand sanitizer, old ketchup packets, some Tic Tacs, and, to my disgust, a desiccated fried chicken wing. That had almost certainly come from Nathan—he loved BBQ chicken wings, which were not easy to find on the reservation. He'd probably taken my truck on one of his jaunts with Shawna to get food. I searched for another minute and was about to give up when I found the pill bottle, stuck inside an old Subway sandwich bag. I must have put it there to hide it from any potential thieves.

The bottle had one of those childproof caps, which proved impossible to open with only one hand. I couldn't hold it firmly with my left hand, so I wedged it against the door with my right and twisted. It was tricky, but I was finally able to awkwardly screw it open, and a half dozen pills fell out onto the floor of my truck and rolled underneath the seat. I cursed, opened the door, and started digging around. After a couple of minutes, I was able to find three pills, still relatively dirt-free.

I wiped one of them off and dry-swallowed it, then took another. I knew how potent the pills were, but the pain was getting worse by the minute. Fuck it. I popped a third one in my mouth, this time chewing it for maximum effect. It tasted bitter and sharp, like harsh vinegar. From past experience, I knew these painkillers took about twenty minutes to kick in, so I decided to start driving to take my mind off my misery.

As I pulled out back on the road, I remembered the boarding school, the place where my auntie Josephine had apparently died. Charley had said there was a small cemetery there. I'd check that first. Whatever I found, it was important for me to visit the site and pay my respects.

I drove into a Maverik gas station, turned around, and headed for the highway. After a few miles, I switched on the radio, hoping for a song or some news—anything, really. I was too far away to pick up KOYA, the Rosebud radio station, but was happy to discover that I could get KILI, the Pine Ridge rez radio.

There was a short commercial for the Black Hills Beauty College, then the DJ came on. "Hey everyone, it's Giggles, coming at ya! Let's get some positive energy and blessings going for the oyate today! Spread the love, laughs, hugs, and cuddles, am I right? This first song's goin' out to Warfield Poor Moose! If y'all ain't heard, he's the center for the Topeka State b-ball team. Ain't no room for disrespect in the Oglala Nation! Stay strong, Warfield!"

I'd heard about this. The basketball player was Lakota from Pine Ridge and played on a college team in Kansas. The game had been on national TV, and the announcers had apparently misread his last name, thinking it was "Pooh" rather than "Poor." They'd mocked him, calling him "Pooh Bear" and "Winnie the Pooh." Even after they were informed about the correct pronunciation, they'd continued to laugh about him, feeling entitled to disrespect someone whose name differed from the European standard. Just another example of the invisibility of Native people.

The twangy opening chords of Aretha Franklin's "Respect" began playing, and I turned the sound way up. I was a heavy metal guy, but it was impossible not to love Aretha's incredible singing. I jammed with the song, singing along with the chorus, grateful that no one could hear my fractured voice and off-key shouting.

After a few more tunes, I arrived at the grounds of the old

boarding school. I'd heard from Charley and others about the sad history of the place. Apparently the school had been shut down many decades ago, then converted into a Native tuberculosis sanitarium. To no one's surprise, the Indian patients received crude, primitive treatments and often died terrible deaths. After researchers learned how to treat TB, the building became an Indian Health Service hospital, but the care provided there was so poor that the federal government shut the whole thing down. Now the place looked deserted, a bitter reminder of the government's abandonment of Natives.

I parked my truck in the empty parking lot. My pain began to subside as the meds coursed through me. I got out of the truck and immediately felt dizzy, lightheaded. It struck me that maybe I'd taken one too many of the pills. I steadied myself, then looked around the area. There were a few generic modern buildings, all boarded up, and a larger structure at the far end of the complex. A badly maintained lawn and a path off to the side, littered with trash. A sense of sadness, desolation. Near a crumbling set of stairs an old metal plaque, stained green and tarnished by age, was installed on a brick post.

GROUND IMPROVEMENTS SIOUX SANATORIUM

BUILT BY U.S. INDIAN SERVICE AND WORKS PROGRESS ADMINISTRATION

NINETEEN THIRTY-NINE

I stared at the plaque for a moment and started walking. I didn't have any idea where the cemetery might be, so I followed the dirt path past the newer buildings and a storage shed. I kept going to the end of the trail, feeling more and more anxious and disoriented, and then spotted an imposing old building in the distance. Made of red brick and granite, it had a large stairway leading up to the entrance and several boarded-up windows. A small turret jutted from the top of the structure, which looked like the guard tower of a prison. Off to the side, there was a wooden signboard with the words RAPID CITY IHS HOSPITAL spray-painted on the plywood with stencils. It looked cheap, as if someone couldn't be bothered to have a real sign installed. I'd found it.

I stared at the building for a while, trying to imagine what it had been like for the children there, far away from their family and friends, forced to abandon their language and way of life. I wondered how I would have fared. Would I have fought against the teachers and staff, or would I have stayed quiet, biding my time until I could get out? I wondered which path my auntie Josephine had taken. The fact that she'd died at the school suggested that she may have been one of the rebels, defying those who'd tried to force her into a foreign culture. Or perhaps she'd simply died of disease and poor medical care, which was often the case for Natives then and now. Again, I regretted never asking my mother about Josephine, as well as a hundred other questions about our family's history.

I sat with my thoughts for a moment longer, then decided to get moving again and find the cemetery. As I started walking, I realized my hand had stopped hurting; it felt like I was gliding as I moved. My body felt weightless, and I noticed a slight distortion in my vision, the edges of objects around me fuzzy. It was like looking through an old children's kaleidoscope, but I didn't really mind. I circled the complex a few times, scanning the grounds for graves or tombstones, but didn't see anything.

After ten minutes of wandering around, I realized that the cemetery might have been located somewhere away from the school itself, so the children—and the teachers—wouldn't be reminded of what had happened there. Walking toward the outskirts of the facility, I spotted a large grassy area to the south, about a quarter mile away in a small valley. Something clicked in my head when I looked that way. Perhaps it was the pain pills, but I had an overwhelming feeling that the children were there, the shame of their deaths hidden away by the school's leaders.

I started jogging down the hill, letting the momentum carry me. As I moved, my instinct grew stronger, and I broke into a run for the final stretch. Once I got to the bottom, I stopped to catch my breath. The air felt different, as if it were denser, heavier, holding more than just oxygen molecules. There was a strange smell, also—a clotted, oppressive must, redolent of charred hair or feathers. I stood up and looked around. There was a stand of trees to my left, Black Hills spruces and an American elm, ominous in the morning light. I took a deep breath and made my way over there, my legs rubbery and unpredictable.

The gravestones appeared before me, barely visible in the shadows of the trees: dozens of small, flat grave markers in two long rows. They bore names only, no dates of birth or death, as if the children had been born out of time, an epoch unto themselves.

I walked between the stones, careful not to step on any, and looked for my auntie's name. The engravings on some of the markers were nearly worn away, eroded, difficult to read. I bent over each one, struggling to make out the words, unable to go forward until I'd identified each child, pausing a moment to say a prayer in my head.

HAZEL WHITE FEATHER

CLARA SHORT HORN

CHESTER BAD HAND

NED FALLS APART

EMMA JANIS

ROSE PRETTY HAIR

THOMAS RED NOSE

JOHN TWO BULLS

SOPHIA GUNHAMMER

MARY PENEAUX

FEMALE CHILD

MALE CHILD

UNNAMED CHILD

INFANT

I walked back over to the markers again, looking for a Wounded Horse, but didn't see any. If the list from the Land Project was correct, then Josephine could be in one of those unmarked graves, buried in the ground with no gravestone, no testament to her humanity, the joys and fears and hopes and dreams she'd had, all of which had come to an end right here on this soil. I bent over, my hands on my knees, the elegies for the dead still ringing in my head, overcome by all I'd witnessed. These children, buried and forgotten for decades, forced to rest near their tormentors.

I looked up. The trees were swaying, but there was no wind. The rocks on the ground seemed to be moving, too, but that didn't make any sense. Then I glanced to my left and saw, to my amazement, a group of children. They were walking slowly past me, in the direction of the old building. The girls were wearing long skirts, and the boys were clad in old-fashioned quasi-military uniforms, with matching jackets and pants. A couple of the boys carried shovels, and some of the girls had buckets. They looked sad, heads down, shoulders curved forward. A Native man with black hair and double-pierced ears walked behind them, pausing for a moment to glance at me before moving on.

As they marched past, I tried to speak, but no words would come. The group continued slowly moving toward the old school, and then one girl stopped. She began speaking to me, but I couldn't hear her words at first. Then I started to understand what she was saying. She was asking if I could help her go home. I asked her where she was from, but she turned away and rejoined the other children. She looked back and gestured with her hand. I saw a fresh grave there, a mound of dark soil torn from the earth. I asked her to stop, but she kept going. I tried to run after them, but my legs didn't seem to work. I called out, but the children were gone. Suddenly exhausted, I sat down on the grass, the world swirling, and then a black curtain descended upon me.

"Hey, you all right?"

I opened my eyes and saw a woman standing over me. "What happened?"

"I don't know. I saw you lying here—thought I'd see if you were okay."

I sat up and looked around, slowly remembering that I'd come to the boarding school cemetery to find my auntie. The sky was overcast, and I realized I must have been out for some time.

"Yeah, I was just, uh, visiting . . ." My thoughts were scrambled as I tried to reorient myself. The last thing I remembered were the children by the graves. Had that been a dream?

"You sure you're all right? You don't look so good."

I suddenly felt self-conscious. I'd been passed out in the dirt—maybe from the pain pills—for who knows how long. The woman probably thought I was drunk or worse.

"No, I'm good, really. I hurt myself earlier, took some pills. They hit me pretty hard; I must have dozed off." I looked down at my hand. The swelling had gone down, which was a good sign. "Thanks for checking."

"No problem," she said. "We don't get many people around here, so I noticed you right away."

"You work here?" I asked, then glanced at her. Native woman about thirty years old, medium-length black hair, lots of tattoos and jewelry—kind of an Indian goth look, maybe leaning more toward punk. She carried a large black bag etched with drawings of a giant moth and images of the sun and moon.

"No." She smiled. "Nobody's worked here for a long time. I'm with a group that's trying to stop some development on the site."

Something clicked. "The Land Project? For the old boarding school?"

She set her bag down on the ground. "Yeah, you know about it?"

"Kind of. I've been driving my friend Jerome Iron Shell to some of the meetings. He's been telling me about it."

She flashed a big grin. "I love Jerome! Are you Rocky?"

I shook my head. "No, that's his grandson. I'm not related, but I help out when Jerome needs me. Most everybody on our rez does."

"Oh, you're from Rosebud! That makes sense. I'm Oglala from Pine Ridge, but I live in Rapid now. What's your name?"

"Virgil. Wounded Horse. How about you?"

"Valerie, but call me Val. Val Tobacco. Stupid, right? I don't even smoke."

Neither did I anymore, but even the mention of tobacco gave me a little craving. "That's not stupid. And props for not smoking. I quit this year."

"Hey, right on! I know that's hard." She paused for a second. "So, if you don't mind me asking, what are you doing out here? Like I said, it's usually pretty deserted."

I wondered how much to tell her about the process serving. "Uh, it's complicated. I had a job in Rapid today, then decided to stop by and look around. See, I think my auntie might be buried here." I gestured toward the school. "A friend of mine got some list and told me he saw her name on it."

"You mean the list of deceased kids? The one they just re-leased?"

"That's right," I said. "I thought I'd check this place out, pay my respects if I could find her grave. Didn't see it over there, so I don't know. I heard some were buried here with no, uh, tombstones or anything."

She nodded. "We're looking for those. We've got people using ground-penetrating radar to find them. It's the best method, because radar doesn't disturb the ground so, you know, it protects the dignity of the deceased. But it's slow going; the entire site is five miles square."

I took a deep breath and tried to clear my head. "Thanks for sharing that. Sounds like I'm out of luck."

She smiled. "Not necessarily. Most people don't know this, but a few Native kids are buried in the town cemetery, a few miles away. We think the boarding school was burying the dead children there, but someone in the city objected. That's when they probably started dumping the poor kids in the unmarked graves."

"Wait, you're telling me there's another cemetery?"

"Yeah, it's called Meadow View, but I don't want to get your hopes up. If your auntie was on that list, then she's likely here at the school somewhere. But there's only one way to be sure. Do you want to take a look?"

"How far away is it?"

"Just a few miles," she said. "I can take you there if you'd like."

"Sure, if you don't mind."

"No problem! What was your auntie's name?"

"Josephine Wounded Horse."

She nodded. "Follow me. You're okay to walk, right?"

"I think I'm good," I said, and stood up. I felt a little shaky, but Val had already started moving toward the parking lot, chatting as she went.

"Originally, we thought around forty or fifty kids died at the school. Twenty were buried at Meadow View, and the rest of them were supposed to be here. Now we're finding out that a lot more children died, and the bastards didn't tell anyone. Do you know how old Josephine was when she made her journey?"

"Sixteen, I think." I tried to remember anything else my mother had said about her sister. It had been decades, and I had only fragments of conversations with my mother left in my memory, nothing substantial about Josephine. I closed my eyes and tried to block everything out. Images of my mother floated in my consciousness as I traveled into my memories. "That's all I know. I'm sorry."

"No, that's helpful. Sometimes really young kids died—you know, babies—and they buried them without including their name. You probably saw the markers that just say 'Infant.'"

"I did. I didn't realize there were babies at the school. Does that mean that some of the girls were getting pregnant here?"

She shook her head and frowned. "Not sure. Maybe they came here pregnant, or maybe that happened later. Either way, it's a tragedy. The state wants to sweep all the history under the rug. You know, they're trying to get a permit to demolish the old school and put up some new building."

We reached the parking lot where I'd left my truck, and I waited while she got her vehicle. After a few minutes, an old orange Volkswagen Rabbit pulled up. She rolled down the window. "Just follow me! This car doesn't go too fast. I think you can keep up in that big-ass truck."

I gave her a thumbs-up, and she took off. We drove for a few miles before turning into a small parking lot, right next to a large sign that read MEADOW VIEW CEMETERY. I parked next to Val and looked around. The place was nicely kept up—no weeds or overgrown foliage. A far cry from the cemeteries I was used to on the rez.

"Their graves are at the far end," Val said, and started moving forward. "Like I said, we don't know why they buried a few Native kids here, or why they stopped. Probably someone objected to Indians being put to rest among the wasicus."

"Shit, that sounds right. I'm surprised they even let 'em stay buried." I walked a few steps behind Val. I noticed she was wearing bright-purple Converse Chuck Taylor sneakers.

She raised her hands, palms up. "We do know the first student buried here; her name was Esther Swift. It's a really sad story—she actually survived the Wounded Knee massacre as a little kid, only to die at the school when she was eighteen."

"That's terrible," I said.

"It gets worse. The people at the school didn't even tell her family that she'd died. And they misspelled her name on the gravestone here. Talk about salt in the wound."

I shook my head. "Hard to believe."

"Not so unbelievable. You know how they treated those students, right?"

"I know enough. They forced them to give up their families and beat them if they spoke their own language, right?"

"Yeah, but so much more. The children weren't allowed to hold on to their culture at all—no spirituality or traditions. If they were caught doing anything Native, they were punished. Abused, really. The boys would be hung up by their thumbs. The girls were sometimes assaulted. You know what I mean."

I felt my anger rising, even though this was many decades ago. "Those poor kids."

"Yeah, and they were sometimes abused even away from the school. There was this thing called the 'outing' program. The students—both boys and girls—would be sent to local farms to work as unpaid labor during the summers. You can imagine what happened to some of them at those places. An Indian girl, all alone, no way to contact anybody . . ."

"I never heard about that," I said. "How could they let it happen?"

"Sad thing is that some of the students really wanted to go to the farms because they knew they'd at least get fed. The school never provided enough food; some kids died of malnutrition."

"Did people from the government know about this? Or were they in on it?"

Val raised her eyebrows. "It's tough to say. There were always a few decent people advocating for Indians. But it was a different time—communication was so much slower, obviously. The newspapers would only cover stories about us if there was something unusual. Like the two Native boys who got hit by a train after they ran away from the school."

We made it to the end of the cemetery, where there were about a dozen small grave markers and one larger memorial. Val saw me looking at it.

"That's the new monument for Esther. The Land Project donated it." She pointed with her lips to the other graves. "Let's see if your auntie's here, just in case. I doubt it—most of the people on that list you saw are buried at the school—but you never know."

We walked alongside the children's graves in silence, stopping to check each tiny marker. I thought of Nathan when he was a small child, and how horrendous it would have been to have him taken away; the pain the parents must have felt was unimaginable. I paused and glanced back at the markers, barely visible in the shadows.

"No," Val said. "It doesn't look like she's here. I'm so sorry. Like I told you, we've got people combing the school grounds for the graves. You want to exchange digits? You can give me a shout in a week or two; hopefully, there'll be some good news."

I was touched by her kindness. "Hey, that's really cool of you. Means a lot." We entered our numbers on each other's phone.

"No problem," she said. "This is my passion. I've been with the Land Project since the beginning. We're the ones who filed the lawsuit against the city—you know about that?"

"A little, mainly from Jerome," I said. "And he told me about that building burning down over there. Construction site, whatever."

She grinned. "Yeah, that's just a few miles down the road. Can't deny I wasn't too upset about it. I was hoping they might delay construction or maybe even cancel it, but word is they're moving full steam ahead."

"Really?"

"Oh, yeah. Don't know if you heard, but those jerks are planning to develop the entire site—tear down the old school, put up a whole bunch of tacky apartments, build some open-air shopping mall. Assholes. We're going to hold a giant Ghost Dance at the site—completely surround it and dance for twelve hours. Should be a ton of media there."

"Jerome mentioned that. Sounds like it could get some attention."

"That's our hope," she said. "Drive them jerks off our land."

We started walking back to the parking lot. "How'd you get involved with this?" I asked. "The Land Project."

"Always been an activist, I guess. My mom raised me to fight for stuff I care about. Rage against the machine, right? I actually ran for city council a few years ago."

"Oh yeah? That's cool. Did you win?"

"Nah, I got crushed. But the point was to show that a strong winyan could run for office in this wasicu city."

I flashed her the horns sign with my hand. "Right on. What are you doing now?"

"I teach a class over at Oglala Lakota College, do computer stuff, too. And I work part-time at the Life Center downtown. You know about it?"

"Is that the shelter for, ah, people who are—" I wasn't sure if the word *homeless* was still being used.

"Unhoused," she said. "But we're not a shelter. We're a day center. We offer a place to make calls, get mail, store personal belongings. The stuff most people take for granted. It's dignity, really. That's what we provide. But not for much longer."

"Why's that?"

"We lost our lease. The city wants us out of the downtown area so that the tourists don't have to see people who need help. Like poverty is some condition that needs to be hidden away. It's racism, really. They don't want to acknowledge that this is our land." She glanced over at me, then began twirling her hair. "What about you? You live in Rosebud, right?"

"Born and bred. Sicangu strong, like the kids say."

We made it to the parking lot, which was still deserted except for our two vehicles.

"So, what do you do?" she asked. "That's a pretty fancy truck. You on tribal council?"

I laughed out loud. "You might be the first person to ever think that. They wouldn't let me within ten miles of their offices."

She smiled and touched my shoulder. "Okay, so what is it then? You hit the jackpot at the casino and win that thing?"

I wondered how I could explain the events of the last year. The drugs that had been smuggled to the reservation, the kidnapping of my nephew, the fact that I'd been shot and nearly died. After I'd recovered, my girlfriend Marie had insisted that I get a safer vehicle, and Charley Leader Charge had sold me the truck for next to nothing—a gift of sorts for what I'd done to help the reservation.

"No, I just got a pretty good deal. I work part-time for a lawyer here in Rapid. He sold it to me."

"All right," she said, looking skeptical. "Hey, you want to grab a cup of coffee or do you need to get back to work? There's a good place—"

My cell phone began buzzing, and I looked at the screen. It was Marie. She usually didn't call me when I was on a job, so I excused myself to Val and hit the answer button.

"Virgil, can you hear me?"

"Yeah, I hear you fine. Listen, I'm at the old boarding school, trying to find—"

"You need to come back. Right away. Something's happened."

My mind immediately went to Nathan.

"Is Nathan okay? Did he—"

"It's not Nathan. It's Jerome. He was attacked. They're not sure if he's going to make it."

told Val what had happened to Jerome. She was as shocked as I was and made me promise to call when I knew more. I agreed, then quickly drove off. Marie had told me that the attack happened at Jerome's house, but she didn't know anything beyond that. I needed to head back to the rez immediately and find out what was happening. It was a long two-hour drive back, and I resolved to keep my driving speed under control. Getting pulled over would just slow me down, not to mention that there was always the possibility I'd be hauled off to jail by a racist cop.

As I drove, I thought about Jerome. In many ways he'd been like a father to me, given that my own dad had passed away early in my life. Jerome had guided me when I needed it, and he'd never hesitated to let me know when I was making a bad choice. But he had a way of showing me things without telling me directly. He'd share a Lakota story, and I'd eventually grasp the meaning of it, sometimes days or weeks later.

I'd heard similar comments from others. Jerome had been helping the Lakota people for his entire life. He'd been a spiritual leader and medicine man since he was thirteen, and he'd spent a year in prison for running a Sun Dance decades ago. Most people didn't know this, but Native spirituality and religion had been outlawed by the federal government since the 1800s. Holding a sweat lodge or other Indian ceremony was a felony, punishable by a year in prison. And that's exactly what happened to Jerome. He'd been active in the American Indian Movement, and the feds had their eye on him. Someone tipped off the FBI that there was an illegal Sun Dance being conducted on the rez, and Jerome was arrested. There was an outpouring of support for him from across the country, and numerous lawyers offered to represent him, but Jerome refused to fight the charges, readily admitting that he'd organized a Lakota ceremony and telling the judge that he planned to do it again.

Indigenous spirituality remained a criminal offense until the American Indian Religious Freedom Act was passed by the US Congress in the late 1970s. That law gave Natives the right to practice our spirituality without fear of arrest, but Jerome had never stopped healing people and practicing traditional Lakota ceremonies. I'd asked him about prison once, and he'd told me that he used his time on the inside to help the other Native prisoners and educate the guards about Indian spiritual traditions.

Who would want to hurt Jerome? He was beloved by nearly everyone on the rez. Yet there were always jealous people who wanted to bring others down, especially those who had earned the respect of the community. Still, it was heartbreaking to realize that someone harbored such hate for a person who'd devoted his life to helping the Lakota nation.

I tried calling Marie, but she didn't pick up, so I dialed Tommy. He answered right away.

"Yo, Virg."

He sounded despondent, not his usual exuberant self. "I guess you heard," I said.

"About Jerome? Yeah. What the hell, man? Can't believe it."

"Is he all right? Marie said it was bad."

"He's at the hospital in the emergency room. Melvin said they ain't allowing no visitors right now. I was thinkin' about going over there later, maybe burn some sage."

"Do you know what happened?" I asked. "Marie said he'd been attacked."

"Nope. Ain't heard nothing yet."

"They're sure it wasn't an accident? He didn't just fall or something?"

"I don't know, but I hear there's a fuckton of cops out at his house. Don't sound like no slip and fall to me."

"Yeah, but who would want to harm Jerome? He's like everyone's tunkasila."

"Homes, I know you two are tight, but there's plenty of people who got a beef with him."

This didn't sound right. I'd never heard him complain about others or mention any feuds. Not once. "What? He never said anything about that."

I could hear Tommy sigh. "Virg, that ain't Jerome's style. He tries to stay above, you know? But they out there. Some bad blood, for sure."

"Like who?" I asked.

"Well, the one family who was all pissed off that Jerome couldn't cure their guy. Their dad was sick—I think cancer—and they went to Jerome for medicine. He died a few months later, and they blamed Jerome. Not his fault! But they been talkin' shit for a while, sayin' that Jerome caused it and they gonna get their revenge."

"They said that?"

"Ayup."

"Who was this?"

"Ah, the Brown Bulls, out in Two Strike. Joe Brown Bull, the guy's son, he the one making all the noise."

"Damn," I said. "Didn't know about any of this."

"A lot you don't know, my man! People don't tell you shit 'cause they afraid of you. They don't wanna get the OG stirred up!"

This stung. I didn't see myself that way, but I kept quiet and let Tommy speak.

"And I been hearin' for a while that the whole Yellowhawk clan done swore revenge on you and Jerome, but they trying to keep it on the down-low," he said.

This was news to me as well. I thought I was done with Guv Yellowhawk and his bunch. He was a true scumbag who'd been assaulting children and selling illegal pain pills on the rez for years until I kicked his ass and sent him to prison. I hadn't heard anything about him in a long time, but apparently his people still held a grudge. Typical. Instead of holding their own accountable for spreading poison and hurting little kids, they blamed me and Jerome for shutting down their pill operation.

"Appreciate the heads-up," I said. "Sounds like I need to keep my eyes open."

I offered to pick up Tommy later and drive him to the hospital. But first I decided to go to Jerome's house and see what I could find out. I tried making a few more calls, but I'd entered a dead zone for cell phones. I tried to make my mind go blank so I could focus on my driving. Traffic on the highway was light, for which I was grateful. A few miles down, a guy on a motorcycle pulled up in the left lane. I glanced over and saw that the rider was a young dude, maybe in his early twenties. He looked familiar, like someone I knew. I looked over again, and I realized who he reminded me of. My closest friend in high school, Rob Turning Heart.

Rob and I had been tight back then—classmates, best friends, comrades. We'd taken the same classes, hung out after school together, and cruised up and down Main Street endlessly on the weekends, hoping that someone would notice us. When my mom died, the first place I went was Rob's house, where they gave me food, burned some sage, and helped me through the roughest days. Not long after that, Rob and I did our own informal Hunka ceremony, where we pledged to be bonded forever. The Hunka is traditionally conducted by a medicine man or spiritual leader, but we just made it up. No horse tails or ribbons, no feasts or give-aways. But after we finished, we were Hunkayapi, bound together more tightly than brothers, connected in a way that transcended traditional family ties.

In our last year of high school, Rob and I talked about getting some money and opening up an auto body shop on the rez. But I'd started drinking and listening to heavy metal music and couldn't get my shit together. Rob joined the army, got shipped out to fight in the war, and came home in a body bag. I'd always felt massively guilty over his death and thought it was my fault, somehow. I didn't go to the funeral. Instead, I hopped on my motorcycle and rode flat out to the Black Hills, pushing the bike to its limit, the road just a blur beneath me, riding until I couldn't see anything, couldn't feel anything, stopping only when I ran out of gas.

I hadn't thought about Rob for a while, although I'd helped his little sister out of a jam once. And now he was back in my mind, no doubt triggered by my fears about Jerome. Over the years, I'd been able to avoid ruminating about Rob's death, as I'd had to focus on what was in front of me. Money, jobs, paying the bills, Nathan's issues. The sharp edges that filled our days.

But now here he was, vivid in my memory, and I welcomed him. I remembered the goofy way he smiled, the ratty ball cap he always wore with the old-fashioned Seattle Seahawks logo. His relentless teasing—he loved to tell me to get off my lazy Native ass and do some work. And I remembered the last time I ever saw him, right before he shipped out, both of us too embarrassed to say anything meaningful, instead just giving each other an exploding fist bump.

I wondered what would have happened if he'd survived. Would he still live on the rez, maybe married with some kids? Or would he and I have finally opened that body shop? In that world, maybe I'd have spent my life happily pounding out dents, fixing the damages in people's lives instead of inflicting new ones. It was overwhelming to think about the thousands of choices we had to make in our days, never knowing if the path we were taking would lead to happiness or grief. It was said that Indians had a duty to always think ahead—that all decisions should be focused on helping the next seven generations. But right now I didn't even know if my actions would help me in the next seven hours.

After another stretch of driving, I arrived at Jerome's house. There were numerous cars parked in front, including four Rosebud Sioux Tribe police vehicles. A number of people were milling around, including half a dozen tribal cops, the most I'd even seen together at the same time. There was no crime scene tape posted anywhere, so I decided to walk around and scope out the situation.

The police were gathered in two separate clusters in the yard, chatting among themselves. Other people were entering and exiting Jerome's house. I didn't see any of Jerome's family around, which seemed strange until I remembered that he was at the hospital. I circled the place, looking for someone I knew. I recognized some of the tribal police officers in one group, but my gut told me to leave them alone. I walked back to my truck and saw a tribal cop standing by himself, staring down at his cell phone. Ty Bad Hand. I didn't know him well, but he was friends with Marie and might tell me something.

"Hey, is that Ty?" I asked.

"Yes," he said, looking up and frowning. "Who are—"

"It's Virgil."

His face relaxed. "Hey there, didn't recognize you at first. Sorry."

"No worries, man. I just got here. Trying to get some news about Jerome."

He shook his head. "He's in the ER at Rosebud. Wouldn't be surprised if they moved him to the big hospital in Rapid."

I didn't like the sound of that. "So what happened?"

"Blunt force trauma. Somebody hit him in the head."

It took me a second to process this. "You're sure?"

He smiled ruefully. "We're sure. You don't get a skull fracture like that from tripping on a rug. Can't find the weapon, though."

"How bad is it? You hear anything?"

He shook his head again. "No word yet. The family's at the hospital. Rocky's in pretty bad shape. He's the one who found him on the porch."

"Damn, that's terrible."

"Lucky, really. He could have died out there if no one had come by." He gestured with his chin toward the front porch, where I'd spent many hours.

"You guys have any idea who did this?" I asked.

Ty looked around, checking to see if we were alone. "Not a clue, man. Jerome is the last person you'd think would be hit."

That's what I'd thought, too, until Tommy told me about Jerome's enemies. I wondered if I should say something to Ty about that. "Any evidence?" I asked. "Fingerprints or whatever?"

He looked at me like I was stupid. "Man, there are probably hundreds of prints out there, and we don't have an investigator yet." He must have seen my face, because he looked apologetic. "Look, we got a call in to Pierre. You know, FBI. Might see them later if we're lucky."

He was referring to our screwed-up criminal justice system. Serious felony crimes on the rez had to be referred to the FBI, but they declined a large number of cases, which meant that offenders went free, or possibly faced prosecution in tribal court for a misdemeanor offense, which carried a maximum sentence of one year in jail. One year, for all assaults, rapes, and murders. It was because of this that people would hire a private vigilante like me. But even I couldn't do anything if there was no suspect.

"So what's next? You know, to catch the person who did it."

"Not a lot of options yet. Best hope is that Jerome wakes up soon and gives us the perp's name. But, I'm not sure what his, uh, mental status will be. Hopefully he'll make a full recovery, Creator willing."

The more I learned, the more my anxiety increased. I started to ask Ty another question about Jerome's injuries, but he pointed toward the house. I looked over, and then I heard.

"What the fuck is he doing here! Wounded Horse, I'm talking to you! I want you out of here!"

R ose Charging Cloud. The chief of police for the Rosebud Sioux Tribe. And she was standing on the porch, screaming at me. This was not a complete surprise, as Rose had never liked me, and had made that point abundantly clear in the past. She was an old-fashioned nuts-and-bolts cop, and she didn't want any vigilante justice on her turf. We'd butted heads several times over the last few years, and apparently I was still on her shit list, even though I was no longer taking jobs as an enforcer.

Rose had been hired as the police chief four years ago. She was originally from Rosebud but was adopted out as a kid and raised in North Dakota, where she'd had a rough childhood. Being both Black and Native, she'd experienced a fair amount of discrimination, but she'd fought back against the bullies and racists. People often recounted a story from her teenage years, when she was accosted by a drunk worker from one of the man camps at the oil field. The legend was that he'd tried to kidnap her and take her back to the camp, but she'd fought back and broken his nose and two ribs. The irony of her own vigilante past wasn't lost on me.

Later, Rose had worked as a BIA police officer, making her way up through the ranks and then taking a job on the police force at Pine Ridge before being hired as the first female police chief at Rosebud. She'd commanded respect right from the start on our rez. She was a tall, imposing person and carried a big Glock 40 handgun. Surprisingly, she was also known as being one of the best star quilt makers in the state.

Quilting was taught to Lakota women and girls in the first missionary schools, and quilts replaced buffalo robes after the bison herds were decimated. But these women had taken the craft and made it their own by incorporating the morning star design in the quilts. The morning star represents the dawn of a new day, but also the link between the people and the spirits. I remember my mother telling me that the eight points of the star quilt stand for the primary directions of the earth as well as the four stages of life. Star quilts were given at the birth of children and to honor significant achievements, weddings, and funerals. People on the rez respected quilt makers, and Rose's skill and devotion to the craft only enhanced her standing in the community. In short, everyone loved Rose.

But she hated me. And now she was headed in my direction.

"Why are you here? This is a crime scene!" She glared at me, then at Ty Bad Hand. "Did you call this numbnuts?"

"No, I was just—"

"I came here on my own," I said. "Jerome is my friend."

She swiveled and locked her eyes on me. "I don't give two shits if he's your goddamn BFF! We have work to do and don't need you fucking it up."

I took a breath. "Look, I'm not fucking anything up. I just stopped by to find out what happened."

"What happened is police business! Now get your ass out of here."

I glanced at Rose, who looked like she was about to detonate. "Okay, I'll go. But can you tell me anything about the attack? I was just talking with Jerome. Maybe I can—"

"Talking with him? When?"

"I don't know—uh, maybe two days ago."

"What was the nature of your conversation?"

"Our conversation? What does that have to do with anything?"

"If you were speaking with Mr. Iron Shell recently, I'll need you to provide a statement. Tell us anything that might be useful."

"Sure, I'm ready."

She rolled her eyes. "Not now. Look around you. Notice anything? We're busy!"

Actually, most of the cops here didn't look too busy to me, but I knew that observation wouldn't go over well. "Yeah, okay. But there's some stuff about Jerome's enemies you may want to know—"

"Later! You think you're the fucking Indian Sherlock Holmes? Christ, call me in a few days."

She turned around and strode off, her gun bouncing off her leg.

Talking with Rose always left me feeling awkward. I left Jerome's house and started for the hospital, feeling like I'd been banished.

As I drove, I thought about Rose Charging Cloud and what I'd done to earn her hostility. It stemmed from a job I'd taken a few years back. A guy on the rez named Cal Swiftwater had been hunting bald eagles and trafficking their wings, their feathers, and even their heads to people outside the state. Only enrolled Natives were allowed to possess and use eagle feathers for ceremonies; it was a felony for anybody else. The Lakota people viewed eagles as sacred, making it especially heinous for Swiftwater to hunt and kill these beautiful creatures. Everybody on the rez knew about this asshole, but it had proven impossible to prosecute him. So I was approached by a couple of people who wanted me to persuade Swiftwater to stop, by any means necessary. I readily agreed and asked only for gas money. I visited the guy and convinced him by breaking all the fingers on his right hand and telling him that I'd come back for the other hand if I heard of any more eagle parts being sold on our rez. When I left Swiftwater, I felt like Super-man, protecting the rez against villains and wrongdoers.

But Rose came to my house and told me that there'd been a two-year undercover operation into Swiftwater and his associates. I'd screwed everything up by putting a beatdown on him, she said; now out-of-state buyers—the investigation's main targets—would find someone else on another reservation, and the sale of eagle parts would continue. I was to blame for the future murder of hundreds of eagles, she screamed at me. I yelled back at her, telling her it shouldn't have taken so long to catch the guy. She called me an immoral thug, and I said she was a useless chicken-shit, which pretty much ended any chance that we could coexist. I'd been trying to stay out of her way since then, but that had ended today.

I turned the radio on, but the rez station was off the air, which was somewhat unusual. I turned onto Circle Drive and soon passed the bend in the road where handmade protest signs had been posted: JUSTICE FOR DRAVEN; JUSTICE 4 GEESKA; NATIVE LIVES MATTER. These billboards memorialized tribal members who'd been killed in shootouts with state or reservation police. Some of them had been there for years, the paint fading and vanishing over time. As I passed the signboards, I spotted the escaped bison herd over by the creek. They turned their heads to watch me as I drove by.

Ten minutes later I arrived at the IHS hospital, where tribal citizens received health care at no charge. This was the bargain that had been struck over a hundred and fifty years ago: The US government took all the land, but promised us free health care, food, and education forever. Of course every single treaty and promise made by the federal government had been broken, which led many Natives to believe that the only fair solution was to revoke the bargain and get our land back. Indeed, there were numerous LAND BACK murals and stickers popping up on the rez, along with other slogans, like THIS IS NDN TERRITORY, DECOLONIZE NOW, and DEFEND THE SACRED.

The hospital parking lot was filled with potholes, the sidewalks and curb strips overrun with weeds. The building itself was circular in the Native tradition, not the usual Western square design. But the paint was peeling on the large beams at the front and sides of the building, and a few of the windows were cracked. I wondered if hospitals in cities looked like this.

I walked up to the main entrance, where a brown rez dog slept peacefully by the door, and went in, past the small dental services waiting room and down a long hallway. A flyer was taped on the wall by the restrooms:

**EMPLOYEE ASSOCIATION SNACK SALE! IN THE FOOD SERVICES DINING ROOM.**
    **BANANA BREAD: $4.00 PER PAN**
    **"TRASH" BROWNIES: $1.00**
    **WASNA: $2.00 EACH**
    **FRYBREAD: $0.50**
    **REZDOGS: $5.00 EACH**

I was tempted to find the food services dining room and get a rezdog, a hot dog encased in frybread dough and deep fried. Greasy but delicious. But I didn't want to waste any time, so I kept going to the big waiting room. This was the general reception area, where people waited to pick up their prescriptions or for their doctor's appointment. It was also a place where people would simply hang out and talk with their friends, even if they didn't have an appointment with one of the clinics. Our reservation had exactly one snack shop, two fast food joints, the casino restaurant, and a small coffee shop, which was rarely open. There was nowhere, really, to sit with friends and talk. So, folks would go to the gas station, grocery store, or hospital to see people and exchange gossip. The rez social circuit.

The waiting room had about forty seats in two rows, seven pieces of Native art on the walls, and large globe lanterns mounted on poles, which felt out of place with the rest of the decor. I looked around the waiting area but didn't see any of Jerome's people.

I went outside and walked around to the separate entrance for the emergency room, where there was a much smaller waiting area exclusively for emergency patients' families. It hadn't changed since I'd last been inside—a few plastic chairs and two cloudy windows. The hills and valleys of the reservation were barely visible off in the distance, due to the accumulated dirt and grime from the outside world. There was no one in the small reception booth, but a sign had been posted next to the window:

**VERBAL, PHYSICAL AND/OR THREATENING GESTURES WILL NOT BE TOLERATED IN THIS FACILITY. REPORT ALL INCIDENTS TO SECURITY.**

Jerome's family was there. I saw Rocky, Pudge, and a couple of other people. I lifted my hand, and Rocky and Pudge stood to greet me. I gave them both a hug, and Pudge sat back down, his head in his hands.

"Thanks for coming, Virg," Rocky said. "Glad you're here."

"Of course," I said. "How's he doing?"

"Not so good. They're planning to fly him out to the big hospital in Sioux Falls. They said he needs surgery to relieve the pressure on his brain. Right away."

This didn't surprise me. Our little rez hospital wasn't equipped for major surgeries, so they'd airlift people to the major hospital in Rapid City or Sioux Falls. But this meant that Jerome was in bad shape. They only had the resources to fly out the most distressed patients. Everyone else went by ambulance on our fractured and broken roads.

"When are they taking him?" I asked.

"Don't know. They're trying to stabilize him while they figure this shit out. They say there's a problem getting a helicopter. Air ambulance or whatever they call it. I guess they're working on it."

Typical. No doubt they were worried about the cost, or maybe all the air transports were tied up with other patients.

"Damn. I'm sure they'll find one. You gonna fly with him?"

"I think so. They said one person can go along. If not, I can just drive out there, really haul ass."

"Hey, you need me to give you a lift, I'll do it."

"Thanks. Might take you up on that."

"So, do you know what happened?" I asked. "Ty Bad Hand told me someone hit him in the head."

"That's what they said. It was terrible, man. I went to his place to give him a lift to the Allstop and he was passed out on the porch. His head was all bloody." Rocky's jaw started vibrating, and his eyes were trembling.

"That's okay. I get it." I patted him on the shoulder. "The cops have any idea who did it?"

He shook his head. "No. It doesn't make sense. He's always been wicasa wasaka, you know, one of our strong men. I've been praying nonstop. What else can I do?" He looked away so I couldn't see his face.

I stood there for a few moments, trying to think of something to say to comfort him but failing. At that moment, I craved a cigarette more strongly than ever. I put my hand on Rocky's shoulder and held it there.

Then someone tapped me on my back. It was Pudge, who looked at me strangely.

"Hey, you want to go outside and talk?" he said.

"Sure." I was happy for any distractions. We left the waiting room and went out to the parking lot. I followed him out to the concrete parking barriers, brushed away some dirt, and sat down. Pudge looked around to make sure we were alone.

"So, uh, this has been driving me crazy. I think it's my fault Jerome got hurt."

I glanced at him, but he wouldn't meet my eye. "What? How?"

"I-I should have told him," he said. "But I was embarrassed."

"Told him what?"

"Those guys from Pine Ridge. Remember?"

I didn't know who he was talking about at first, then it dawned on me. "The gangbangers?"

He nodded. "Yeah. One of them called, said they were gonna kill me. And you. Because of what happened."

No surprise there. I knew those jackoffs would make some noise. "Okay. What does that have to do with Jerome?"

"He said they'd get my family, too. Jerome is my uncle."

The dirty bastards. It was one thing to come after me, but to go after a holy man was some evil shit. I'd make them pay. "Why didn't you say anything earlier?"

"I was scared! And, you know, I thought they were just talking smack. I've had drunks call me up and make threats before."

"Did they mention Jerome by name?"

He shook his head. "No, they said they'd cut me up, my family, and everyone I knew. Then I hung up."

I went back inside, more confused than ever. If the Pine Ridge gang wanted to get back at Pudge and me, it seemed like the most likely move would be to come after us directly, rather than hitting an elderly medicine man on the head. Everybody knew that hurting a holy person not only was morally wrong but could disrupt the spiritual balance of an entire community. But I'd track them down and find out for myself, once Jerome was back on his feet.

Back in the waiting room, Rocky and the others were quiet, most of them looking down at their phones or listening to music on their earbuds. I grabbed one of the open chairs by the restroom and sat down, suddenly exhausted. I stretched out my feet and closed my eyes, hoping to rest for a moment. Then I nodded off, the sounds of the room serving as a white-noise backdrop to a deep, dreamless sleep.

An hour later, I began to emerge from my nap. I looked around the room and saw that everyone was still there. Rocky was dozing, Pudge was staring off into space, and the others were still clicking on their phones. I used the opportunity to text Marie.

> Hey, I'm at the emergency room with Jerome's family.
> They're waiting for a helicopter to take him to surgery at
> Sioux Falls.

Marie sent back a worried emoji and a message.

> Praying to the Creator that he's all right. Let me know
> any news.

I went over to Rocky and asked him if there'd been any news about a chopper. He raised his hands and shook his head. It was frustrating, but there was nothing we could do. For the next hour, I read an old *Lakota Times* that someone had left behind— the news stories, the editorials, the local sports news, and even the classified ads.

My stomach began to protest, and I realized I hadn't eaten in a long time. I decided to run out to the lobby for some snacks from the vending machine. I was about to ask Rocky if he wanted anything when one of the big double doors swung open and a tall man in a white coat came in. The doctor. He had short brown hair, a patchy beard, and bloodshot eyes. He looked around the room, then down at the floor.

We waited for him to say something.

# Jerome

When a bison dies, it looks back one last time, seeing into the heart of the hunter before entering the passage to the spirit world. When a person dies, he travels the Spirit Road to the place where the Old Woman judges each soul. The Fork in the Road. If the soul is not worthy, it is sent to the left, where it must attempt to be purified in a second life. If the person has lived a life in a sacred manner, the soul is deemed worthy and sent to the right on the Good Road to join the spirits.

Jerome opened his eyes and saw the doctors and nurses around him. He saw his family and his friends and tried to speak to them. He wanted to let them know he was fine and that he loved them. And then he felt as if he were rising, drifting into the sky like a waca'zi in the sun.

He saw his até and iná, speaking quietly in Lakota. Jerome couldn't make out the words, but he knew they were talking about him, his mother concerned because he hadn't started speaking by age three. His father told her not to worry, that he was just observing the world in his own way.

He witnessed his grandparents, walking side by side, taking him to the boarding school he'd entered when he was ten years old. They told him not to be scared, that he'd be all right and would come home soon. His classmates were there, playing outside in the grass. Some were happy and some were troubled, missing their homes and families. He tried to comfort them from above, but they couldn't hear him.

Then he was in the Paha Sapa, the Black Hills where he'd had a vision during his hanblecheya. He'd fasted in the mountains for four days and nights before a deer spoke to him. He knew then that he was meant to be a healer like his father. He saw himself as a young man, learning the traditions, practicing them in secret, away from the reservation agent and police. Then he witnessed his time in prison after being arrested for conducting the ceremonies. He saw the men he lived with, their anger and their miseries, and those who came to him for help. The countless hours of prayer while in his cell, the guards eventually leaving him alone.

The visions began to speed up. Jerome relived the pipe ceremony that bound him to his wife, Ella, then the birth of his son, Wayne. His sorrow, decades later, when Ella made her journey. The year he spent alone, taking part in the Wanagi Yuhapi, keeping Ella's spirit close to him while he grieved. The joy when his grandson was born. The sadness, again, when Wayne walked on just four years after Rocky was born. Teaching Rocky the ceremonies and the culture. The silence in the evenings, alone with his memories.

Then there was darkness all around him, a dense obsidian space, and he entered an open plain where he could see shimmering colors, all the hues the world had ever known and shades never before seen. He heard sounds, echoes of the people he had loved, their lives and his life, the words they had spoken, the music of their voices, the hum of the land, the beginning of the tatuye topa, the four directions.

Jerome turned and looked back at the world of the living. Rocky, Pudge, Virgil, and all the others in his tiospaye. The people. He waited for a moment and watched them. The good and the bad, the young and the old. Those he had helped and those whom he had failed. He felt every wounded and lost spirit, those who still needed him. But it was time. He turned and began walking, the world of the living becoming fainter as he traveled.

He entered a familiar space, the meadow by the small house where he'd been born. He recognized the rolling hills off in the distance, the trees and the bushes, the wildflowers and the creek. And then he saw his people. His mother and father, grandmother and grandfather. His wife and his son. All of his relations gathering in the valley, just steps away. His journey was finished.

He raised his arms, and he went to them.

The memorial service for Jerome was being held at Sinte Gleska University's Wakinyan Wanbli multipurpose student center, one of the few spaces on the reservation suitable for a large gathering. The service would begin at noon with a feast of wohanpi, frybread, and coffee, followed by speeches and tributes from community members. Later there would be a vigil at the creek. Jerome's body would be wrapped in a ceremonial blanket and placed on a cedar scaffold outside. Family members would stay up all night, talking, singing, and praying.

Most importantly, there would be ceremonies to prepare Jerome's soul for his passage to the spirit world. Rocky would conduct the keeping of the soul ceremony, the Wanagi Yuhapi, even though he too was grieving. He'd serve as the soul keeper for the next year, mourning and honoring Jerome in the traditional way. He'd hold Jerome in his memory as well as conduct himself with dignity. No fighting, cursing, or socializing. In a year, Rocky would release the soul and return to normal life.

Marie was with me, and I'd persuaded Nathan to come along. He claimed he was tired, but I told him to drink some coffee and pay his respects. He'd made a phone call and agreed to join up with Shawna at the service. Marie had brought a basket of wasna, which she'd prepared with Tommy at the casino restaurant. Over the last several days, they'd labored with the bison meat, tallow, and berries using a food processor and dehydrator. Given the short time frame, they couldn't use the traditional method of preparation, which would have taken over a month.

We pulled into the parking lot at the Wakinyan Wanbli building, where there were already forty vehicles or more ahead of us. I found a space in the corner, and we made our way to the entrance. Inside, dozens of people were gathered near the back, where the food was. Marie headed off to drop off the wasna, and Nathan left in search of Shawna. Alone, I wandered over to the other end of the space, where several folding tables and a small podium with a microphone were set up. Jerome's medicine and pipe bags were displayed, along with about a dozen photos of him. I'd seen a few of them, but most were new to me. I stared at the photos of Jerome as a young man, then at the ones with his wife and family. Pictures of him by his house and a sweat lodge. Shots of him dressed up and looking serious. The final picture was him sitting on his porch, smoking a cigarette and looking perfectly content. That was how I'd remember him. I looked at the photos again, but then I had to move away.

More people were streaming inside, and I made my way over to the other side of the room. Jerome's people were camped at one table near the front. I saw Rocky, various cousins, nieces and nephews, and other folks I didn't recognize. At the next table, numerous tribal council members were chatting, along with our tribal president and local business leaders, a veritable who's who of the Rosebud reservation.

People were setting up the food tables for the meal, and I spotted Marie helping them. She caught my eye and gave me a smile. I saw Tommy across the room and went over to him.

"Hey, homes, how you doing?" He leaned in and gave me a big hug.

"Okay, all things considering," I said, and continued scanning the crowd. Mitch Gagnon was walking in, looking somehow somber and gleeful at the same time.

"Marie bring the wasna?"

"Yeah, she's back there."

"Goot, goot. That stuff was a bear to make. Gonna grab some chow myself after the elders eat. If there's any left! There be some wateca wars today, for sure."

I surveyed the room again. It seemed like the entire reservation was here, young and old, rich and poor, healthy and sick. I didn't know all of them, but they were all familiar to me. The oyate, my people. For now, they were chatting with each other, happy to be together and share a meal. The mourning would come later, although it had never stopped for me.

I noticed a group of men sitting off to the side, not speaking or eating. They were solemn, unlike everyone else.

"Hey, who are those guys?" I asked Tommy, pointing with my lips at the group.

"You don't know? Them's the other medicine men. The one closest to you is Leon Bellmore. He ain't from Rosebud—moved out here a year or two ago, I think. Guy with the cap on is Floyd Left Hand from Pine Ridge. I think him and Jerome was friends. Good dude—gave me some medicine a while back."

"Yeah, I think Jerome talked about Floyd."

"No shit? We should say hi."

Tommy led the way over to the men. As we approached, they all turned their heads and looked at us.

"Hey Floyd," Tommy said. "Remember me? You helped me out once."

The one named Floyd looked to be around eighty or ninety years old. He was dressed in a weathered blue flannel shirt, ancient brown corduroy pants, and a battered cap embossed with the words DEADWOOD SALOON. He looked at Tommy for a full five seconds without saying anything.

"Yes. I remember your face but not your name. You came to me because you were having problems with a woman. In the bedroom."

Tommy looked embarrassed, perhaps the only time I'd ever seen him that way.

"Uh, yeah, but you fixed me up! All good now, for real." He coughed, swallowed, then coughed again. "I'm Tommy, and this here's Virgil Wounded Horse. Virg was tight with Jerome."

Tommy shook the men's hands and spoke a few words with each of them, then it was my turn. I held out my hand to the man closest to me, the one who wasn't from our reservation. He smiled at me and shook it, using a powerful grip, not the usual soft Indian clasp. He looked to be around fifty, with short black hair and lighter skin. He was wearing jeans, a chambray shirt, and a faded black jacket.

"Sorry, I didn't catch your name," I said.

"Leon Bellmore. Who are you?"

"Virgil Wounded Horse."

"Oh, yeah. I heard about you."

"Really? Hope it was all good."

He chuckled. "You know how people talk. I don't pay no attention to bullshit."

Bullshit? I decided to let it go. "Tommy tells me you're new here."

"Not really. I'm from Cheyenne River but got tired of the crap up there. Thought I'd try it out here. You know, change of scenery. Thought you all could use another *wicasa wakan*."

*Holy man.* Jerome would never refer to himself that way.

"Did you know Jerome?" I asked.

"A little bit. He came out and talked to me a few times. Very sad, what happened to him. He was a good man."

"Yeah, he was. Never be another one like him."

"So I've heard!" He smiled again.

"Are you helping people out here now?"

"That's right," he said. "I run a sweat, a few ceremonies. Lend a hand if I can."

"Good to hear."

"Why don't you come out to my place? You can sweat if you'd like. Every Saturday night. Got a place off White River Road. We could talk about things."

"That might be nice," I said. "Thanks for the invitation."

Leon nodded and winked at me. I turned to the older medicine man, Floyd. I'd seen him before, but we'd never spoken.

"Nice to meet you, sir. I'm Virgil."

He looked me up and down. "Yes, I know. Jerome talked about you some," he said. "His name for you was Takini."

Survivor. Someone brought back to life.

I was quiet for a moment. "Oh, wow. Really glad you told me. Thank you."

He nodded, and I turned away, lost in my thoughts.

Tommy nudged me. "Virg, let's get you a soda, yeah? Take your mind off shit. Might even be a Shasta over there."

"Sounds good."

I glanced back at Floyd to say goodbye, but his eyes were closed.

We made our way over to the plastic coolers, where I had to settle for a Best Choice cola, the off-brand soda sold at Turtle Creek, our rez grocery store. It was all right but lacked the unique corn syrup bite of Shasta.

I sipped my drink, and then I saw Rocky, Jerome's grandson, step up to the podium. "All right, everyone, wana wota! Come grab a plate, elders first."

The elders worked their way through the serving line, followed by everyone else. I waited until everyone had eaten, then grabbed a plate and sat down next to Marie and Nathan. I chatted with Marie as I ate my stew and frybread.

"People must have really loved your wasna," I said to Marie. "The basket was empty."

She smiled and reached into her bag. "Ta-da! I saved you a piece. Nathan already had his."

I hugged her and ate the wasna, which was excellent. People were getting up and throwing the paper plates away and pouring themselves water and coffee. I started to get up for a cup myself, but Rocky began clinking an empty bottle with a bread knife to get people's attention.

"All right, everyone. Everybody? Hey, I want to say a few words, okay?"

Gradually, people quieted down and focused on Rocky.

"Thank you. Uh, I'm not no public speaker, so I just want to thank everyone for coming out today to honor my grandpa, who was a great man. He loved the oyate so much, and he tried to help everyone he could. He was a healer, but also a warrior, you know. He didn't make no big stink about stuff that was wrong, but he always fought to do good. That's how I'm gonna remember him—a man who believed in the pipe, cared about the people, and always did the right thing. His battles are over now, but we got to keep up the fight. I just, ah, I just miss him . . ."

He stopped speaking, and his cousin Bill patted his back and led him away. After a moment, Bill came back to the microphone and spoke.

"Folks, we're going to let anyone who wants to honor Jerome come up and speak. Tonight, the family will be gathering at Jerome's home to pray, so now's your chance. Lester, you want to go first?"

Lester Standing Elk, the Rosebud Sioux Tribe president, came up to the podium. "Jerome Iron Shell was a man who cared deeply for the oyate. I think probably everyone here has a story about Jerome. I'll tell you mine. It was a while back, when I was at the lowest point of my life. I made some bad decisions—we've all been there. I reached out to Jerome, and he got me on my feet again. I'm forever grateful for that. So I honor his memory, but of course he's not really gone. He's right here—outside in the wind and the rocks and the trees. Wopila, Jerome."

I heard people say "Aho" and some light clapping. At the table where the VIPs were seated, an older tribal councilman started to stand, but I saw Mitch Gagnon jump up. He scurried over to the podium so he could speak right after the tribal president. I glanced over at Marie, and she rolled her eyes.

"Lester, that was very moving," he said. "You always know the right thing to say. Friends, we've lost a great man, one of our true spiritual leaders and someone who was a great supporter and friend of mine."

This was utter horseshit. I knew for a fact that Jerome hadn't liked Mitch, even before he was elected to the tribal council. He hadn't trusted Mitch, a feeling that I shared.

"It's important that we use this sad occasion to reflect on where we want to go as a nation," Mitch continued. "As you know, I'm running for tribal council again, and I believe it's time to make some changes. Changes that will make our homeland safer and more prosperous."

Jesus Christ, was he really turning a memorial service into

a campaign event? I knew this guy was shameless, but this was outrageous. I glanced around the crowd to see if anyone else was getting angry.

"I'll share details on my plans another time. Today, we are here to honor a distinguished man. Of course, Spotted Tail—Sinte Gleska—was the great chief and leader of our tribe. But I'll submit that Jerome Iron Shield was perhaps one of the greatest spiritual leaders our nation has ever known! Please join me by applauding him!"

He began clapping enthusiastically, and the crowd joined in. Then people began standing up, giving Jerome—and Mitch—a standing ovation.

Marie stood up but didn't clap, then she turned and left the room. I didn't hesitate to follow her outside.

"Can you fucking believe that?" Marie said. I knew she was furious; she rarely dropped an F-bomb. "I am so angry. He used Jerome's death for a campaign speech!"

"What a jerk," I said. "Not the time or place. Unbelievable."

"And I can't believe people actually applauded! They should have stormed the stage and knocked him down."

"I hear you. I think everyone just got carried away by his words."

"Carried away? What, you think he's some great orator? He's a half-wit loudmouth." She glared at me.

"Take it easy; I'm on your side. I'm saying that people were responding to Jerome, not anything Mitch said."

She sighed. "I don't think I can go back in there. Did everyone see me walk out?"

I shook my head. "Don't think so. It was pretty chaotic."

"Well, I still don't want to go back inside. You mind if I take off?"

"No, I'll go with you. Nathan can catch a ride with his friends."

I moved closer and embraced her. She resisted for a second, then fell into my arms and started sobbing quietly.

"I-I just can't do anything right. . . . No matter what I do, it always goes wrong."

"Hey," I said. "You are amazing and brilliant and beautiful, and everyone knows how devoted you are to our people. Why don't you and I go home and just be together—no kids, no friends. What do you say?"

Her breathing slowed down, and she looked me in the eyes. "Yes, absolutely. Let's go, now."

The weeks after Jerome's death were some of the hardest in my life, as I cycled nonstop between denial, grief, and anger. Even worse, I was plagued by the fear that, in my failure to keep my temper when confronted by the Pine Ridge gang, I might have been to blame. I didn't know if they were the ones who had murdered Jerome, but I planned to find out. I had to stay peaceful while the preparations for Jerome's spirit journey were being made, so I bided my time. I strongly craved nicotine, booze—anything that would dull my emotions. It was hard, but I stayed clean.

A few days after the memorial service, Rocky conducted the keeping of the soul ceremony, the Wanagi Yuhapi. After a year of restrained behavior, Rocky would release the soul and return to normal life. For now, he had retreated to his house in Norris, where he'd have to refrain from any thoughts of vengeance.

But I was under no such restriction.

A week after the service, I gathered with Marie, Nathan, and Shawna at our house. Marie had insisted that we have dinner together, and Nathan reluctantly agreed. He and Shawna—whose hair was now bright purple—liked to go in the evenings to the new skate park, where they'd meet with their friends, listen to music, and complain about teachers and school.

Marie made deer soup with wild onions, dried corn, and turnips, Nathan's favorite. We all sat down at our little kitchen table, and I poured water into our clear plastic tumblers, which I'd owned forever, having bought them at the dollar store years ago. Marie hated those cups—they reminded her of drinking glasses from a crappy all-you-can-eat buffet, she said—but I loved them, as they were practically indestructible. Our little dog Ava sauntered over, hoping for some scraps.

"I've got salad to start," Marie said. "Who wants some?"

"I do, please." Shawna passed her plate to Marie.

"What is it?" asked Nathan.

"Curly dock—picked it down by the creek today. I got some nice young leaves and stir-fried them to get rid of the bitterness. They taste good by themselves, but I made some vinaigrette if anybody wants it."

"We got any ranch?" Nathan asked.

Marie winced. "No, this is much better and healthier. It's olive oil and vinegar, with a little wild garlic and some honey I got from the youth lodge."

One of the local organizations had started teaching beekeeping, and they sold jars of the stuff. I liked it, and put it on my bread every morning.

"Try it," Marie said, and brought a small bowl of the vinaigrette to the table.

We each ladled some onto our salads, although Nathan took only a tiny amount. I stirred the salad and the dressing together and began to take a bite.

"Wait!" Marie said. "I have something to say before we eat."

Everyone put their forks down.

"Just a few words, okay?" She glanced around the table, then looked right at me. "We offer this food as thanks for the honor of knowing Jerome, and for his journey to the spirit world. Jerome was a good man—no, a great man! He believed in our culture. He knew that our ceremonies and our prayers would protect the people. Waohola and woksape, wisdom and respect, not violence and hostility—that was how he lived his life."

After a pause, Shawna spoke. "That was really beautiful, Marie. Thank you for sharing, and for cooking this meal."

"You're welcome," Marie said. "Everyone go ahead and start, please. I'll get some bowls for the soup."

The salad was excellent; the vinaigrette added a tanginess to the slightly sour taste of the leaves. The deer soup had an excellent flavor, savory and salty with hints of a spice I couldn't identify. I told Marie the soup was fantastic and asked her what herbs she'd used. She beamed.

"You can taste them? That's great. I added a little oregano, some Worcestershire, and a splash of red wine. Those aren't Indigenous, but I couldn't resist. They really add to the flavor, and the alcohol cooks out, Virgil."

Although Marie no longer worked at our fancy casino restaurant, she still loved to cook when she had the time. I'd learned quite a bit from her over the last year, although I was still a novice in the kitchen. I devoured the rest of my food and noticed that Shawna—who didn't eat much meat—was slipping pieces of deer to Ava, who'd stationed herself right below her.

Shawna caught me watching and gave me a half-smile. "The soup is amazing, Marie!" she said. "I want to get the recipe for my mom."

"No recipe. I just use what I have on hand. But I can show you how to make it next time."

Shawna smiled. "I'd like that! I can help, too. You know, chopping or slicing or whatever."

"That would be nice." Marie got up and brought the water pitcher to the table. "So, what are you doing this summer, Shawna?"

"Just the usual. Probably work a little at the Boys and Girls Club. They always need help with the kids."

"I did that myself, a long time ago," Marie said. "They're a good group."

"They're starting a lot of new programs this year. Lakota language, baseball, there's even a cooking club. Lots of stuff."

"Really?" Marie said. "That's good to hear."

Nathan cleared his throat and glanced at Shawna. "You still planning on that other thing? Out in New Hampford or whatever?"

Shawna looked exasperated. "That's not the name, and you know it. And I told you I'm just thinking it over."

"What's out there?" I asked.

Nathan chimed in. "Shawna's planning to leave me and—"

"I am not! This is just a visit. We've talked about this."

Marie squinted at me, puzzled. I shook my head a little to signal that I didn't know what the kids were talking about. I looked over at Nathan, who was staring down at his plate.

"It's no big deal," Shawna said, "just a visit to a college. It's called the Indigenous Fly-In Program at Dartmouth College. Which is in *New Hampshire*," she emphasized, looking at Nathan. "It's for Native high school students to learn about the school. They pay for you to go out there and everything. Meals, stay at a dorm, meet professors. I'm thinking about it. It might be cool to visit before the whole college application thing starts."

"My sister went to Dartmouth," Marie said. "I could have you talk to her about the college. I'm sure she'd be happy to if I asked her."

I wasn't so sure about that. Marie and her sister Julie hadn't been on good terms since their father's death. Apparently, Julie had blamed Marie, even though none of it was really her fault. I suspected that Ann, their mother, had fed some lies about the extent of Ben's wrongdoing on the reservation to Julie, although I had no proof of that.

"That would be excellent!" Shawna said. "I mean, graduation is still a ways off, so I have time to think about this stuff. You know, I've never even met anyone who went to college out of state. Maybe you should talk to her too, Nate."

"Why?" Nathan said. "I ain't going to college."

"Hold on," I said. "I thought you were going to go to Sinte for a few years."

Sinte Gleska University was our local tribal college, located just a few miles from our house. The tuition was very affordable, so students could attend without going into debt. Nathan had told me he wanted to take general classes there after high school, and he'd decide later what he wanted to do with his life. This sounded like a good idea, and I had a little cash hidden that I'd use to help pay for it.

"No point. Don't need to waste my time."

"Okay," I said. "So, what's the plan? If you don't have time to waste."

Nathan was silent. I looked over at Shawna, who wouldn't meet my eyes. I waited for someone to say something.

"You might as well tell him," Shawna said.

I looked straight at Nathan. "Let's have it."

"Okay. So, I been thinkin' that I want to, you know, go after people. Like you. Be an enforcer or whatever you call it. Put the hurt on people."

Marie and I both started talking at once. We glared at each other, and I motioned for her to go ahead.

"That is completely unacceptable!" she said. "Beating people up is not a career! And it's not in the Lakota tradition."

"He does it," Nathan said, and pointed his chin at me.

"He used to!" Marie said. "But that's a completely different thing. You have a chance to do something with your life, honor your mother and your ancestors. We need to talk about—"

"There's nothing to talk about," I said. "You are going to college, and that's it. You don't just decide to become an enforcer. It's not like becoming a plumber or whatever. People have to come to you, and you're not exactly a brawler."

Nathan smirked. "There's a lot you don't know. Kids at school don't mess with me since I got jacked."

I didn't understand what he meant at first. *Jacked* used to mean getting kidnapped or being high, but then I realized he meant what we used to call "buff"—muscular and strong. I'd noticed that he'd been going to the gym religiously, and I'd seen giant cans of protein powder and creatine around the house. He'd grown about two inches in height over the last year and put on at least twenty pounds in muscle.

"Don't matter if you're jacked or ripped or whatever. You gotta be a fighter to do what I used to do, and that ain't you. You're going to Sinte or somewhere else and learn stuff. That's final."

Shawna shook her head. "Nate, I told you this was a dumb idea."

"What's dumb about it? I don't want to deal cards at the casino or pump gas. I whoop some clown's ass and get a little paper, that's a win-win, bro."

I was stunned that Nathan thought being a vigilante was a valid career choice. He had no idea what it was like to get slammed in the head and feel your grasp on life loosening. It wasn't like in the movies, where the hero shakes off a punch and goes on with his day. After some of my fights, I'd be dazed and spitting up blood and could barely use my hands for days. That wasn't the path I wanted for him.

"Nathan, you know I respect you," I said. "But you aren't cut out for this, okay? You take on some guy who knows how to throw a punch, you'll end up brain-damaged or worse. This is a hard no."

"I can handle myself," he said. "I'll knock out any joker who wants to throw down. You hear me?"

I laughed. To my knowledge, Nathan had never been in a fight, and now he was boasting like he was an MMA champion. "Buddy, give it a rest. You want to do a little sparring, I'll show you some moves. But you are going to college, and that's final."

"Yo, it's my life! I'm not a kid anymore." He stood up and walked out of the house without saying goodbye. Shawna looked at us apologetically and followed him out.

"Did you know about this?" I asked Marie.

She shook her head. "First I've heard. I know he's been working out and drinking protein shakes lately. Did you say anything to him?"

"What do you mean?"

"I don't know. Maybe telling him that being a vigilante is a good way to make money?"

This pissed me off. I'd never done anything but encourage Nathan to get a real job, and Marie knew that. "Of course not! You think I want him to go out there and get his ass beat? He needs to go to school and learn stuff. Economics, engineering, I don't care."

Marie put her hand on my shoulder. "Take it easy. I'm just trying to figure out what's going on. You think this has something to do with Shawna?"

"How? You think she's encouraging him to do this?"

"No," she said. "I mean, the fact that they're fighting a lot."

This was news to me. "They are?"

Marie raised her eyebrows. "Jeez, you haven't noticed? Maybe because you haven't been around much lately."

Again, I didn't know what she was talking about. "What? I barely left the house this week."

"Yeah, but you haven't really been here. You know, mentally. You've been pacing around, not talking to anybody. I understand you're sad about Jerome. I am, too."

Was this true? Had I been preoccupied? I guess I had, but I hadn't realized it was a problem. "Look, I'm sorry if I've been ignoring you and Nathan. It's just that—"

"No need to apologize. Really. But I do want to talk to you about Jerome."

"What is there to say? He's gone."

She turned her chair and faced me. "Yes, he's gone. It's a tragedy for this reservation. The oyate. I know you're angry over his murder. Enraged. You're so upset, you're practically radioactive. And I don't blame you. But we have to talk about what happens next."

"What happens next is that we move on. What else can we do?"

"Come on, Virgil. You and I both know that you want to go after the person who did it. I heard you talking to Tommy on the phone the other night."

"You were listening? That's not cool."

"I didn't mean to, but you were practically shouting. But I didn't need to hear your call—I know you. Do you deny that you want to go after those guys from Pine Ridge?"

There was no point in hiding it. Confronting the gang was pretty much all I could think about. "Yeah, I do want to find out if they had something to do with it. And if they did, I guess I'll—"

"You guess? Quit bullshitting me. If they did it, you'll probably end up killing them. And then what? You end up in federal prison, or maybe some other Pine Ridge gangbanger comes after you."

"You know I can hold my own."

"That's not the point." She got up, took out her special tea,

Sparrow's Tears, and turned on her electric teakettle. This was a signal that things were serious. "If you take revenge on them, what makes you think they'll just stop? You can't take them all out. Maybe they keep coming after you. Or they go after Nathan— or me."

"I don't think so," I said, shaking my head. "They have a beef with me, not you guys."

She measured some tea leaves and put them into the tea strainer, which looked like a forceps clutching a tiny metal globe. "Jerome is Pudge's uncle, right? Seems to me that those jerks are willing to go after family members."

She had a point. "Okay, I see what you're saying. But those assholes don't know we're together. They have no idea who you are."

"Come on, Virgil. You're pretty well known around here. Not to mention, Mitch Gagnon has been screaming about you in order to hurt me in the election."

"Is that what this is about? You winning a seat on the tribal council?"

"Of course not. This is about ending the circle of violence. And about you making changes. You promised last year you'd stop fighting, do something else. Right?"

"I did what I said I'd do! I'm not taking jobs no more—I got that gig with Charley."

She got a cup out for herself. "You want some?"

I shook my head.

"Look, I'm proud of what you've done. I know serving papers for Charley isn't your dream job, but you stuck with it." She poured hot water into her cup. "But you got into that brawl with the gang and came home all bloody."

It wasn't my blood, but her point was taken.

"And your last job for Charley didn't go so well. You got into a fight there, too, right?"

I paused for a second and thought about how to respond. "Yeah, but it wasn't my fault. The guy came after me. I had no choice."

She poured boiling water into her cup, immersing the tea leaves. "Really? You couldn't have just walked away?"

I started to deny it but stopped. She was right. I could have gotten away from the situation somehow, but I didn't. I wanted to hit the guy. He was a scumbag who'd hurt his own kid, and I'd forced him into a brawl so I could show him what it felt like to get thumped.

"Okay, I admit it. It was a slip. Relapse, whatever."

"You're entitled to make mistakes. Forgiveness, waunsila, that's part of our teachings. But I'm worried you're going back to your old ways. And you see the example you're setting for Nathan? Now he wants to be a thug."

This was a low blow. Marie knew how much I hated to be called that. "Is that how you see me?"

"No. Of course not. I'm just worried about him, and you." She removed the infuser from her cup and laid it on a saucer, then took a drink of the tea. "I don't want him getting into that life, and I want you to honor your promise. Doing the right thing. That's what you said, isn't it? 'I'll do what's right, no matter how hard it is.'"

I'd made that promise to the Creator a year ago when I was laid out on the floor of an abandoned slaughterhouse, wounded and waiting to die, and I'd repeated it to Marie in the hospital. The problem was that I didn't know what was right anymore. Was it justice to let Jerome's killers get off scot-free, or to let my loved ones get injured? These were the sort of questions I used to discuss with Jerome.

"Yeah, I did say that, and I'm trying to keep my word. But it's complicated. You have to trust me."

She took another sip of the tea. "I do trust you. But I need to know that you'll keep your promise."

I stared at her teacup, which was embossed with flying butterflies on the cup and saucer. "It's not that simple. I don't know if it was them Pine Ridge guys, but I got to find out. Like you said, they could come after Nathan or maybe you. I can't let that happen. That's not the promise I made."

She looked out the window into the distance. "Okay. I understand what you're saying. I appreciate you wanting to protect us. But here's what I'm asking. Go find who did it. But don't do this on your own. Work with Rose Charging Cloud if you can. Show Nathan what it means to be Lakota."

She finished the last of her tea. "Can you do that?"

The conversation with Marie hit me hard. I felt like I'd failed her, Nathan, and the entire community. Every week, someone who'd been screwed over by the government asked me to get justice for them, but I'd turned them all down. The people sometimes got mad and didn't believe I'd quit. To them, I was a bad guy or lazy or just an asshole. Yet I'd also let Marie down by getting into some fights again. Even worse, I'd learned that Nathan wanted to follow in my footsteps as an enforcer and skip going to college. My sister Sybil—Nathan's deceased mother— had especially valued education, and it seemed Nate was turning away from that. On top of everything, the Pine Ridge gang might be coming after us if I didn't do something.

All of these issues weighed on me, and it felt like I was carrying the Black Hills themselves on my back. I'd tossed and turned all night, barely able to sleep and waking before dawn, reeling and unsteady. I brewed some strong coffee and tried to clear my mind. After a few cups, I realized what I should do.

Since I bought the truck from Charley, I hadn't ridden my beloved old Kawasaki motorcycle. I hadn't even winterized it but simply stuck it outside, behind my little house. That was stupid, but there'd been other things on my mind.

I wheeled the bike out to the street, then went inside and grabbed my tool kit and a rag. I cleaned the spark plugs with some fine-grained sandpaper, then took a look inside the fuel tank with a flashlight. I didn't see any rust, so I decided to leave the gas in the tank and fuel up as soon as I could. After checking the fluids, I reconnected the battery, hoping there was enough charge left for it to start. Then I rotated the wheels and checked the brakes. I didn't hear any squealing, and the brake fluid looked okay. The tires were low, but I'd fill them up at the gas station. Finally I wiped down the bike, removing months of dirt and grime.

There was a lot more maintenance that needed to be done, but I decided to roll the dice and hope the bike was safe to ride. To my surprise, it started on the second try. I let it run for a few minutes, then cautiously pulled out onto the road. I rode slowly for the first few miles and stopped at the gas station in town, where I drained the old fuel, filled the tank up with fresh gas, and pumped up the tires. I rewarded myself with a Reese's Peanut Butter Cup from the candy rack and ate it while I gave the bike a final check, then headed west on Highway 18.

It felt good to be on my sled again. The engine ran smoothly without knocking, which was a relief. I focused on the road, not thinking about anything, simply enjoying the ride. I rode past the Keya Wakpala community garden, the Turtle Creek grocery, and the propane company, and then the road opened up. I rolled the throttle back, going full out, weaving around cars, trucks, and SUVs. I smelled the trees, the grass, and the wildflowers, each scent vivid and distinct. I saw every animal and bird, and I felt the weight and heft of the air. The roar of the wind and the hum of the tires created songs and symphonies in my head as I hurtled across the prairie. It felt like I was flying over the surface of the earth, barely touching the pavement. All of my anxieties and worries dissolved as I entered a Zen-like state, the g-forces the only thing tethering me to the ground.

I rode for over an hour, feeling better and lighter with each mile I traveled. I crossed over to the Pine Ridge reservation on Highway 18 and then turned right on County Road 7, going north. I stopped at a gas station for some beef jerky and fuel and decided to keep going as long as I could.

An hour later, the stratified rock formations of the Badlands appeared in the distance. In Lakota, this enormous area was known as Mako Sica. Native people had been traveling through the eroded buttes and pinnacles for thousands of years. I couldn't remember the last time I'd been in the southern area, which was comanaged by the Oglala Lakota Nation along with the National Park Service. I slowed down to enjoy the eerie beauty of the formations, then suddenly realized exactly where I was.

Just down the road was Oonakizin, known in English as the Stronghold Table. This was a sacred place for the Lakota people, one that I'd visited with my family when I was just a small child. It was at Oonakizin that the last Ghost Dance had taken place. The Ghost Dance—also known as the Spirit Dance—was the ceremony established by the Indigenous prophet Wovoka, who'd had a vision in the late 1800s that the land would be returned to Native peoples if they danced nonstop in the way he proposed. The Lakota people were powerfully attracted to the Spirit Dance, especially the idea that all Europeans would be removed from North America.

Wovoka's vision of the return of all lands to the original owners had come at the lowest point for the Indigenous people in the United States. The US government had been successful in forcing everyone to the reservations, and then had proceeded to cut food rations by half. Natives were forbidden to leave the reservations; starvation and malnutrition were rampant, so it's no surprise that the Spirit Dance became popular almost immediately. The American authorities were threatened by the ceremony—they believed that it was a war dance and signaled the resumption of hostilities, and the US Army sent fully one-third of all of its troops to the plains in an attempt to put down this presumed uprising.

The final Ghost Dance took place on the Stronghold Table in 1890, just a mile from where I was standing. Some of the most devoted believers had gathered to dance, even as the army approached. The South Dakota Home Guard opened fire on men, women, and children, killing seventy-five and then tossing their bodies off the Table into the ravine. Later, the captain of the unit returned to the scene and plundered seven loads of clothing, ceremonial items, and even body parts—items displayed a few years after at the World's Columbian Exposition, along with the corpse of an Indigenous infant, which a billboard announced as a "Mummified Indian Papoose, the Greatest Curiosity Ever on Exhibition."

The Stronghold massacre didn't end the violence against the Lakota people. Just two weeks later, army troops detained Chief Big Foot's band at Wounded Knee and murdered hundreds of Native people, primarily women and children. The brutality shown by the American military at Wounded Knee shocked the Native world, and symbolized the end of the traditional Indian era.

But one more act of violence would take place at Oonakizin. A Sicangu man, Plenty Horses, was so outraged by the Wounded Knee massacre that he killed US Army Lieutenant Edward Casey in revenge, just one week after the tragedy. Plenty Horses never denied the murder, instead arguing that the lieutenant had come to their camp and threatened to kill even more Natives. There was a state of war between the Indians and the whites, he maintained, and so the killing of Casey was justified; he—and other Indians— had the right to protect their lives from those who wished to cause them harm. Surprisingly, a federal court in Sioux Falls agreed with Plenty Horses, and entered a verdict of not guilty at his trial for murder.

I parked my bike by the side of the road and began walking up to Stronghold Table, keeping an eye out for snakes, my head buzzing with memories. I'd learned some of this history in school, but most of it from Jerome and Marie. When I was here as a kid, this was just a big rock hill to me, but now I understood the significance of what had taken place. Hazy images of our visit so long ago bubbled up in my thoughts, and I realized that our visit to Oonakizin was probably the last time we'd traveled together as a family. In the valley leading up to Oonakizin, I passed an ancient tipi ring, the stones placed in a circular pattern. Someone had camped there long ago, perhaps a lone traveler or family.

I thought about my mother, father, and sister, now all gone to the spirit world. The death of my sister Sybil had nearly broken me, but I'd had to keep it together for Nathan's sake. My mother had passed twenty years ago, and I'd lost my father when I was just ten. And now I had to face the loss of Jerome, who'd been my spiritual father for years.

I was panting heavily by the time I reached the top of the plateau. There was a good amount of grass and brush there, so I sat down and caught my breath. Far below, some mule deer grazed, and a prairie falcon circled in the sky. Except for the wildlife, the landscape was completely deserted, quiet and peaceful, and I felt like the last person on earth. My motorcycle ride had refreshed me and cleared my head. Perhaps now I could think more about the challenge Marie had made to me—that I seek justice for Jerome's death by working with Rose Charging Cloud, rather than on my own. Let law enforcement handle the investigation and focus on my own problems.

Few people on our rez completely trusted the criminal justice system, federal or tribal, for a lot of reasons. There'd been some protests against the tribal police, and the FBI agents—who had the sole authority to investigate felony crimes—weren't viewed any more favorably by the people. I had no idea if the feds had already started investigating Jerome's murder, or if they'd even arrived on the reservation yet.

But the possibility of the FBI taking over the case didn't change my dilemma. I had far better knowledge of the reservation than the FBI agents, who usually came to the rez and cycled out after a few years. Most of them had just learned how things worked on the rez when they were assigned somewhere else, and the new agent would have to start from scratch. I could talk to Natives who wouldn't speak to a government agent, and I wasn't bound by stuff like search warrants and Miranda warnings. If I got lucky, I might find the piece of shit who'd attacked a holy man, and perhaps I'd even be able to resist stomping the life out of him.

Suddenly exhausted after my long ride, I stretched out and closed my eyes. When I opened them, I was surprised to see a Native man standing over me. He was tall, with dark skin, medium-length black hair, and brown eyes. His ears were pierced with large shell earrings, and a tattered blanket was wrapped around his shoulders.

"Who are you?" I asked.

"You know who I am."

"Tasunka Ota."

"Very good. I thought you'd say Plenty Horses. Or His Horses Are Plentiful, which is a better translation."

My Lakota language skills were minimal at best, but somehow I'd known his name. "What are you doing here?" I asked.

"I wanted to talk to you."

"About what?"

"Jerome Iron Shell, of course. What you must do."

I sat up. "Yeah? And what is that, exactly?"

"You don't need me to tell you."

"Looks like I do. Because I'm getting dumped on by everyone. Marie, Rose, even Nathan. I can't catch a break."

"All right, fine. Get out there and do the right thing. It's not that hard. Quit moping around like some damn sad boy."

"Who are you, Casper the shit-talking ghost?" I said. "I got better advice from that robot at the Wall Drug. How about being a little more specific?"

"Jeez, figure it out. You don't need to go on a darn vision quest, okay? Just go get some justice. It's not difficult."

Now I was getting steamed. This punk-ass wanagi had the nerve to talk trash to me when he'd been dead for a hundred years. "All right, tell me about it, loudmouth. I know you murdered that army guy. Was that justice?"

He sat down with his legs curled beneath him. "I didn't murder Casey; I killed him. There's a difference, chum. We were at war with the Long Knives. Maybe we still are. They rounded us up into prison camps—the reservations, right?—and wouldn't let us leave. Damn mutton shunters. We couldn't hunt or fish; we had to eat the rotten food they gave us. Then the army killed Big Foot's band at Wounded Knee. Get it? When you're in a battle, you have the right to strike back. Put 'em in a pine overcoat."

"Not really sure, but I think you mean revenge," I said. "You're saying it's all right to get vengeance."

The ghost rolled his eyes. "You're not listening. State of war, get it? Active hostilities. It's not revenge if someone's trying to wipe out your people."

"So, you didn't feel the slightest bit of triumph when you killed the dude? Not even a little?"

"You got me there." He smiled, and a neon-blue butterfly landed on his shoulder. "Sure, I got some satisfaction from dispatching him. You know, I was only human. But that doesn't change what I'm saying to you, pal."

"Still not clear what you mean," I said. "Maybe drop the mystical Indian shit and tell me if I should go kick some ass or not."

He smiled and shook his head. "I'm just your guide, kemosabe. That's what Tonto said, right? The TV show? A little after my time."

"I'll say. You need to upgrade your lingo, homes. Ain't nobody said that in about fifty years. So, what's it gonna be? You give me some real advice, or am I just waking up with a bad headache?"

"I'd put my money on the headache. You want some help? Okay, here goes. You're trying to decide to walk the Lakota path or go out and lay down a whipping, right?"

"No shit," I said. "I promised to get on the Red Road and stay cool. I got to honor that."

"I take your point. But look at it this way. You know what wasicu means, right?"

"Uh, duh. A white person."

"Wrong answer! It means someone who takes the fat. Somebody who hoards food or money or whatever. Being greedy. Any scoundrel who takes more than they need is stealing from the community. You get it?"

"Not really. You're saying that white people are thieves?"

He stood up and started walking away, but turned and looked back at me.

"No. It's not that simple." He raised his hand. "When somebody—white or Indian—dishonors the community, they're declaring war. Understand? Now put that in your pipe and smoke it."

I rode back to the reservation in a daze, not sure if I'd been dreaming, hallucinating, or both. If it was a dream, it was the most vivid I'd ever had. As soon as I got some cell phone reception, I called Tommy; I wanted to tell him about my experience in the Badlands and get his thoughts. He was at the tribal college but told me to stop by.

Two hours later, I pulled into the Sinte Gleska University parking lot. Tommy was at the Lakota Studies Building on the Antelope Lake campus. The building was circular, with large girders extending beyond the roof and meeting in the middle to suggest a tipi. I opened the doors and entered the lobby. Tommy and Professor Cortings were sitting at the conference table inside the reception area. I'd hoped to talk with Tommy by himself, but there was nothing I could do.

"There he is!" Tommy said. "You rode all the way out to the Badlands, Virg? Dang."

"Yeah, I'm hurtin'. Haven't ridden that hard in a long time. Needed to empty my head." I noticed Rich was waiting for me to acknowledge him. "Hey, Professor."

He raised his hand in greeting. "Just Rich, please. Good to see you."

"Grab a chair and take a load off," Tommy said. "We just been talkin' about them old monster movies. Frankenstein, remember him?"

"Actually, Frankenstein was the scientist," Rich said. "He created the monster in the lab. Correct wording is 'Frankenstein's monster,' or just 'the monster.'"

Tommy shook his head. "Hold on, prof. If the scientist made the scary dude, then he's like his dad, right?"

"I guess so, although—"

"Then the monster has the same last name! He's Frankenstein Junior, am I right?"

Rich gave a half smile. "Not exactly. I suppose I could ask my friend at Santa Cruz, who does monster studies. We used to talk about this stuff."

"He gets monsters and studies them?" Tommy said. "He take 'em from a museum or what?"

Rich chuckled. "No, he writes academic papers about how monsters in film represent the cultural unease in our collective unconsciousness. The liminality of monsters and mythical beasts."

"I don't know what the fuck you just said." Tommy scratched his head. "Maybe in English, prof?"

"All right, sure. Start with the word itself. In Latin, the word *monster* means an evil omen, something that evokes fear. Makes sense, right? A monster is a creature with some deformity that scares us—a warning that something is morally wrong. So, monsters represent the metaphysical disorder in our society. Get it?"

Rich sat back in his chair, a look of satisfaction on his face.

"Prof," Tommy said, "you got some crazy shit in that head of yours. Yo, you want real talk?"

Rich raised his eyebrows. "I'm all ears."

"Aight, Dracula is an asshole for sure, and Frankenstein—okay, the monster, whatever—he's like some crazy drunk comin' out of the bar at two a.m. He all loco and shit, throwin' people around and stirring stuff up. The only one of them monsters that's any good is the werewolf. He got like, uh, a sense of right and wrong. He feels bad when he fuck someone up. The rest of 'em don't give a damn."

Rich grinned. "All right, you win. Dracula's a jerk and the Wolfman's a hero. I'll tell my friend out in Cali to write this up."

"Is this what you're studying at Sinte?" I asked Tommy, smiling. "Dracula and Frankenstein? Thought you were gonna major in business."

"Naw, changed my mind on that; switched over to Lakota studies after I met the prof here. His class was the bomb. First thing we read was this old law case. What was it, Rich? *Johnson v. McDonald's?*"

"Uh, that would be the case of *Johnson v. McIntosh*. US Supreme Court, 1823. You remember what the court said, Tommy?"

"Yeah, pretty much. That skins can't own land, right?"

"Not exactly," Rich said. "The court said Natives can't sell their tribal lands because—get this—they don't own them. John Marshall, shithead in chief, ruled that Natives have absolutely no title to their ancestral territory, even though we'd been living here thousands of years."

This didn't make sense. "I don't understand. If Indians don't own their land, who does?"

Rich gave a half smile. "Give you three guesses. Marshall stated that the US government owns the land because of the doctrine of discovery. That comes from the Catholic Church in the 1400s—it proclaimed that Christian colonizers automatically acquire any lands they discover if those lands are occupied by non-Christians."

"Hold up," I said. "Columbus and those guys didn't discover America, right? We were already here. Everybody knows that."

"Doesn't matter, according to the Supreme Court. Because

Indigenous people weren't Christians, they lost their rights the moment Columbus set foot in the Bahamas. This meant that the European powers who came later had established claims on the land, which eventually passed to the US government. Basically, Native territory was converted to trust lands, which means that the feds have sole authority over them."

I'd known that the government supervised our reservation, but I'd never heard of any of this. "That's messed up," I said. "Just plain wrong."

"Right?" Rich said. "The decision set the stage for the expansion of the good old U.S. of A. Since we didn't own our lands—even though we'd been there since the beginning of time—the government could force us to leave our homes and move to reservations. And that's exactly what occurred in the nineteenth century. So much for the idea of property rights, which only exist for white people, apparently. Game over, boys and girls."

"See what I'm sayin'!" Tommy said. "The prof knows his shit."

Rich waved him off and stood up. "I've been a bad host. Virgil, can I get you some water? I might be able to scare up some instant coffee or a soda."

"Some water would be great, thanks."

I looked at my phone. No calls or messages.

Rich returned to the conference room with three bottles of water. "Virgil, sorry to hear about Jerome. How are you holding up?"

"All right, I guess. Still hard to understand how it happened."

"The police have any leads?" he asked.

"Haven't heard anything," I said. "But nobody tells me nothing. Tommy, you got any news?"

"Naw," he said. "Only thing I heard was that the FBI ain't taken the case yet. Typical." He yawned. "My money's on the family mad at Jerome 'cause he couldn't cure their dad. Told you about them before. The Brown Bulls. The son been mouthin' off for a while."

"Hold on," Rich said. "If this person could be a suspect, why don't you call the tribal police?"

Tommy and I looked at each other. I motioned for him to go ahead and explain. "Well, prof," he said, "our police chief ain't exactly a fan of me or Virgil. I got picked up a few years ago, and she called me a born loser. Joke's on her, right? Cause *The Born Losers* was Billy Jack's first movie!"

Tommy was obsessed with the 1970s Billy Jack movies, which featured a Native guy who kicked the crap out of racists in a small town.

"And Virgil here," he went on. "Well, that's a whole other thing. Rose hates on him 'cause he fix shit the police won't touch. She always tryin' to shut Virg down."

Rich raised his eyebrows. "Sounds like a piece of work. But is she a good cop?"

I decided to jump in. "Tommy's being a little harsh. I don't think she hates me; she's just used to being the boss. And she's a decent cop—that's my opinion, anyway."

Tommy looked skeptical but kept quiet.

"Maybe I'll get a chance to talk with her some time," Rich said, and turned his head to me. "Virgil, what about that Land Project thing? Tommy told me that Jerome was involved with it."

"Sort of. He was their spiritual leader, I guess, given that he'd actually been a student there. He never talked much about the place."

Rich looked interested. "These Rapid City people, they want to tear down the old boarding school, right?"

"Yep. And build a shopping mall and apartment complex. But I guess the Land Project found some records of dead children. Kids who died at the school and they just dumped them in the ground, no headstones or nothing. They're using radar to find where the bodies are buried."

Rich shook his head. "I read about that. Pretty terrible."

"I found out my auntie might be one of them," I said. "I went out there and looked around."

Tommy touched his chest with his hand. "Dang. That's really sad. Any chance you might find her?"

"Yeah, I think so. I met this woman named Val who's with the Land Project group. She said she'd try and help. She's really involved with the whole thing."

Rich got up and threw his empty water bottle in the recycling bin. "Interesting. Is the discovery of the buried children impacting the project?"

"I don't know," I said. "There's a lot of stuff going on there. Not only the dead kids, but there was a fire at one of the construction sites a few weeks ago."

"Fire?" Rich said. "A bad one?"

"Not sure. Val says they're moving forward with the construction, fire or not."

"Is it an arson situation?" Rich asked. "You know, sabotage by the protesters?"

"You know as much as I do. Val didn't say anything about arson, but who knows?"

Rich raised his eyebrows. "Could be some good old-fashioned monkeywrenching. Decommissioning, ecoterrorism, whatever they're calling it these days."

"The only thing Val said is that her group is planning a big protest at the site. They want to have a giant Ghost Dance there, get the media involved. But maybe they canceled that now, you know, because Jerome . . ."

"We get it, homes," Tommy said quietly. "Maybe somebody else can step in."

"Yeah," Rich said. "Keep us in the loop, maybe we can help."

I flashed a little peace sign with my hand, thinking it might be familiar to Rich.

"I'll send some of my students there. Hell, I'll run up myself and join in. Be like the good old days." Rich looked off into the distance, no doubt lost in his memories of demonstrations and protests in the past. I wondered what I'd remember when I was his age. Times with Nathan and Marie, or something darker?

"I got to run, guys," Rich said. "There's a pile of exams on my desk that won't grade themselves." He stood up and gave an ironic salute. "Tommy, you're going to show up for class tomorrow, right?"

"Yes, sir!" Tommy exclaimed. "Might do the reading, too."

Rick shook his head and walked away.

"What class are you taking?" I asked.

"American Indian Political Systems. It's some good shit. Not too much to read; Prof Rich mainly just talks." Tommy drank the last of his water. "You hungry, man? I know where they hide them power bars."

"No, I'm good."

Tommy went over to the reception area, where the departmental assistant held court on weekdays. He started opening and closing drawers until he found what he was looking for.

"Score! Check this out: Crunchy Peanut Butter! Walmart brand, nice." He opened the package and devoured it in two bites. "Listen, I been meaning to ask how you doin'. Been a little worried."

I nodded. "I'm all right. Trying to stay busy."

"Real talk?" he said. "I ran into Marie at that new coffee place—the drive-through? Over by the auto parts store?"

"I know the place." Last year, an enterprising teenager from the local high school raised some money and opened a little kiosk, which served espresso drinks, coffee, and sodas. I hadn't been by there yet, but Marie swore it was the best coffee on the reservation, maybe even the entire state.

"Had me a Red Bull slushie—dang, that's some rocket fuel! Anyway, Marie was there, so I yapped with her for a bit. She said that you was missin' Jerome bad."

I was surprised—even a little annoyed—that Marie was talking about me to others. "Yeah, I miss him. Don't you?"

"Course, man! Jerome was our tunkasila. But I know you and him was tight."

I nodded.

"The thing is, he ain't really gone, you know? He ain't here no more, but you still got his words, all he taught you. You feel me?"

"Sure, but it still feels strange. Like it's not real. I keep thinking I can drive over there and talk to him about stuff."

Tommy looked out the window. "For sure. I still think about my homeboy Carlos. But it gets better, yo."

Carlos was Tommy's cousin. They'd been inseparable growing up, but Carlos was killed in a car accident like so many here on the rez. My own sister had been killed by a drunk driver while coming home from school one night.

"Thanks, man," I said. "For what you said."

I looked over and saw that a few tears were rolling down Tommy's face. In all the years I'd known him, I'd never seen him cry.

"Hey, you all right?"

He wiped his face with the sleeve of his jacket and smiled ruefully. "Yeah, I'm cool. It just hit me all of a sudden. Sheeit, I ain't usually no weepy willie."

"It's all right," I said. "This is real life."

"Oh man," he said, "You know I miss Jerome, too. I used to purify at his place. Now I ain't got no place to sweat this stuff out."

"Why not go out to Floyd Left Hand's place? He and Jerome were friends, right?"

He shook his head. "Naw, Floyd ain't doing sweats no more. I think it got to be too much for him at his age."

"What about the new medicine man? The one from Cheyenne River? He said he was running a sweat out at his place."

"Leon?" he said. "No, don't think so. I ain't heard about none of our people going out there. I think his sweat's for out-of-towners."

"You mean white people?"

"That's what I'm hearing. But hey, none of my business, right? He wouldn't be the first one to grab some cash from the wasicus for a little enlightenment, you know."

"Interesting," I said.

He took another pass with his sleeve over his face. "So what you gonna do?"

"What do you mean? About—"

"The killer, man! Guy who offed Jerome. You going after him?"

"How can I? Don't have any clue who did it."

He raised his eyebrows. "You'll figure it out. I got faith in you."

If Tommy had faith in me, then he was the last one.

awoke the next morning to find Marie sitting at our kitchen table, drinking coffee and looking at her phone. I wondered if she was still pissed off at me.

"Hey there," I said. "Where were you last night? I passed out around nine; didn't hear you come in."

She smiled, which was a relief. "Oh, I stayed at my parents' place, came back early this morning. I needed to pick up some clothes, so it was easier to crash there."

This was a bit surprising, as she rarely slept at her old house. She'd told me that there were too many ghosts inside. I poured myself a cup and sat down.

"Everything all right?" I worried about somebody breaking in at her parents' place, given that everyone on the rez knew it was empty now.

"It was fine, except that I couldn't find the shirt I was looking for. How about you—you have a good ride?"

"Yeah, I rode all the way out to the Black Hills. Needed to clear my head." I wasn't ready to tell her about what had happened at the Stronghold Table. "Then I stopped at Sinte and hung out with Tommy for a while. That new professor was there, too."

"Really? I heard the students like him. What's his name again?"

"Um, Rich. He seems all right. Knows a lot about Indian law and stuff."

"I read that. No one can figure out why he took a job at our little university."

"I think he got tired of teaching the students at his old school. And he said he wrote some article the bosses didn't like—something about his college being on stolen land."

She got up and placed her empty coffee cup in the sink. "That would make sense. Hey, are you coming to the candidate forum tonight?"

I'd forgotten about that. Marie had told me about it a few weeks ago. She'd be appearing with the other candidates running for tribal council, including her opponent, who had it in for me.

"You sure you want me to go?"

She paused. "I won't lie—it crossed my mind that it might be better for you to stay away. But I think we need to show Mitch we've got nothing to hide."

Mitch Gagnon had posted more statements on the local Facebook group, denouncing me for associating with bootleggers and for contributing to the violence on the rez. Naturally, I'd been pissed off about those posts, but Marie had made me promise to let it go.

"Okay, if you're sure."

"I am," she said, then leaned over and kissed me. "Just promise that you won't cause any trouble there."


WE WERE OUT OF white bread, milk, and cereal, the foods that Nathan ate in prodigious quantities. I had some time to kill before the debate, so I decided to drive to the grocery store. I took my keys and walked out to the truck. As I did that, Nathan pulled up in an old car. Somebody I didn't recognize was next to him. They both got out and walked over, and then it came to me.

"No way," I said. "Is that Jimmy?"

"You know it!" He grinned and shook my hand. "How are you, sir?"

"Not too bad." I hadn't seen Nathan's friend Jimmy Two Elk in a long time. He'd grown half a foot, put on forty pounds, and looked like a young Jim Thorpe. "Dang, you done grown up. I hear you're over at St. Francis now."

"Yeah, on the b-ball team—made varsity this year! And helping this guy out with his business." He mock-punched Nathan on the arm, and I saw Nate look at Jimmy and shake his head a few millimeters.

"Business? What?" I looked at Nathan, who avoided my gaze.

"It's, like, uh . . ." He trailed off, and I glanced over at Jimmy, who had the look of a white-tailed deer in the headlights.

"Jimmy, why don't you go run inside—the door's open. Give me a minute with Nathan."

Jimmy nodded and gratefully scurried away. I turned to Nathan. "All right, what's going on?"

He still wouldn't meet my eye. "Nothing. Just some stuff at school."

"What stuff?"

A pause. "I'm, like, protecting kids."

I waited for him to explain, but he kept silent. "You want to tell me more?"

"It's no big deal. I'm looking after some kids in the elementary school. Making sure no one bothers them."

"Who's bothering them? I don't understand."

"You know, like, bullies."

"You're stopping kids from getting bullied? How?"

He scratched his nose. "Uh, they come and ask me for help. So, I help them."

I didn't like where this was going. "Okay, you're helping schoolkids. That sounds nice. And what do you get out of it?"

This time he scratched the side of his head. "They, you know, pay me a little."

"Pay you! How much!"

"Like, five dollars a month."

I could feel my temper rising but kept my voice under control. "How long has this been going on?"

"A few months."

"And what do they get for their five bucks?"

"You know, I spread the word that nobody should mess with them."

"Uh-huh. What happens if some kid does mess with them?"

Another scratch. "I ain't had to do nothing, but I guess I'd scare the, uh, bully. Or Jimmy would."

"But none of you two have threatened anyone?"

He shook his head and grinned. "Like I said, not necessary. Everyone knows to leave our peeps alone."

Jesus Christ, my nephew was running a grade-school protection ring and was apparently proud of it.

"All right, here's the deal," I said. "You are not going to do this anymore. And that's final. People around here don't got cash to spare, and you know that."

He grimaced. "I ain't forcing no one! They come to me!"

I struggled to keep my composure. I knew he probably believed he was helping these children, but the thought of him taking money from them disturbed me. "Nate, little kids don't have enough, ah, maturity to make their own decisions. It's not cool."

He raised his hands up. "Shit, I wish I had somebody like me when I was in grade school! I would have paid two bills to stop them assholes from beatin' my ass!"

"These kids can go to their teacher or the—"

"Oh, come on! You know they won't do nothing! Bullies go

after the weak ones—always been that way, always will. Teachers can't stop shit."

He had a point, but the entire enterprise was a bad idea.

"Look, even if that's right, you'll get kicked out of school if you hurt some fifth grader. And you absolutely can't take no money. That's the part I don't like."

"Oh, really! How is this different from what you do?"

How was it different? It was true, I *had* made my living from clients who'd paid me to get justice when the police wouldn't do anything. But I'd only dealt with adults—people who'd had real harm done to them, not a schoolyard quarrel.

"Nathan, this is not the time or place. My work, whatever you think about it, don't involve no kids."

"Same damn thing, yo! Keeping people safe. If this is good enough for you, how come it's wrong for me?"

"It's completely different." I was struggling to keep my temper. Nathan was pushing all of my buttons, and I was already stressed out enough. "Look, you two are going to stop this shit right now. My work—it's not the same. I'm on the side of the good guys, okay?"

"Keep telling yourself that!" He stormed off and didn't look back.

I went and sat in my truck for a few minutes, trying to collect myself. Marie had warned me that Nathan was getting increasingly aggressive, but I hadn't wanted to believe it. I desperately wanted to speak with her about this, but that wasn't possible right now. In a weird way, I approved of Nathan's intentions—to protect younger kids from being harassed or bullied—but he shouldn't have taken any money from them. I considered going back inside and talking to him, but I knew that no good would come of that. I needed to let him have some space, which I could use as well.

When my blood pressure had returned to normal levels, I started the Ford up and began driving to the market. Memories of Nathan as a kid crowded into my head. Nathan as a baby with my sister Sybil; the look on his face when he moved into my house after her tragic death. The way he'd spread out on his bed with a library book, completely immersed in some fantasy saga or science fiction tale. The friends he'd bring over to our place if they were hungry and didn't have any food at home. His voice, which had deepened in puberty almost overnight. His love for Shawna, and the sweet way he spoke about her. I focused on these and began to calm down.

LATER THAT EVENING, I arrived at the Tribal Building for the event. It was being held in the council chambers, a large conference room seating about fifty people at four long tables positioned parallel to each wall. The table nearest the entrance was reserved for the tribal president, vice president, and secretary; they had padded leather chairs, not the cheap plastic seats strewn about the room for the other participants. Two flags—Rosebud Sioux Tribe and American—stood like sentries along each side of the leadership table. Large television sets were mounted on the east and west walls, and video cameras were positioned in the corners of the room. This event would be televised on YouTube and local cable television, broadcast on the rez radio station, and even streamed on Facebook.

I sat down directly across from a large, framed print of Sitting Bull, the words TWELVE LAKOTA VIRTUES displayed next to his face. The first virtue listed was "unsiiciyapi," translated in English as humility. I wondered if we'd see much of that tonight.

There were two candidates from each of the five districts speaking on this night, all of them seated in front of white placards displaying their names and communities. I glanced at the order posted on the whiteboard: Antelope, Bull Creek, He Dog, Ring Thunder, Soldier Creek. Marie and Mitch Gagnon were running in the Soldier Creek district, so they'd be speaking last. Marie was across the room from me, right next to Mitch, who was holding a conversation with someone in the audience. Marie was quiet and looked uncomfortable, but she smiled when she saw me.

We all waited while the camera operators set up their gear. After a few minutes, the tribal secretary introduced herself and spoke a little about the event. She said that each candidate would be given five minutes to speak, and there would be no questions from the audience. She closed by encouraging everyone to vote in the election, especially young people who had just turned eighteen. With that, she called on the first candidate, who was from the Antelope community. I realized I'd have to sit through at least forty minutes of speeches before I got to hear Marie. Resigning myself, I sat back in my chair.

The first couple of speeches were mildly interesting. The candidates spoke mainly about their history on the reservation, their family connections, and their desire to help the oyate. A few mentioned substantive issues, such as the need to improve medical care at the IHS hospital. Another talked about increasing revenues at the casino. The candidate from He Dog spoke heatedly about the need to improve the roads on the rez, many of which had become nearly impossible to drive or even walk on. Toward the end of the speeches, I was getting sleepy, but fought it off by pinching myself. Finally we came to the Two Strike candidates. Mitch was up first, by dint of his last name.

He stood up and cleared his throat. Unlike the other candidates, he was wearing a suit, capped off with a beaded medicine-wheel bolo tie.

"Good evening. It's nice to see everyone here tonight. I'm

Mitchell Gagnon, and I'm running for representative for the Soldier Creek community as the incumbent. Now, as many of you know, I had the honor of previously serving our tribe as treasurer." He looked around at the audience and smiled. "I was honored to be elected to the tribal council for the Two Strike community in the last election, and I hope to continue my service to our people."

He paused and took a drink of water. "I think everyone knows this, but let me remind you that I was born on the reservation, and I've lived here my whole life. The other thing I want to share is my background. Now, I don't have anything against multi-tribal people, but I think it's important to know that I'm one hundred percent Lakota—mainly Sicangu but a little Oglala in there too! Please forgive me for that."

The crowd laughed, and I saw Marie wince. This was a shot against her, as she was both Osage and Lakota. It was pretty nasty to go after her for something beyond her control.

"Now, I've heard some good things tonight." He gestured toward the other candidates. "Like Stanley, I fully agree that we need to prioritize our elders. We should recognize and take care of them always, not just on Tribal Elder Day. And I'm with Maxwell regarding transparency and accountability for the council. If I'm reelected, I'll lead the charge to provide written minutes of our sessions immediately. We represent the people, and they have the right to know what we say at our meetings."

He took a step forward and scanned the room, trying to make eye contact with each person. "But I want to talk about the issue that's most important to me. Economic development, which really means *jobs*. J-O-B-S, if you need me to spell it out. We all know that jobs are scarce here—last year, we hit eighty percent unemployed. Friends, that is outrageous! We need to create good jobs right now!" He made a fist and raised it in the air. "For too long, we've relied on the federal government to give us funding.

Money to open a tribal-owned grocery store, golf course, you name it. Why does the tribe have to own and operate every business? We need to open the gates to development! Let's stop being dependent on the federal government and become sovereign, independent."

He paused again. I saw that Marie was looking straight ahead with a blank face.

"So how do we do that? Well, we need to stimulate the business environment. Let's become a place where wasicu businesses *want* to come and hire our people! Instead of driving the white people away, let's bring their jobs and take their money! Why should they hire workers in China or India, when we've got people who want to work right here in South Dakota?" He stopped for a dramatic pause. "You might be thinking that this is a tall order. And you'd be right! It's going to take bold action to create a business-friendly environment. And that means changing the culture."

He took a deep breath. "Tonight, I'm proud to propose a brand-new tribal law, which I call the Get Rid of the Criminals Act. This law will impose a mandatory five-year jail sentence for all drug dealers, bootleggers, violent criminals, and their enablers. It's time to lock up the troublemakers who hurt our citizens. We've got to go back to the old days when we didn't have brutal lawbreakers roaming the streets. No wasicu employer wants to deal with that."

He paused and lifted both hands. "The law will target all of the dealers, bootleggers, and vigilante thugs on our land. And to make this stick, their relatives will be held responsible for their crimes as well."

*Vigilante thug.* Mitch was threatening to jail me. And it sounded like he was also threatening Marie, the child of a pain-pill dealer.

"This is how our ancestors handled crooks and lowlifes, and it's time to bring it back. Once we put these parasites behind bars, we'll create new businesses and new jobs. Not to mention, it'll be safe to walk the streets again. I think we can all get behind that. And there are other components of this law that I'll be announcing later."

He put his hand over his heart. "Wopila. I truly mean it; thank you for listening tonight. I've got a lot more to talk about, but I'm out of time! My complete platform is coming soon, so keep your eyes open. Again, I'm Mitch Gagnon, and I'm asking for your support for tribal council rep."

I glanced over at Marie, who looked stunned. My mind was racing with a thousand different thoughts. Could he actually imprison Marie and me? I'd never been convicted of any serious crime, and Marie was the person who'd actually brought down her father's drug ring. Not to mention, there were dozens of violent gangbangers and drug dealers on our rez; did he intend to jail their families as well?

After a moment, Marie stood up and took the microphone from Mitch. Her long hair was braided, and she wore a modest blue blouse and colorful beaded earrings. Although she looked great, I could tell she was nervous.

"Hello everyone, I guess it's my turn. I'm Marie, and I'm running for tribal council representative for the Soldier Creek community against Mitch here. But I guess you all know who I am." She was quiet for a moment as she looked down at her notes. There was a peculiar look on her face, which I knew was usually a precursor to her bursting into tears. She held the mic but didn't say anything.

The audience was quiet, waiting for her to speak. Seconds passed in silence, which seemed like an eternity. She started to talk, then stopped. Then she began again.

"I had some words prepared, but I'm not going to use them. I just want to be honest, all right? No politics, just truth." She looked over at me. "My name—my name is Marie Short Bear.

My father was Ben Short Bear, and I loved him. He's gone now. I shot him, because he was about to murder my partner, Virgil Wounded Horse."

She closed her eyes for a second, like she was trying to block out the memories of that terrible night. "For the last year, I've tried to forgive myself. For shooting him, yes. For not knowing enough. For being stupid and trusting and naive. The night of the shooting, I found out he'd been selling pills—drugs—to our people. I had no idea, and I hate myself for not being smarter. Not being able to figure out what was going on. For that, I am very sorry."

A tear appeared on her cheek. "My father betrayed our trust. I've tried to understand why, but I don't think I ever will. Selling that poison—hurting families, kids, everyone, it's . . . unforgivable. Unforgivable."

She stared down for a moment, then looked up. "But I did love him. He was my father. My dad. I have so many memories, you know. Riding with him in his car. Watching cartoons together. Laughing at his dumb jokes. I miss him, every day. And I miss my mom, who won't speak to me, and I miss my friends who've turned away. But you know, I guess this is the price I have to pay."

She wiped her face. "I don't expect you to forgive my father. And I know some of you blame me. I accept that. But I'm asking for a chance to make things right. I can't go back and undo the damage he caused, but I can work to make things better around here. Yes, we have problems, but I believe in our culture, our values. The Lakota way means working together, not against each other. The oyate, our tiwahe, that's what matters."

She stopped for a moment. "I love it here, and I'm not going to hide anymore. No more secrets." She gazed around the room, then stood up straight. "My father was Ben Short Bear, and he did some bad things. My boyfriend is Virgil Wounded Horse. He's a good man who helps this community. And I'm Marie Short Bear. I've made mistakes in my life, but I promise that I will work as hard as I can to serve the people. I promise you that I will help to make our community stronger, the Lakota way. Thank you."

I glanced around the room. Some people had tears in their eyes; others looked angry. Mitch Gagnon looked furious. He caught me looking at him, and his expression changed to a false smile. I sat back and listened to the tribal secretary give some closing remarks.

When the event ended, a group of people came up to Marie and started asking her questions, so I decided to wait in the parking lot. After twenty minutes, she appeared, carrying her canvas briefcase and a notebook. I could tell from the way she walked that she was in bad shape.

"Do you want to go to the Depot?" she asked. "I need a drink. Badly."

Marie was not normally a drinker, but these were special circumstances.

"Sure, I'll meet you there."

The Depot was the area's only Indian bar, located in Valentine, Nebraska, ten miles from the reservation's border. I usually avoided the place, given that I didn't drink booze anymore, but it was clear that Marie needed to blow off some steam.

Within twenty minutes, we were there. The place was busy, but not too crowded. Someone I didn't know was playing the old Black Knight pinball machine, which only had one working flipper, so games tended to be short. I saw a few people I knew sitting at the bar. Harold Charging Eagle was talking to Sharlene, the bartender. A couple of guys from my high school were there, nursing their beers. I spotted the new medicine man, Leon Bellmore, and he motioned for me to join him.

"Hey there, Virgil," he said. "Still haven't seen you out at my place for a sweat. Looks like you need to be purified."

"Oh, right." I remembered that he'd invited me to his sweat lodge. "When do you hold it?"

"Most Saturday nights. Come early and we'll talk, before all the crazies get there."

"Crazies? What do you mean?"

He chuckled. "You know, the New Agers from the city looking for some wisdom. I get a ton of 'em."

Tommy had mentioned that Leon was probably taking advantage of white people looking for some Native spiritual guidance. I wanted no part of that.

"I better get back to my lady," I said, motioning toward Marie. "Good luck with everything."

"Okay, then," he said. "You take care. Stay safe."

He stuck out his hand, and I shook it, noticing again his very firm grip, different from Jerome's gentle handshake.

I joined Marie at the back of the bar, near the pool table. "You all right?" I asked. "That whole thing was pretty rough."

"I think so," she said. "I nearly lost it when it was my turn to speak. What an asshole Mitch is!"

"Agreed. What do you want to drink?"

"Something strong. A shot of vodka?"

"You sure? That stuff can go to your head."

"That's exactly what I need."

I made my way to the bar and returned with Marie's shot and a Shasta cola for myself. I handed the drink to her, and she downed it in one gulp, followed by a brief coughing fit. She grabbed my soda and had a big drink.

"God, I needed that," she said, after she recovered. "I feel human again. Starting to, anyway."

"Mitch's speech was crazy," I said. "Did you notice he used the words *vigilante thugs*? It sounds like he was threatening me."

"Yes, totally." She pointed with her lips at her cell phone. "I read a little while you were getting the drinks. This proposed law is completely unconstitutional! I've never heard of threatening to jail people if someone in their family commits a crime. I think it's just propaganda to get votes. I mean, the law would have to be enacted by the whole council, and I can't imagine they'd support it. Some of them have kids who've done real shady stuff."

"But you're saying it's possible? If the tribal council approves it."

"Well, yeah. I'm no lawyer, but I think it's something they could pass. If they—"

"Hold on," I said. "You're saying they have the authority to jail anyone they want? That ain't right."

"No, it's not right," she said, "but that's never stopped Mitch. We just have to hope that he's bluffing. But who know?"

"Yeah, I get it. Nothing we can do at this point." I had enough problems right now without worrying about Mitch Gagnon's plans.

My cell phone vibrated, and I glanced down at it. It was Pudge, who rarely called me. I excused myself to Marie and went outside.

"Virgil! Oh man, really glad you answered. Listen, we need to talk."

He sounded stressed out, not his usual chill self. "Sure, no problem," I said. "I'm actually at the Depot. You want to come down? I'll be here for a while—"

"I can't get there," he said. "It's my ride."

"What's up? You out of gas?"

"No, man. They fucked up my car."

"What?"

"Tires are slashed. All four of 'em."

"You sure they're slashed? Not just flat?"

He laughed, bitterly. "Yeah, I'm sure. Four punctures in the goddamn sidewalls."

"Damn. That's messed up. Who did it?"

Another sour chuckle. "Who do you think?"

The Pine Ridge gang. The idiots who wanted Pudge's business.

"Okay," I said. "How do you know it wasn't some stupid kid?"

I heard the sound of a bottle being opened. "They spray-painted '705' on my car door in big numbers."

The name of their gang. The 705. They'd gone after Pudge and declared war. And this meant that Pudge had been right—these dimwit gangbangers must have been the ones who'd murdered Jerome. I hadn't wanted to believe it, but it was now clear that these evil fucks were out for blood. I felt my anger rising through my spine.

Pudge continued. "Shit, Virgil, what am I supposed to do? I can't make my deliveries now."

Pudge was one of the few bootleggers who'd make home deliveries, which had contributed to his success. "Man, I'm sorry. You able to get some new tires?"

"Eventually. Maybe some retreads. No point in spending good money—they'll probably just slash 'em again."

"Uh, do you need some help? I can maybe give you a little money—"

"I don't want your cash. That's not why I'm calling."

I waited for him to say more.

"These guys—these *assholes*—been coming after me for a while. And it don't look like it's gonna stop."

He paused, and I heard him take a drink.

"Virgil, you got to help me. Hey, I don't want to, you know—" He stopped, and I could hear the sound of his labored breathing over the phone. It sounded like a busted muffler on a junk car.

"Look, I don't want to blame you or nothing, but that fight

with the gangbangers, that was bad. Real bad. I mean, you cut that one guy's face open. I'm not sayin' he didn't deserve it, but now they're coming after me. Us. I don't want to end up like my uncle. This shit has to end."

He stopped speaking, and there was silence on the line.

"Virgil, you got to do something."

The conversation with Pudge hit me hard. I didn't tell Marie any details about the call, as I didn't want to add to her burdens. It had already been a brutal evening for her, so I kept quiet at the Depot and just listened. She was still annoyed by Mitch Gagnon's grandstanding, and I let her vent. But inwardly, I was thinking about the 705 gang and how events had spun out of control.

I felt miserable, guilty, embarrassed. None of this was Pudge's fault. He'd been unfairly targeted by the Pine Ridge gang when he'd been minding his own business. I'd gone along to that meeting hoping to protect him, but it looked like I'd made things worse. He seemed to blame me, rather than the guys who'd bullied and threatened him, for the fight at Wisdom Corner. And hanging over the entire thing was the grim likelihood that the 705 guys were responsible for Jerome's death.

I didn't like it, but it was clear I had no choice in the matter. I had to find the Pine Ridge guys and get some answers.

The next day, I got up early and started planning my strategy. My goal was to find out which of the gang members had murdered Jerome. The big question, of course, was what to do after I found out who it was. The best option would be to incapacitate him and deliver the asshole to Chief Rose and the FBI. But I knew that this would be a difficult—maybe even impossible—

task. They'd have the advantage of numbers and their own turf. I had only my wits and my Glock.

As I gamed out the various strategies and scenarios, I kept coming back to the possibility that I could be forced to take out Jerome's killer. These guys weren't like the half-smart, half-drunk idiots I usually battled. The 705 gang were morons, but they'd shown themselves to be vicious morons—guys willing to murder an elderly holy man in cold blood. I had to assume they'd come after me the same way. Could I kill one—or more—of these assholes? That was a line I'd never crossed and never considered. In the end, the best I could do was to plan my counterattack as carefully as possible, and minimize the chances of having to use deadly force.

Ultimately, I decided that I'd try to find their leader—the one called Bear—and catch him alone, preferably where he lived. If that happened, I was confident I could persuade him to tell me which gangbanger had harmed Jerome. The problem was that I didn't have the guy's real name, or even the town he lived in. But there was one person who might know. I picked up my cell phone and punched in the number.

"The fuck are you doing up so early?" Tommy said. His voice sounded like a failing muffler on a rez car. "Shit, what is it, four a.m.?"

"Try eight o'clock. I thought you might be working today and getting ready for your shift."

He yawned. "I go in at two. Doin' prep work, then gettin' on the line."

"Shit," I said. "Sorry if I woke you. I can talk later—"

"No, it's cool. Hold up for a sec. Let me grab a Rockstar."

He'd become addicted lately to Rockstar Energy drinks, which he claimed tasted like traditional Lakota tea. I suspected the insane amount of caffeine in them had something to do with it.

"Yo, I'm back. Couldn't sleep well; think I had some bad Taco John's. That Super Hot Sauce done tore me up, if you know what I'm sayin'."

"Yeah, I get it. I'd lay off that stuff if I was you. Why don't you go to that taco stand out by Soldier Creek? Their stuff is better."

He sighed. "Yeah, I know. Thing is, I got a beef with the guy at the food truck. Last August, I told him his refried beans were soupy, and he got all bent out of shape."

"Really? That don't sound like a big insult."

"Yeah, right? I think that guy who owns it—his name Red Pipe or something—was pissed off at someone else. The lady in front of me told him he was disrespectful for advertising wet tacos."

"I don't understand—what's a wet taco?"

"Yo, it's a taco you dip in some soup. It's good shit! But this lady be goin' on and on, sayin' children shouldn't be reading that. Taco guy tells her to fuck off, then he goes off on me when I ask for more beans. I think he was, you know, prolapsing."

I paused for a second. "You mean, projecting?"

"That's it! He was projecting and taking out his anger on me. I just wanted more beans, man! So we got into it."

"Sorry to hear about your taco dramas. Tell you what—you help me out and I'll buy you ten cans of Old El Paso."

He snorted. "Now you talkin'! So, what's going on?"

"Well, I need to find a guy from Pine Ridge. One of the gang-bangers."

"From that brawl you had? With Pudge?"

"Yep, those assholes."

"What you gonna do? You plannin' to throw down?"

"Most likely, yeah."

I heard Tommy take a big gulp of his Rockstar. "You want me to ride along? You know I got your back, son."

I was touched by Tommy's willingness to come with me, but

I didn't need him to get involved. This was my mess and my responsibility. "Thanks, dude. Appreciate it, but I got this. I just need to find out where those guys are."

"If you say so. Who are we talkin' about here? They about forty gangs over there."

"The 705. You know them?"

"Yeah, I heard some. Split off from the Tres, I think. Mainly sell hooch, a little weed. They not the worst, but they got some boys."

"All right, cool. Their leader is a guy called Bear. Mato. You know where he lives?"

Another drink from his can of caffeine. "No clue, homes. Sorry. Never heard of him."

Shit. I'd been hoping that Tommy could give me some info, given his prolific knowledge of the Native players and hustlers in South Dakota.

"Damn. You sure?"

"Yeah. Only thing I heard is they do they thing at Big Bat's. You want to find this Bear, that's the place."

Big Bat's, of course. The gas station and convenience store that was at the center of life in Pine Ridge. It had been around for decades, the place to get fuel and oil, but also T-shirts, drinks, strong coffee, and a large assortment of fried foods. The place was named after Baptiste "Bat" Pourier, a French trader who'd lived among the Lakota in the 1800s and been friends with the great Oglala leader Red Cloud. According to legend, Big Bat had carried the body of Crazy Horse to the Sun Dance grounds after his murder. He later married a Lakota woman and spent the rest of his days on the reservation.

Poirier's descendants had named the gas station after him and spared no expense in creating a Lakota-style convenience store, with Native art on the walls and Lakota language used on the signs and labels. During the day, Big Bat's was an informal community center, a gathering place and village square. But for the outlaws of Pine Ridge, the action occurred just outside. Panhandlers would accost anyone who looked their way, and drug dealers and gangs would appear when the sun set. If the 705 gang had in fact cornered the bootlegging market on Pine Ridge, it made sense they'd sell their stuff there.

So it was settled. I'd go out to Big Bat's in Pine Ridge and see if I could smoke out Bear. If he wasn't at Big Bat's, I'd engage with whoever was there and persuade them to tell me what I needed to know. This was not the best plan, but it was my only option.

I decided to go out there that night.

The planning for the trip was fairly simple. I drove to the gas station and filled up my tank. While I was there, I bought a couple of energy drinks, some candy bars, and a banana. At home, I grabbed my handgun and some extra ammo, my Spyder knife, pepper spray, rope, zip ties, and a wooden bat. I put everything into a bag and then stashed it in my truck.

There was only one thing left to do. I sat in our little living room, brewed some coffee, and waited for Marie. She was out campaigning but returned in the early afternoon.

"Hey there," she said as she put away her purse and jacket. "Didn't expect to see you here."

"There's some coffee left," I said. "Enough for a cup or two."

"A little late for me," she said, and then sat down. "Is everything okay?" She'd sensed something in the air.

"Not really. You remember that phone call I got last night at the Depot?"

She nodded grimly. "Uh, I'm thinking I should brew some tea."

While she did that, I told her about the call from Pudge. The damage to his car, the graffiti on the vehicle. The threat to go after Pudge and his family, which included Jerome. My plan to find out who had committed the cowardly attack on our holy man. My intention to subdue the killer and bring him to Rose.

"Oh, come on, Virgil. What makes you think you'll be able to catch that guy, if you can even find him? Not to mention, nobody's going to admit to anything. This whole thing makes no sense."

She had a point. "Look, you're right that I might not find the guy or get any information at all. But I need to try."

She set her cup down, and tea splashed out on the table. "No, you don't! The only thing you need to do is to call Rose Charging Cloud and let her handle this."

"I thought about that. But what can Rose and the tribal cops do to those guys? They'll need a search warrant or whatever, and I don't think the Rosebud cops can do anything at Pine Ridge. I mean, it's a different nation."

She picked up the teacup, and I saw it was shaking. "Then you let the goddamn FBI get the warrant."

"I heard they haven't even taken the case yet. You know as well as I do that they're slow. Might not even take the case."

She sighed. "That's true, but there's still no reason for you to be the one who handles this. Why not Rocky, or one of Jerome's other grandkids?"

"Come on, Marie. You know that Rocky ain't no fighter. Plus, he's in mourning. I'm the only one who can do this. And it's the right thing, too. You know, Pudge blames me for all this, and he's not wrong."

Marie stood up. "No! None of this is your fault, and you can't carry that weight. The blame is one hundred percent on those jerks who tried to bully Pudge and then murdered Jerome."

She turned away from me, went over to the window, and looked outside. "Is there anything I can say to convince you to not do this?"

I saw there were tears running down her face. "Marie, I'm sorry, this is—"

"When are you leaving?"

"Right now," I said.

"Then come here."

She turned and embraced me. "I love you. Whatever happens, never forget that."

I felt her love and fear course through me like an electric current. I held her, this woman who had placed her life with mine, who'd stood by me when so many had not. This woman, whose strength and goodness I could never hope to match. We stayed there for a long time, neither one of us wanting to let go.

As much as I hated to leave, it was time. The weather was good, but I saw dark thunderclouds off in the distance. I turned on the engine, backed out of the driveway, then stopped and looked at the house for a moment, wondering when I'd return. Then I hit the gas and sped off to my destination.

I had a long drive ahead of me, so I turned on the rez radio station and listened to the DJ spin some old country and rock music played by Natives. Buddy Red Bow, the Wingate Valley Boys, Jesse Ed Davis, John Trudell. I was a heavy metal guy, but this was music that calmed my spirit and helped me center myself.

I soon found myself near the Pine Ridge reservation and forced myself to focus on the road. Highway 18 turned into Main Street in the village of Pine Ridge, the largest town on their reservation. I passed their grocery store, an Ace Hardware, and a Subway shop. There was a parking spot on the street a block down from Big Bat's, so I pulled in and looked around. It was still light out, so I had a good view of the area. There were a few people walking about, some teenagers on bikes, and a couple of panhandlers. No sign of any bootleggers, dealers, or gang members. I locked my truck and walked over to Big Bat's.

It was a few years since I'd been there, but nothing much had changed. The standard coolers full of drinks, racks of candy and snacks, jugs of windshield fluid and cans of motor oil, a wall of T-shirts behind the cash registers. There was a food counter and a dozen tables and booths, currently occupied by some elders drinking coffee. It could have been any convenience store in America, except for the mounted bison head on the wall, the paintings and murals depicting Lakota legends on the walls, and a bronze plaque on the floor that proclaimed, I SEEK STRENGTH, NOT TO BE GREATER THAN MY BROTHER BUT TO FIGHT MY GREATEST ENEMY—MYSELF.

I ordered a coffee and sat down at one of the tables by a window, so I could keep an eye on the people outside. I sipped my drink and watched the sun set. Scores of people came inside and bought sodas, Starburst candy, Doritos, ramen noodles, chicken sandwiches, Indian tacos, chewing gum, toilet paper, diapers, drain cleaner. Cigarettes, too—each pack sold spurring a brief moment of longing. As it grew darker, the activity on the street outside steadily increased. I kept a close eye on the people beginning to mill in the parking lot. A few cars and trucks parked across the street, but no one came in. Small clusters of people mingled for a few minutes, then left. Groups of teenagers passed by, sometimes stopping to speak with each other, sometimes not. The traffic increased exponentially, and I saw the same vehicles cruising up and down the avenue.

I spotted one dude standing alone on the sidewalk, not talking to anyone, just waiting. I focused on him, watching to see what he was doing. After a while, another man wandered up to him and began speaking. They walked away together, then the first guy came back by himself. Five minutes later, the same thing happened.

This was my guy. I didn't know if he was selling drugs or

hooch, but he certainly wasn't giving tourists directions to Mount Rushmore.

I exited Big Bat's and walked over to my truck, taking my time and making sure no one was watching me. Then I took another look at sidewalk guy. He was staring at his phone, paying no attention to me or anyone else. Rather than approach him right away, I wandered over to the Subway sandwich shop and gazed inside. There were a few people there, although it looked like they were getting ready to close. A little kid saw me through the window and waved. Then I ambled back to the parking lot, keeping my head down.

Sidewalk guy looked to be in his twenties, sporting a black Adidas hoodie and a light blue ball cap, worn backward on his head. Short black hair, a scraggly mustache trying to survive on his lip. Some tattoos on his arms, although I couldn't make them out.

I walked closer. "Hey man, what's up?"

He stared at me from the corner of his eyes and nodded a millimeter or two.

"Looking for a water bottle," I said. "I got cash."

He took a step back and looked me over slowly, then shook his head. "Can't help you."

I was surprised. Skips and water bottles were usually easy to come by. Bootleggers looking to make easy money would buy a gallon of cheap Karkov vodka in Nebraska, water it down, and pour it into sixteen-ounce plastic bottles, then sell them for $10 each. The real shithead bootleggers would bamboozle the bottle, mixing it with rubbing alcohol—or worse—to maximize their profits. Savvy drinkers knew to shake a water bottle and watch the bubbles, as the bubbles in bamboozled pints wouldn't rise the same way as in genuine booze.

"You can't hook me up?" I asked. "Big wopes if you can. Or point me to a house."

Another pause. "Where you from?"

I thought about whether to bullshit him but decided against it. "Rosebud. Just passin' through, need a little something for the drive back."

He nodded. "Pretty fancy truck you got."

Shit. He'd seen my ride, which was my error. Although the Ford wasn't new, it was light-years better than most of the vehicles around here.

"Yeah, right? Friend sold it to me cheap." I lifted my hand up. "So, you help a brother out with some hooch?"

"Sorry," he said, then turned away.

"All right, cool," I said. "You have a good one."

There was no point in trying to hide my truck anymore, so I walked back and climbed up into the front seat. I figured I'd sit in there for a while and figure out my next move, given that I had all night to find the 705 guys.

I spent the next hour monitoring the street and mindlessly scrolling on my cell phone, trying to stay awake. Teenagers and a few tweakers strolled by. People on their way to parties, lonely people looking for a little company, harried parents came and went. The parade of Natives wandering the streets continued, and at some point I dozed off, my dreams taking me back to my childhood, the idyll of youth when I had no worries, my mother and father with me, speaking to me, telling me to have fun but return home before dark, my sister and I off on an adventure.

I jerked awake when I heard a rapping on my windshield. I struggled to focus as I looked outside into the darkness. The clouds in my head began to clear, and I was able to see better as my eyes adjusted to the dim light. A group of guys were standing right outside of the door to my truck, none of them smiling. Then I saw it.

A handgun pointed straight at me.

Bear and his gang buddies. The 705. I'd found them. Or I guess they'd found me.

Jolted awake by the sight of the weapon, I immediately felt foolish. I'd lost whatever element of surprise I might have had. It was the kind of mistake that could get me killed.

Bear motioned with the gun for me to exit the truck. "Get out, motherfucker!" he said. "Hands up."

I complied and climbed down from the vehicle on to the street, then put my hands up halfway. I took a few steps back, keeping an eye on him and the gun. It was too dark to clearly identify his weapon, but it looked like a cheap PSA Dagger. A Glock clone—inexpensive but serviceable.

I didn't say anything and kept my hands in the air. I glanced over at the guys standing behind Bear. One of them had a nasty red wound across his entire left cheek, just under his eye. Shorty. The one I'd cut open during the gang's attempted shakedown of Pudge.

Shit.

Bear kept the handgun aimed straight at me.

"Move your ass! Over there!" He pointed with his weapon, indicating that he wanted me to walk behind the building into the alley.

I took a look and saw that the alley was dark and deserted; no one could hear or see us there. I peeked down the block at Big Bat's. The place was still open, and there were a few people mingling outside, but they weren't paying any attention to us.

"I said move!" His arm was shaking as he pointed the weapon at my chest.

I slowly stepped into the dim alley.

"Down there," Bear said, pointing to a large garbage bin.

I did what he said, stopping by the dumpster, which was embossed with the words WHITE OWL WASTE AND DISPOSAL. I quickly surveyed the area to evaluate my situation. Bear was in front of me with a gun. A few other men, including Shorty and sidewalk guy, flanked me on the left and right. It didn't look good.

"You got a lot of motherfuckin' nerve, coming to our patch."

"Yeah, just like you assholes came to Rosebud. You think I don't know about that?"

Bear sneered. "I don't give a fuck what you know. But we glad you came. My man Shorty here been beefin'."

I looked over at Shorty, who was staring at me with hatred.

"He been hopin' to get a chance to see you again, and you show up just like damn Santy Claus."

I motioned with my head at Shorty. "You got something to say, go ahead."

Bear laughed. "Shorty ain't much of a talker."

Shorty didn't take his eyes off me. "Fuck you," he said. "All I got to say."

"Thing is," Bear said, "you done fucked up his face with a cheap shot. Shorty here think he deserve revenge. Vengeance, yo."

"Yeah, right," I said. "You guys started that shit with Pudge, and I ended it. If Shorty wants to throw down, bring it on. But you motherfuckers are gonna pay for what you did to my people."

"Shorty, what you say? You got a knife?"

He shook his head.

"Any y'all got one?" Bear asked.

One of the guys pulled out a small knife, opened it, and handed it to Shorty. It looked like a three-inch blade.

"Shorty, you decide," Bear said. "I can shoot this mofo, or you can carve his face up. Eye for an eye, right? Maybe you take out one of his motherfuckin' eyeballs with that thing."

Shorty took a step toward me. "I'll do it."

"Aight! That's what I'm talkin' about. Jay Jay, Woodsy, hold him." He raised the gun to my face. "You fuck around, I gonna blast yo' ass, feel me?"

The gang members looked at each other, then began moving toward me. In a second I'd have to make a move for Bear's gun and hope to overpower him. I had to assume the other gangbangers were carrying, but if I could get Bear's weapon, I'd have a fighting chance of getting out alive.

"You ready, Shorty?" Bear said.

"Why don't you fight me like a man?" I said. "Either one of you."

I was trying to bait Bear to come closer to me with the gun so I could make my move. If he came just a foot or two closer, I'd grab the barrel of the gun while shifting out of the line of fire. The key would be to pull the firearm down hard and rotate it away from me. If I got the right angle, his trigger finger would break, and I could use that moment of shock to take his weapon. After that, I'd have to improvise. I estimated the odds of success at about 30 percent.

"Come on!" I shouted at Bear. "You afraid of me?"

His face darkened, and he started moving toward me, the handgun pointed at my chest.

Here we go, I thought. The sound of cars and people speaking in the distance echoed in the night, and I wondered if that was the last thing I'd ever hear.

Then a blinding light lit up the alley. We all turned and faced the flashlights aimed at us.

"Drop the weapon! Now!"

After my eyes adjusted, I saw who was shouting at us.

Two uniformed officers, guns drawn and pointed at us.

The tribal police.

Bear put his gun down on the ground, and one cop snatched it away.

"Hands up! All of you."

One officer kept his firearm trained on Bear, and the other one pointed his flashlight at us. "Any other weapons?" he said.

No one responded.

The cop with the gun motioned toward us. "Mike, start cuffing these guys."

I was able to get a better look at them. One younger guy, one middle-aged. The younger cop was thin, the older one was a little beefy. Short black hair on both, the Oglala Sioux Tribe flag emblem embossed on their shirts above their right pockets, their badges on the left. Sidearms, radios, batons, and mag pouches on their duty belts. The older cop's name badge read WILLIAMS, the younger one's was marked TWO EAGLES.

Two Eagles handcuffed Bear first, then Shorty, then the other Pine Ridge boys. Then he asked the older cop for his cuffs and restrained me. I didn't resist.

The older cop—officer Williams—spoke first. "Okay, what's going on here?"

None of us said anything.

"Kerwin, is that you?" asked the cop, looking at Bear. "We got a call about suspicious activity. You know anything about that?"

Kerwin? No wonder he wanted to be called by his nickname.

"No," Bear—or Kerwin—said, his face stoic.

"Then what's happening here? You want to tell me why you had a gun pointed at that guy?"

Bear stayed silent.

"Somebody else want to tell me what's going on?"

Nobody said anything. As much as I despised Bear, I wasn't going to rat anyone out.

"Okay, looks like you need some encouragement," he said. "If nobody talks, we're taking you all in."

Everyone stayed silent.

"Okay then, jail it is. Let's see some IDs," he said, looking at me first. "You got one?"

"Back pocket," I said.

The cop pulled out my wallet, got out my tribal identification card, and looked at it.

Officer Two Eagles looked at the other cop and nodded. "This is the guy."

What did that mean?

"Rosebud?" Two Eagles said. "You're a long way from home. What are you doing here?"

"Just visiting," I said.

"Visiting, sure. Taking in the sights. A tourist. We'll hang on to this for now." He gave my card to his partner, then turned to the others. "You all have IDs?"

"I left mine at home," said one of the guys.

"Me, too," said another.

"Uh-huh. What about you, Kerwin? You got a driver's license?"

Bear stayed impassive. "You know who I am."

"Yeah, I do. That's why I want to see some ID. You got it on you?" Williams glanced at Two Eagles.

"I don't got to show you shit, 'cause I ain't done nothin'."

"Looked to me like you had a firearm pointed at Rosebud over here."

"Fuck you," Bear said.

"Done deal," Williams said. "You just got yourself a charge for felony menacing and assault. Disorderly conduct for the rest of you."

"How you want to do this?" Two Eagles asked.

"You take Rosebud, and I'll take the others."

The cops shepherded us down to the end of the street, where there were two big white SUV hybrid trucks, the doors stating OGLALA PUBLIC SAFETY and AKICITA on the front fenders.

I watched as the cops loaded the Pine Ridge guys into one of the vehicles. Bear was the last to get in.

Before he got in, he turned to me and said, "This ain't over, fucker."

I just stared at him.

The younger cop pushed me into his vehicle and shut the door. Within minutes, we arrived at the Pine Ridge correctional facility, a huge building with a large granite marker in front, emblazoned with the words OYATE KI WOOPE OGNA TIPI. Justice Center for the People. The Oglala Sioux Tribe had received funding from the Bureau of Indian Affairs to build a combined courthouse, police headquarters, juvenile center, and jail. The local newspaper had even reported that the facility had a peacemaking room, where people with legal disputes could sit in a circle and discuss their disagreements. I'd driven by the building before, but now I was going to experience it from the inside.

Two Eagles drove around to the side of the building and parked, then opened the back doors of the vehicle and told me to get out.

"What's the deal?" I asked. "Can I bond out?" If they wanted a cash bail, I'd have to call Marie for help, but there was no other choice.

He snickered. "It's eleven thirty—there's no judge here now. Telephonic arraignment is tomorrow afternoon."

Shit. Looked like I was spending the night in jail, which hadn't happened since I was nineteen years old.

The cop took me inside, where we entered through a sally port and then were ushered to the booking station. He pointed to a plastic chair and told me to wait. I didn't see any sign of the Pine Ridge guys. I closed my eyes and tried not to think about anything.

Finally, they called my name. The booking officer took off the handcuffs and brought me up to the desk. He asked me where I lived, my date of birth, and whether I had any medical conditions. After entering my information on his computer, he took an inventory of my possessions, which consisted of my wallet, car keys, cell phone, and some month-old Altoids. After more questions and typing, I was moved to another room, where I was forced to strip off my clothes and submit to a search. Following that humiliation, the cop gave me a jail uniform consisting of canvas slip-on shoes, trousers, an orange T-shirt, and a dark gray V-neck pullover shirt. Then he moved me to the photo stand for my mug shot, both front and side photos. I wasn't sure if I should look friendly or stern, so I compromised and tried to look neutral.

"Okay, that's it," he said. "Let's get you down to the tank."

"Hold up," I said. "Don't I get a phone call?" I needed to contact Marie, even though I dreaded it.

"Tomorrow," he said.

"Any way I can do it tonight? I'm from Rosebud and need to get in touch with my people."

"Sorry, no. Unless you're having a medical emergency."

I sighed. No point in arguing. "Okay, so what time do I get in front of a judge?"

"Depends. We'll let you know."

With that, I resigned myself to a night in a holding cell with the others. No telling what would happen once I was locked up with the gangbangers. The guard led me to another part of the facility, and we passed through several security gates before arriving at our destination. I was surprised, as this wasn't the large holding cell with the other prisoners but appeared to be a small lockup.

"What's this?" I asked. "Solitary confinement?"

"Drunk tank," he said. "You get the royal treatment." He opened the door, and waited for me to go in.

I walked in and sat on the bench. A small toilet, nothing else. There was nothing to do but lie down and try to relax. I stretched out on the bench as much as I could, closed my eyes, and listened to the sounds of the jail. After a while, the lights were dimmed, which made it easier to calm down.

In my head, I reviewed the events of the last twelve hours. The argument with Nathan, the drive to Pine Ridge, nearly getting stabbed by Shorty, and the grand finale of ending up in jail. Not one of my stellar days.

I tried to think about positive things, but it was hard not to focus on the fact that I'd been arrested, which had always been my mother's greatest fear. Every Indian knew that the slightest incident with police could have deadly results, especially in the border towns of Nebraska. Not long ago, a Sicangu man had been arrested in Omaha by state troopers, then punched repeatedly and tased thirteen times before dying in custody. Then there was the case of Raymond Yellow Thunder back in the 1970s. He'd been walking on the street in Gordon, Nebraska, minding his own business, when he was abducted by a group of local men, who'd earlier bragged about "busting an Indian." He was beaten, stripped naked, and forced to dance at an American Legion Hall before dying of a brain hemorrhage.

The noise level in the jail grew louder as the night wore on. I slept fitfully, and began to hear sounds in my own dreams, the sobs and moans of those who had been in the cell before, their pleas for release, their calls for deliverance. I felt the presence of all the people who'd been here before me, their pain and fear revisited, the depths of their sorrows becoming my own. I felt lost and helpless as I swam through the currents of my visions.

"Hey, you all right?"

It was Tasunka Ota, the crazy ghost from the Stronghold Table. He was sitting cross-legged on the floor in front of me.

"How'd you get in here?" I asked.

"Same way as always. Magical Indian, right? Thought I'd pop in and lend a hand."

"You gonna get me the fuck out of here? That would help."

He waved his hands in a circle. "Your wish is my command. But maybe just quit feeling sorry for yourself and take your ease. You're not the first Injun to get locked up. Wait, do we say 'Injun' now?"

"Ah, no. Not at all."

"Sorry," he said. "How about 'savagerous'?"

"Never heard it."

"All right then. Look, I got to pull foot and move out. There's an Indian out in Cheyenne River I'm looking after—he thinks he's in a paper town. Just be patient, okey dokey?"

None of this made any sense. "Wait, I'm dreaming, right?"

He held two fingers up. "Are you?"

THE FLUORESCENT LIGHTS SWITCHED on again. I opened my eyes and then closed them.

"Wounded Horse! Get your ass up."

I jerked forward, now fully awake. It took me a moment to focus, then I saw the correctional officer standing at the cell door.

"What's going on?" I asked.

"You're getting out. Let's go."

I stood up, unsteadily, and tried to collect myself. I wondered if Bear and the others were also being released, and if I'd have any trouble on the way out. I followed the guard down several corridors to the same desk where I'd been processed the night before.

The officer was busy entering information into his computer system. From a clock on the wall, I saw it was 6:44 a.m. I needed coffee and some food, not to mention that I was jonesing for a smoke pretty badly. After a few minutes, the officer walked over to a locked cabinet and came back with a large plastic tub.

"Here's your clothes and personal items. Leave the uniform in the basket."

I took the tub with my stuff, sat down on the bench, and stripped off the jail wear. I changed back into my clothes, then put my wallet, keys, and cell phone into my pockets.

"So, what's the deal with the charge against me? Is there a court date or what?"

He shook his head. "The case was dismissed. You're good."

"Wait, I'm clear?" I didn't understand. "What happened?"

He pointed to the door. "Somebody's outside for you."

He buzzed me through the sally port, and I entered the waiting area. A dark-haired woman was sitting there, staring at her phone.

Rose Charging Cloud. Rosebud's police chief.

o-lah!" she said. "Been waiting forever."

I was dumbfounded. Rose was the absolute last person I'd ever expect to find waiting for me at seven a.m. at the Pine Ridge jail.

"I-I, um, what are you doing here?"

She gave a half smile. "Getting you out of jail. What does it look like?"

I still couldn't make sense of this. Rose was not exactly an admirer of me or my work.

"That is—I mean, thanks, really. But why?"

"Because your girlfriend called me last night, half out of her mind. She told me you were likely to get killed threatening some idiot gangbangers. So I called my friend Clyde and had him put out a BOLO."

"What's that?"

"Be On the Lookout. It's an alert to patrol officers. And I told Clyde to keep you safe if you were picked up—keep you out of the holding cell. He do that?"

This explained why I was locked up by myself. "Yeah, I was in solitary, I guess. No one in there but me."

"Sounds like they threw you in the tank. Serves you right for being an idiot. Come on, let's get out of here."

"Sure. But where are we going?" I was trying to catch up with everything Rose was saying.

"Back to your vehicle—what do you think?" She started walking ahead of me toward the door. "But you're going to talk to me, tell me some things."

This was fair. I followed Rose out of the building to the parking lot. I was surprised to see that she had brought her own vehicle, not a patrol car. It was a metallic blue Mini Cooper, perhaps the least rezzy auto I'd ever seen.

"Hop in," she said.

"Not sure I can fit."

"It's roomier than it looks."

I squeezed in. "Got to admit, didn't see you driving one of these. Had you pegged for a pickup."

She chuckled. "I love this clown car. It's fast and handles like a dream. And it goes off-road way better than some giant truck. You should get one."

I was pretty satisfied with my Ford, but I appreciated her love for her ride. She started the car, and we were on our way.

"Where are you parked?" she asked.

"Over by Big Bat's."

"Sounds good. But we're going to have us a chat on the way there."

I noticed that Rose drove very fast, which could be a problem if we hit one of the many enormous potholes on Pine Ridge roads. I tightened my seatbelt.

"Did you see Clyde at the jail?" she asked.

"The police chief?"

She nodded without looking at me.

"No, I only saw a couple of guards and the booking officer."

"Too bad. Clyde's a good ol' boy—met him at the federal police academy a million years ago. He'll talk your ear off about Indian tacos."

I was confused. "You mean, where to get the best ones?"

"Yeah, sure," she said. "But mainly about who invented them. Everybody thinks it was a Navajo, but Clyde swears the Indian taco was made here first. He says a cook here figured out to use frybread instead of tortillas. That's why Clyde gets his back up whenever someone calls 'em 'Navajo Tacos' instead of Sioux Tacos."

I was surprised to hear the word *Sioux*, which was hardly used on the rez, as it was an Ojibwe slur that had unfortunately stuck. In any case, all of this talk about tacos was making me hungry. "Any chance we can stop somewhere and get a candy bar?"

"No! You can do that on your own time. You need to start talking and tell me what the hell happened last night. Why the fuck were you going after some Oglala gang?"

I didn't know where to start. "Short answer is they murdered Jerome Iron Shell."

"What? Why do you think that? Those Pine Ridge gangbangers can't even tie their own shoes."

I told her about the incident with the 705 gang at Wisdom Corner, the call to Pudge where they threatened to kill him and his family, and how they'd vandalized Pudge's car just days ago.

"Okay, fine," she said. "But why didn't you tell me and let me question them? For shit's sake." She shook her head in exasperation.

"Uh, I didn't think you could get a warrant in Pine Ridge. You don't got authority there, right?"

"You let me worry about that! I could have gone with Clyde and checked them out. Now they're on alert. This is just like that eagle-feather case you fucked up."

Apparently she was never going to let me forget about that. "I also thought the FBI probably took the case away from you, and I'm not gonna talk to them."

"No, the FBIs haven't stepped in yet; that's why you should have come to me first. I'm trying to track down as many leads as I can before they get here and mess it up. Point is, the clock is ticking."

"Look, I thought I could persuade the Pine Ridge guys to tell me the truth. I admit I miscalculated."

"Miscalculated! That's the goddamn understatement of the year." She slowed the car down. "There's the Handi Stop if you want to run inside for some food."

"Yeah, great."

I went inside the gas station and checked my wallet. Thankfully, I had a few bucks, just enough to buy a snack and some coffee. I wandered over to the section with the chips and dried meat snacks, where I saw some MegaBuff-brand snacks on the shelf. Owned and distributed by a giant corporation, these were protein bars made from dried bison, fruit, and seeds. The bison bar trend had actually started right here on the Pine Ridge reservation, where a small start-up company, Wasna Bars, had reinvented beef jerky by using locally sourced bison and Lakota workers to create a new product that was both healthy and a boon to the reservation. But of course, a competitor—MegaBuff—came along and coopted the product, using inferior ingredients at a processing plant in Texas. That company was soon bought out by the multinational corporation, which spelled doom for Wasna Foods. Their sales plummeted, and now you couldn't even get the original Wasna Bar on our own lands. I bought some old-fashioned Jack Link's beef jerky and a Styrofoam cup of coffee and quickly snarfed both down, wishing I had enough cash to buy more.

"You good?" Rose asked when I got back in the car.

"Yep, thanks. They didn't give us any chow at the jail."

"Consider yourself lucky. They probably would have given you some cereal or a bologna and cheese sandwich."

Right now, that didn't sound so bad, but I kept quiet.

"We've got a little time left," she said. "Tell me more about that boarding school land thing in Rapid. I know Jerome was involved in that."

"Yeah, he was a part of it. Don't know if you knew, but Jerome had been a student at the school, way back when. That's why people listened to him. See, the land was supposed to be returned to Natives when the school stopped—"

"Yes, I know. The city ignored some federal law and sold the land to private citizens. Big surprise. I want to know what role Jerome had with the protesters."

"He was one of the people talking to the media. That's all."

"He say anything to you about that fire out there?"

"No, not at all. Why, you think that could be related to this?"

"Just asking," she said, as she signaled and passed a slow-moving car on the road. "Gathering information."

"I know the builders are going through some shit. Not just the fire, but I heard the protesters found out about some children who died at the school, and they're planning to raise a stink about that. What's weird is that I found out my own auntie was one of those kids."

"Wait, she was a student there?"

"Yeah, a long time ago. I saw her name on some list, so I went out there to try and find her grave."

"You find it?"

"Not yet."

Rose shook her head. "That's too bad."

We were back in the town of Pine Ridge. I directed Rose to my truck, which was thankfully still there.

"Look, shitass," she said, "go home. Stay away from Pine Ridge and those dipshit gang assholes. And one last thing. You hear *any-thing* about Jerome, tell me. Hell, you hear anything about any-body, you let me know. Remember, you owe me."

I drove back to Rosebud in silence, alone with my thoughts. On the outskirts of the reservation, I saw the escaped buffalo herd, slowly moving in the distance, their silhouettes ghostly in the morning fog.

An hour later, I parked in front of the house and went inside. Marie was there, sitting on the couch looking at her phone. She jumped up and embraced me. Ava wagged her tail and watched us.

"Oh my god," she said, "I'm so happy to see you. I thought you were dead. I've been calling Rose Charging Cloud's office, but she didn't answer. I had all these terrible thoughts."

We embraced for another minute, then sat down. I told her about the confrontation with the 705 gang, the tribal police, and my night in jail.

"Listen," she said, "I don't want to lie to you. I called Rose last night and told her what was happening. I was so worried. I asked her to help."

"I know. She told me. She called the Pine Ridge police chief and had him put out an alert. You probably saved my life. If the tribal cops hadn't come by, who knows what would have happened?"

She put her hand on my knee. "You can't go back there, okay? Let Rose handle the gang people. We don't need any more trouble. Things are bad enough around here with all the election crap."

"Is there something new?" This didn't sound good.

"You sure you want to hear? You've had a rough night."

"Tell me."

"Well, freaking Mitch Gagnon is ramping up his jail talk on the internet. And people seem to be liking it."

Damn. "He mention any names?"

"No, just general stuff about locking up certain people. Drug dealers, bootleggers, abusers. And their accomplices."

"What does that mean—'accomplices'?"

She shook her head. "Not sure. That's the danger here. He could define it any way he wants. Incarcerate anyone he doesn't like. A bad precedent, for sure."

"I'll say."

She sighed. "I mean, nobody is more opposed to drugs than me. For obvious reasons! But putting them in prison isn't the way. We need to get help for addicts, stop them from taking that junk. Jailing their families wouldn't solve anything."

This was rough terrain to cover, given that Marie's father had been the top pill dealer on the rez for years. Not to mention that she'd shot him when she found out.

My cell phone made a sound, and I picked it up. A text message had come in from Val Tobacco.

I've got some news. Let's talk. ASAP.

I met Val the next day in Scenic, halfway between Rapid City and Rosebud. She'd suggested meeting there, which I found a little odd, given that Scenic was a literal ghost town, with only a gas station and general store still in business. I'd asked if we could talk on the phone, but she insisted on speaking in person. I didn't mind, as it had been years since I'd seen the old buildings; not to mention, there was a drive-in on the way that served a great burger with jalapeños and cream cheese.

I arrived early in Scenic and stopped by the dilapidated buildings for a moment. There was an abandoned dance hall, jail, art gallery, and museum—all now weathered and gray, the wood splitting and cracking, and surrounded by overgrown foliage. On the corner of the main street was the Longhorn Saloon with its famous sign. Like the rest of the town, the bar had been long abandoned, but the large billboard still stood, bordered by dozens of cattle skulls mounted on the frame. The sign proclaimed LONG-HORN SALOON and, just under that, NO INDIANS ALLOWED, although the word NO had been lightly painted over at some point but still visible, creating a mixed message.

The first time I saw the sign, years ago, I'd been angry at the open exclusion of Natives, even though the saloon had failed decades earlier. Jerome had once told me that the bar was no different than any other back in the old days, because of the federal law prohibiting the sale of liquor to Native Americans. The law was finally repealed in the 1950s, and the Longhorn Saloon eventually welcomed the Lakota people to the bar. Jerome said that the tavern had been a decent place to get food and drink, but it became increasingly rougher, and he'd stopped going there after a person was killed at the bar with a fireplace poker.

I drove past the rest of the ancient structures and parked by the gas station, which appeared to be open. There was no sign of Val yet, so I went inside, where an elderly gentleman with an undersized cowboy hat sold me a dusty Mountain Dew. I took my drink outside and sat down in one of the battered metal chairs overlooking the prairie.

Twenty minutes later, Val pulled up in her battered VW Rabbit, which rattled and knocked as she turned the engine off. I was surprised that it had made it all the way from Rapid City. She jumped out of the car and gave me a hug. Today she was dressed in black jeans with holes and a turquoise Western shirt. Her hair was braided into a double ponytail, and her nose ring flashed in the sun. She carried a small handbag adorned with a skull surrounded by lilies.

"Great to see you again," she said, sitting down across from me.

"Likewise. It's been a minute."

"Has it? There's been so much happening, time's just flown by."

I motioned at the buildings behind us. "So, what's up with meeting all the way out here? Why not in Rapid City?"

She turned her head and glanced at the town. "I just like the vibe here. It feels, I don't know, *real*. Not like some stupid strip mall or chain restaurant."

"It's real, all right. I'll give you that. Although I was wondering if the new owners might tear it all down."

"New owners?"

I gave a small smile. "You didn't hear? Some religious cult

bought it a few years ago. I thought they might clear all this out and build something new, but"—I gestured toward the abandoned structures—"it doesn't look like it."

"Interesting, hadn't heard that. A cult . . . Weird." She raised her eyebrows. "Hey, let me grab some water and I'll be right back."

While I waited for her to return, I wondered what she wanted to tell me that couldn't be discussed over the phone. I assumed it was something about the Land Project, or maybe the Rapid City Native community. She hadn't seemed upset when she arrived, so I guessed it wasn't anything too bad.

She returned with a Liquid Death flavored water and sat down. "Much better. I was parched."

"All right," I said. "So hey, what's going on? You said you had news."

"Yeah, I do. And sorry for having you drive all the way out here! I know I'm super paranoid, but I'm kind of, like, worried about somebody listening to my calls or reading my texts. Not that I'm anybody special, but I know how easy it is to do."

"Easy to do what?"

"Hack into somebody's phone. Get their info, yeah? Face-to-face is the only way to be secure."

Hack into a phone? I could barely figure out how to turn mine on and off. "Okay, I get it. That's why you wanted to come out here. No people, right?"

"Yup. Plus, it is nice to get out of Rapid every so often. That place gets me down at times."

"Sure," I said. "But I got to admit, I'm pretty curious now. Sounds important if we need to meet in secret."

"We're not exactly secret here, but it is kind of big stuff, I guess." She looked around, making sure that no one was close. "So, I wasn't exactly truthful with you when we first met."

"Yeah? In what way?"

"Well, I told you I was a writer and teacher. I mean, all of that is true, but I also do internet stuff."

*Internet stuff.* Was she one of those online models? I knew Tommy used to mess around with those websites whenever he won some money at the casino. Was she going to ask me to join her club or subscribe to her service?

"Look, I'm not here to judge," I said. "Photos, videos, whatever you do, it's cool but not really my thing—"

"Videos? What?" She looked puzzled. "Oh my god, you think I'm a porn person! No, no, no! I would never—I mean, I don't look down on that, but oh wow!" She started giggling.

"Sorry, sorry," I said. "I didn't mean anything—I guess I don't understand when you said you're on the internet."

She shook her head again. "I'm not on the internet—I *use* the internet to get data. And sometimes I have to, ah, break the rules."

Then I understood. "Oh, you're a hacker? I didn't get that—"

"No, it's all right. And I'm not a hacker, exactly. Think of me as a security expert. If you really have to use a label, call me a hacktivist."

This was a new one. "I can guess what that means, but I'm not completely sure. All this stuff is way out there for me."

She grinned. "It's just like it sounds; I use information technology for social justice. No profit, no ransoms, no credit card numbers. No black hats. Just trying to do stuff for the Native community."

"Okay, great. But what does that have to do with me?"

"Cool your jets—I'll get there. The thing is, after I met you, I kind of checked you out. Had to make sure you were legit, not one of the bad guys."

"Checked me out? Like a background check?"

She wiggled her hand up and down. "Sort of. Nothing too intrusive. I ran your criminal sheet, court records, your socials." She smirked and took another drink. "You are apparently the very last person in the world who doesn't use any social media. Kind of inspiring, actually."

I felt immediately exposed. "You saw all of that? I can explain the stuff back—"

"Don't worry, you're good. Honestly, there was nothing to be concerned about. You've got a pretty small digital footprint."

"What does that mean?"

She chuckled. "It means you haven't left much of a trail. I mean, there is some chatter about you on a few people's socials—speculating when you're going to start taking jobs again. Clients, whatever you call them."

Shit. She knew about my work as an enforcer. "Uh, so you know what I do? Used to do—I sort of quit."

"Relax. I was impressed. What you and I do is not that different. Helping people. Also, I made a few calls to friends at Rosebud and got the down-low. They vouched for you."

I was a little relieved but also disturbed that it was so easy to learn the details of my life. "Uh, that's good, I guess."

"No worries, okay? Just being cautious."

"So, the news is, you checked me out and I passed? Well, thanks for letting me know, but—"

"No, no. I'm just giving you the background, 'kay? So you know where I'm coming from." She paused. "Here's what I wanted to tell you. I've got some news on your auntie's grave. It took us a while, but we figured some stuff out."

She took a big drink of her water and set the can down.

"So, since I last saw you, our people did find some unmarked graves on the site using the radar and identified those remains.

But I'm sorry to tell you that your auntie and many others weren't found, even though they covered the entire site. We knew they were there from the historical records, but there was no sign of them with the radar. It was a mystery, right?"

I gave a single nod and waited for her to say more.

"That's where my computer skills come in. I was able to hack into one of the builders' email accounts and scan most of the messages. Private chat from Willow Creek Development, the largest real estate developer in South Dakota. Couldn't get 'em all, but I read enough."

"So what did you find out?"

"Well, it's pretty horrible. The developers are building that apartment complex over the graves. Right on top! And they know about the people buried there. Those fucking bastards." She shook her head. "That's why we couldn't find the graves on radar—they were underneath some construction, and our equipment couldn't pick them up."

I tried to process all of this. "Wait, you're telling me that my auntie might be buried underneath an apartment building? That makes no sense. Why don't they just build somewhere else? Or move the graves? Plenty of land out there."

She smiled, ruefully. "Profits. Cash, right? Always comes down to that. They discovered the graves when they began digging but didn't want to start over. Too expensive. I read lots of messages about the fallout if the news got out. They thought Indians would raise massive hell in the media and shut down the project. There was also talk about NAGPRA. You know about that?"

I shrugged. "Not really."

"The Native American Graves Protection and Repatriation Act is a law that protects Native cultural items from graverobbers. Can't buy or sell sacred objects. But the law also protects

Indian burial sites—can't build on those. Makes sense, yeah? If developers find Native graves, the project has to stop while the feds come in to examine it. Review committees, archeologists, the whole thing. Takes years to sort out. But here's the catch: The law doesn't apply to private land."

I didn't understand. "What's 'private land'? Is that different than tribal land?"

She nodded. "Yep. The NAGPRA law only applies to land that's owned by the federal government or by tribes."

"Does this mean they might have to stop construction at the site?"

She shrugged. "That's the question. Do those fuckwads own that land, or is it rightfully ours? Or should it go back to the feds? If the court rules in our favor, we invoke NAGPRA immediately and get them to stop building. You can see why those assholes are scared."

I wasn't completely following all of this, but I understood enough. "So, this is good news, yes? I mean, not the people buried there, but that you can stop the project, right?"

She sighed. "Not necessarily. When I got this information, I went to Henry and Donna right away. I thought—"

"Who are they?"

"They're the leaders of the Land Project. When I told them this stuff, I thought they'd contact the feds or hold a press conference or whatever. But they're lawyers, and I guess they're worried about how I got the emails, like I broke the law or something."

She picked up her water and looked at it like it was her mortal enemy. "They got pretty mad—said it could cause them to lose the lawsuit. I heard they're trying to get the info legally, but I'm not real welcome over there right now."

"Oh jeez," I said. "Seems like they'd be grateful."

She took a deep breath, and her brow furrowed. "It's complicated. Donna was, like, way more mad than Henry—said she could lose her law license. I mean, it seems like there are a lot of lawyers in the world doing worse stuff. But what do I know? To them, I'm just a stupid hacker."

I touched her shoulder. "Sorry that woman is being so shitty to you. Way I see it, you're only trying to get the truth. Fighting the good fight."

I got up to leave. "Anyway, great talking with you. Thanks for telling me about my auntie; this is—"

"Wait," she said. "There's more. Something you should know. Big time."

"Yeah?" I sat back down.

"So, I was reading those emails that I hacked. A lot of it was stupid stuff or like, scheduling or whatever. But there was one thread that was weird."

She paused and crossed her arms. "The developer guys were all talking about 'the problem.' That's what they called it. 'The problem.' It seemed like they were really worried. And they kept talking about how to handle it. Here's where I got freaked out."

She reached into her bag and took out a piece of paper.

"The last email in the thread was really creepy, so I printed a copy. Read this, it's from the CEO of the company."

She handed me a piece of paper. I silently read the words she'd underlined.

> This has gone on long enough. We need to have our person on the reservation take care of the medicine man. Tell our guy to get rid of him. Any means necessary.

My head was spinning as I worked to understand what I'd just read. "Wait, you're telling me that this person wanted to hurt Jerome?"

She threw up her hands. "Well, yeah. Exact wording was, 'Tell our guy to get rid of him.' You tell me what that means."

This was shocking. I knew the Rapid City builders were greedy, but were they killers?

"This is crazy," I said. "Are you sure about this?"

"I guarantee that email came from the president of the company. No question about it."

I was still reeling from the news. Could the Rapid City developers really have been the ones that attacked Jerome? Then I realized something and asked to see the message again.

"This email says they have a 'person on the reservation.' So who is that?"

"No clue," she said. "I read the thread a hundred times. There's no name mentioned anywhere."

"Damn. Can you hack into some other email message? Maybe find out that way?"

Val grimaced. "I've tried. I'll keep trying, but I think I've discovered all I can."

"Shit. I'd like to know who this person is."

She paused again. "Well, there is one way . . ."

"Yeah?"

"We do know who sent that message—the company CEO, guy by the name of Russell Rowfield."

I didn't understand where she was going with this. "Oh, so you're saying you can monitor his emails and find out more?"

"No, I was thinking that someone could talk to him in person. Get more information that way. You know, maybe, uh, persuade him to be truthful."

She looked at me expectantly.

After a moment, it dawned on me. "You want me to go out and question this Rowfield guy. And by *persuade*, you mean beat the shit out of him."

A small smile appeared on her face, and she nodded, almost imperceptibly.

The drive back to Rosebud was a blur. I cycled through what Val had told me, trying to make sense of it. My auntie, buried under some tacky apartment building. Jerome, viewed as a threat by rich developers up in Rapid City who were willing to get rid of him, whatever that meant. And most infuriating was the possibility that someone on our reservation might have been involved in the attack on Jerome. Could the Willow Creek people have been responsible for Jerome's murder? Would they really set up a hit just to protect their multimillion-dollar building project? Not to mention, murder was not something wealthy wasicus tended to commit. But I had a strong—maybe even overpowering—feeling that I needed to check this thing out. My gut told me that something shady was going on with the developers, even worse than the seedy tactics they'd already used.

As I steered the truck back to the rez, I thought about the logistics of confronting and questioning this Russell Rowfield person. It would be problematic, if not impossible. For one thing, how would I gain access to some rich businessman? It wasn't like hanging out at the local rez bar and waiting for some asshole to show up. But more critically, if I got apprehended, I'd get hit with serious criminal charges—menacing, battery, even kidnapping, depending on how it all went down. And this would take place off the reservation, where felony crimes were severely underprosecuted. Criminal charges on settler land could bring massive consequences—ten or more years in the state pen.

The first issue, if I moved forward with this, was where to confront Rowfield. Val had given me a packet of information she'd uncovered on the guy, including an old picture of him, his vehicle's make and model, his home address, and the location of his company's offices. Questioning him at his office was out of the question. Even if I could get past his assistant and any security guards, I'd be tossed out and arrested within minutes. Finding the guy at home was also tricky. Rowfield was married with two kids, Val had noted, so he likely had some fancy home security system. Not to mention that I wouldn't do anything near his wife or kids. It didn't seem there was any way to get the guy alone. He lived in a completely different world than ours, one sealed off from those outside of his income bracket.

Then it came to me. I could possibly detain him at his workplace when he got out of his car—assuming that he drove himself to work. I'd need to find out if he carpooled, in which case this plan was dead on arrival.

When I arrived home, I told Marie what Val had said about the developers and their emails, and my idea to speak to Rowfield in Rapid City. She was as shocked as I'd been, and somewhat skeptical about the email threatening Jerome. I gave her Val's printout, and she looked it over.

"I admit, this looks legitimate. I just don't understand why those guys would do this. I mean, they've got more money than God. Why risk getting arrested just to stop some elderly Native from protesting their fancy new apartments?"

"Not sure, but maybe these dudes are just really arrogant. You know, they've been running things for so long that maybe they think they can do anything. I mean, look at our politicians these days."

"Good point. But do you really think you can get to this guy?"

I told her my idea about intercepting Rowfield at his office.

"Okay, but how do you know he doesn't have a driver? Or maybe he works from home."

I hadn't thought of this. Maybe rich folks used personal drivers to ferry them around, or maybe they didn't bother with offices these days. "I guess I'd need to go check it out, see what his deal is."

"Look," she said. "I'm not saying you shouldn't talk to this guy. If you can find him. But only if you can do it safely. And by that, I mean not getting arrested. You sure you don't want to go to Rose Charging Cloud with this?"

Marie had a good point, especially given that I'd promised to keep Rose informed. But something in my gut told me to keep this to myself for now.

"Not yet. If she contacts Rowfield and his bunch, they'll lawyer up and stonewall. If I surprise the guy, I've got a shot of getting the truth. But I'll tell her if I find out anything."

Marie looked like she wanted to say more, but she stayed quiet.

The next day, I left very early and drove to Rapid City long before the sun rose. Upon arriving, I first surveyed Rowfield's home on the outskirts of the city; I was careful to stay far away from the house itself. It was located on Alta Vista Drive and was predictably large, with a three-car garage and a gigantic four-acre lot. As I'd guessed, there were security cameras mounted all over, and I quickly drove off. Then I made my way to his office.

The Willow Creek complex was surprisingly modest, located not in the downtown area but south of the city. It was an L-shaped structure with three floors and a parking garage located off to the side. I was able to enter the parking area without having to take a ticket and drove over to the main lot, which was deserted at this hour. I saw a row of reserved parking spaces near the elevator, and I guessed these spots were for the bosses and bigwigs.

My dashboard clock read 4:35 a.m. as I parked my truck at the back of the parking garage. I had a decent view of Rowfield's presumed space, so I settled in for the wait. I'd learned from Val that Russell drove a silver Mercedes SUV, which wouldn't be hard to spot. I'd brought a thermos filled with coffee and a bag of Cape Cod kettle-fried potato chips. Nathan had given me a taste of these chips some months ago, and I agreed that they were the best. The bad news was that they were rarely available at the reservation grocery store. I made a mental note to pick some up here in Rapid City on the way home.

A little after five a.m., two cars entered the parking garage, an old Toyota Tercel and a rusty Honda Civic. I kept my head down and watched them park in another area of the garage. These would be the working people, the ones who cleaned the buildings and cooked food for the white-collar folks. Another wave of modest vehicles entered the garage in the next half hour, then it was quiet again.

I glanced at the dashboard clock. It was getting near seven a.m., and the workday started at eight, so there'd likely be a surge of arrivals in an hour. I was staring at my cell phone, reading some news about the Denver Broncos, when I heard the sound of a vehicle. I looked up and spotted a silver SUV driving toward the front parking area. I kept my head down and watched.

The SUV pulled into the spot nearest the elevator, and a man emerged. It was Rowfield, alone. He matched the picture I'd seen, although his hair was different. He was dressed in a white shirt with one of those fancy button-down collars and carrying a blue jacket on his arm, along with a black briefcase. He locked the vehicle and walked away.

I waited for ten minutes to see if anyone else was coming. I left my truck and nonchalantly walked toward the Mercedes, then glanced inside. Nothing out of the ordinary, just a few papers and an empty water bottle in the cupholder. I looked up and scanned the garage for security cameras. I didn't see any, which was another break for me. I returned to my truck and waited again to see when the other employees would show up. As I'd expected, the big group of office workers arrived about thirty minutes later. I now knew that Rowfield drove alone, and that he showed up at his office early. If this was his pattern, it gave me an opening.

I returned to the parking garage for the next two days at the same time. Rowfield arrived each day before everyone else and parked in his assigned spot in the deserted structure. I'd have a window of about half an hour if I was lucky. That was good enough for me.

I decided that tomorrow was the day. There was just one thing I needed to put my plan into motion. I picked up my cell phone, pulled up a contact, and hit the button. He answered immediately.

"Hey Tommy, it's Virgil. Listen, I need a favor from you. Can you—"

"Of course, homes," he said, before I could even finish my sentence. "Whatever you need."

I drove back to the rez, where Tommy had agreed to meet me at the casino restaurant before his shift started in the afternoon. As a gesture of thanks, I'd stopped and bought a bag of Mexican fast food with a dozen extra-super-hot-sauce packets, which were Tommy's favorite. He'd told me that Professor Cortings might join us, so I bought some tacos for him, too. I didn't know the professor's sauce preference, so I had the drive-through lady throw in another five of the mild packets. I arrived at the casino thirty minutes later and parked in back.

Rich Cortings and Tommy were already there in the kitchen prep area, sitting on stools in front of a metal table and chatting.

"Hey Virg!" Tommy said and turned to Rich. "Told you my man would bring the grub!"

I put the bag down on the table. "Help yourselves, guys. Got some tacos, burritos, nachos, and those potato olés you like. Plenty of hot sauce packets and a few milds, too."

"Looks like a feast," Rich said. He stood up and shook my hand. "Many thanks, Virgil." He took one small taco and left the rest for Tommy and me.

I grabbed a chicken taco and bean burrito from the sack and handed the bag to Tommy. "The rest are for you, dude."

He grinned and started eating.

I unwrapped my burrito and took a bite. Pretty salty, but not too bad. I still preferred the stuff from the food truck out by Soldier Creek. By the time I finished, Tommy had polished off the entire sack of fast food.

"Big wopes," he said. "That hit the spot."

I noticed he had nacho cheese on his chin, nose, and even his left ear. I motioned with my head that he should wipe himself off, but he didn't understand.

"Tommy!" Rich said. "Jesus Christ, you are covered with sauce! Go clean yourself before the prairie dogs smell that stuff and attack us."

The area behind the casino was crawling with prairie dogs. On a sunny day, you'd see dozens of the little critters poking up from their tunnels and watching the world go by. Sometimes hunters would come to the rez and shoot them, which seemed pretty unsporting to me. After all, they weren't exactly difficult to track.

Tommy smiled sheepishly and wiped himself clean, although he missed a few spots. "What can I say? I love me that TJ chow."

"Someday you need to try real Latin food, like mofongo or arepas," Rich said. "Best mofongo I ever had was in Long Island, of all places. Little place in Hempstead."

"Mo-what?" Tommy said. "Sounds like a dirty word."

Rich shook his head and smirked. "It's a Puerto Rican dish, you clown. I actually prefer the Dominican style."

"Whatever you say, prof." Tommy took a big drink of his water. "Oh hey, I just remembered! Tell Virgil here about that stuff we were reading in class—how Indians invented football."

"Well, that's not exactly accurate," Rich said. "It's more precise to say that Natives revolutionized the sport. Specifically, the Carlisle Indian School football team."

This was news to me, and I guessed it was probably some sort of academic hokum the professor had dreamed up. I'd never heard of Indians playing football. Everybody knew that basketball and lacrosse were the two sports Natives were good at.

"Okay, Professor, tell me more," I said. "I'm a big football fan, but I never heard nothing about this."

"Happy to. The marginalization of the Carlisle team is a crime against history. Everybody believes it was Knute Rockne and the Notre Dame team that developed the forward pass, but it was actually these skinny Indigenous kids."

"Wait, the pass?" I asked. "When was this?"

Rich smiled. "Way back in 1907. The Carlisle team was the first to really use it effectively. They weren't the first team to throw the ball, but they figured out how to use it in a game. In a sense, they were the inventors of modern American football."

"You're messing with us, right?" I said. "The pass has always been part of the game."

"No," he said. "The forward pass wasn't allowed until 1906, when they changed the rules. But even after the pass was legalized, players would just toss the ball underhand or maybe sidearm it."

Rich stood up and mimed an underhanded throw. "Get it? An overhand spiral pass was unheard of. Carlisle was the first team to use it successfully. They destroyed Harvard and the University of Pennsylvania by throwing these beautiful passes way down the field. Nobody had ever seen anything like it."

Now I was really confused. "Hold on. I thought Carlisle was one of them boarding schools, for little kids and high school students."

Rich fluttered his right hand. "Yes and no. They educated—if you can call it that—small children, but they also took in Natives in their late teens or early twenties."

"And they played college teams?"

"Sure did. Carlisle was one of the earliest football teams. They weren't a great team at first, but then they got this football genius to coach them. Guy's name was Glenn Warner, better known as Pop Warner."

Tommy piped in. "They got a kiddy league named after the dude, yeah?"

"That's right." Rich winked at me. "You get an A, Tommy. Pop Warner's best known for that, but his real claim to fame should be coaching the greatest football team of all time. And I'm including pro teams in that list of the greatest."

This was getting interesting. "Don't leave us hanging, Professor," I said. "You gotta tell the rest of the story."

"Okay, short version is that the rules of football were changed in 1906 to allow the forward pass. But the teams back then— mainly Ivy League schools—were still playing the old-fashioned smashmouth game. You know, running the ball down the middle, trying to overpower everyone. And Carlisle couldn't compete in that style, because their players were much smaller than the guys on the college teams. Remember, these were Native kids from reservations, underfed and underresourced, not like the wealthy kids from Yale or Princeton."

"Hey now," Tommy said, "you ain't dissing us bony skins, are you?"

"Take it easy, man. Point is, these rez kids absolutely destroyed the college teams. Pop Warner developed an offense that used the Native players' speed and brains. Long passes, trick plays, crazy formations. The other teams were so befuddled, they didn't even know where the ball was. At one point, the Carlisle quarterback called out the plays in advance just to embarrass the other guys. And they still couldn't stop them."

"Some crazy shit, huh?" Tommy said, looking at me.

I was surprised. I'd been a football fan my whole life, and no one had ever told me that Indians had once been good—maybe even great—at the sport. "For sure. And you say they were the best team ever?"

The professor shrugged. "Look, you can make a case for the 1972 Miami Dolphins. Never lost a game. Perfect season. But the 1911 Carlisle Indians won eleven games and lost only one game by a single point. Jim Thorpe was their quarterback. That year, they beat Harvard in the greatest upset of all time. Best team ever, and I'll stake my reputation on that."

He chuckled and took a drink of water. "Not that there's much of my rep left. Anyway, the cherry on top was the 1912 team, which had eleven wins, one loss, and one tie. But the thing is, Carlisle played Army that year at the West Point stadium. The newspapers were all over the game, called it a replay of the Wounded Knee battle. And Dwight Eisenhower—yes, that Eisenhower—was the leader of the Army team. You can guess what happened. The Indians crushed 'em, twenty-seven to six."

He stood up and waved his arms like he was cheering. "And that, children, is the story of the greatest football team of all time that nobody knows about."

"Well, ain't that a kick in the nuts," Tommy said.

"Damn, I had no idea," I said. "Why don't schools teach this stuff? You know, something for Indians to be proud of."

Rich shook his head gently. "Just more whitewashing and erasure. We need Indigenous folks writing the history books, telling the real story before everyone forgets. The Carlisle school closed in 1918, so that was the end of that team. Over time, Native athletes drifted to basketball—cheaper to field a b-ball squad, right? And everybody forgot about the Indigenous history of football."

I thought of my friend Rob Turning Heart. He'd been a huge football fan, and his team had been the Seattle Seahawks for some reason. I wondered what he'd have thought about all of this. Native kids tearing it up on the football field, proving that they could compete with anyone.

"Thanks, Professor," I said. "That's some cool stuff. Feels like I'm back in school, but in a good way."

Tommy yawned, then belched loudly. "Dang, ex-squeeze me."

Rich rolled his eyes. "That's my signal to head out. Nice seeing you, Virgil."

"You too." I shook his hand, and he left, waving at Tommy on his way out.

"Oh man, I feel like I could take me a nap, but I gotta get to work," Tommy said. "So anyway, I grabbed that thing you asked for. You gonna tell me what this is all about? Been wondering."

"Look, I got to keep this quiet for now, okay? I'll give you the down-low later."

He shrugged. "You the man. Follow me."

We went to a back room where the canned goods and dry foods were stored. There were plastic bins labeled with tape and markers, giant cans of vegetables and fruits, and large plastic canisters of dried spices. There was a handwritten sign posted on the back wall—it read FIFO in all caps and underlined three times.

I pointed to it. "What does that mean?"

Tommy shrugged. "First in, first out. Means get rid of the oldest cans first, make room for the new stuff."

First in, first out. Kind of like what had happened to Indians since Columbus stumbled onto the Americas.

"There you go," he said, and handed it to me.

"You sure you don't need it back?"

"Nope," he said. "Ain't nobody gonna miss that shit. Just toss it when you're done."

I looked down at the item he'd scavenged from the casino. It was exactly what I'd requested.

One neon-yellow-and-orange safety vest.

The day had come for me to confront Russell Rowfield and find out the truth, whatever that meant. The night before, I'd told Marie my plans, but we didn't talk any more about it. We both knew what was at stake.

I got up before dawn and began getting ready. I wore jeans, a plain blue T-shirt, and a ball cap. Everyone was still sleeping, so I silently gathered the items I needed. Sunglasses, retractable police baton, and pepper spray. My handgun, although I didn't plan to use it. The safety vest was still in my truck. I quietly left the house and managed not to wake anyone up.

I stopped at the rez gas station, filled up the tank, and bought some bad coffee and a couple of energy bars to munch on during the long drive. After taking a few swigs of the bitter java and a bite of the energy bar, I hit the road to Rapid City. As I drove, I thought about my plan, and all the things that might go wrong. I knew from my surveillance that Rowfield showed up at his office around seven a.m., but I hoped there were no eager beavers showing up early today.

The drive passed quickly, and I arrived at the Willow Creek offices right on schedule. The place was deserted. I parked in the outdoor lot, away from the security cameras, and put on my sunglasses, then the safety vest, which would render me invisible. The irony was that reflective traffic safety vests were designed to be highly visible, but they worked the opposite way in upper-class America. The uniforms of working-class America—the traffic workers, custodians, fast-food workers—created a sort of shield; highly paid employees would always look away from their lesser-paid brethren, lest they be forced to reflect too deeply on capitalism's imbalances. Tommy's cast-off safety vest would make me anonymous as well as give me a backup story if events went south.

Next, I grabbed the pepper spray, baton, and gun and stuck them in my pockets. The pepper spray was an insurance policy in the event Rowfield tried something really stupid and I needed to temporarily incapacitate him. The baton would come in handy if I needed to encourage him to be forthcoming with his answers to my questions.

I looked around the parking garage. Still no one around, so I found a spot at the corner of the space. There was nothing left to do but wait. If Rowfield stayed consistent, he'd arrive in about thirty minutes.

I usually wasn't nervous before a confrontation, but this time I felt anxious and edgy. I was completely out of my element, which shifted the odds away from me. There was so much I couldn't predict, like security guards or local police, which were far more numerous here than back on the reservation. On the rez, usually only eight or ten officers were on duty at any given time, and they had to cover a huge area. Most of the time they were dealing with domestic disturbances, drunk and disorderlies, and random car accidents. That meant that I could usually conduct my business as the reservation enforcer without worrying about the police showing up. But the city was different. I had no idea how many cops were on duty at any one time, or if there were private security guards at the office complex. I needed to keep my interaction with Rowfield as short as possible.

My mind wandered as I tried to squelch my cravings for a cigarette, which were intense. My tobacco jones had subsided somewhat over the last year, but it was back with a vengeance. I wondered if people developed an addiction to cansasa, the traditional tobacco Lakota people smoked during ceremonies.

I saw something in the corner of my eye and snapped to attention. It was Russell Rowfield and his silver Mercedes SUV, which sparkled even in the parking garage's dismal lighting. It looked as if it had never been driven on a dirt road or through a patch of mud. He maneuvered into his space, then turned the car off and stared at his cell phone. I began slowly walking over there, waiting for him to get out.

After a minute he put the phone away and climbed out of the SUV, then pulled his key fob out of his pocket. That's when I made my move. I walked over, stopping about four feet away from him.

"Excuse me, sir." I held up my hand in greeting.

"Yes?" He looked startled, not expecting anyone this early in the morning.

I was able to get a good look at him. Short brown hair, clean-shaven, and wearing a yellow button-down shirt and navy-blue fleece vest. A patch on the vest read VINEYARD VINES. I guessed he'd gotten it from some winery in California, not some dusty storeroom, like my safety vest.

"I'd like to ask you a few questions, please."

"What?" he said. "Sorry, I can't—"

"Yes, right now. Get back inside the car." I took the Glock out of my pocket and pointed it at him.

He froze. I could see him struggling to understand what was happening.

"Is this a, um, robbery? I don't have any—"

I motioned with the gun again. "Get in. And unlock the back door. Now."

He didn't move, trying to decide what he should do.

"I'm not here to rob you," I said. "Let's just talk for a minute, then I'll leave."

He still didn't move, but his eye was twitching. If he came at me, I'd have to hit him, or in the worst case, fire a warning shot with the Glock. I couldn't use the pepper spray—yet. He'd be unable to talk for an hour or more because of the pain.

I pointed the weapon at his head and waited for him to make his choice.

He got back in the vehicle, leaving the door open. I pushed his door shut, then opened the back door and climbed in, sitting directly behind him. He turned around to look at me, and I kept the gun pointed at him.

"Turn back around and look straight ahead. Don't watch me in the rearview mirror. Just keep your eyes pointed right in front of you. Now, put your hands on the steering wheel, both of them."

He complied. I watched him closely, as this was the most dangerous moment. He'd had a second to process that he was being threatened and now was running scenarios in his head. There was a chance he had a gun stowed in the glove compartment or under his seat. If so, he was deciding if he should go for it, or attempt to bargain with me.

"Are you here to hurt me? I need to tell you—"

"I'm not here for that, okay? Take it easy."

"Please, don't shoot. We'll pay you whatever you want."

"I don't want your money. I just want to talk to you."

"Yes, sure, let's talk. We can work this out." I could see him looking at me in the rearview mirror.

I tapped the back of his head with the gun, and he flinched. "What did I tell you? Keep your eyes on that wall over there and don't look back."

"Yeah, yeah, sure. I just, it's hard to, you know—"

His face in the mirror wasn't a pretty sight. He was twitching and blinking like crazy, and I realized that this guy was on tilt. I needed him to stay coherent for the next few minutes.

"Calm down," I said. "I need to ask you a few things, then you can go to work. All right?"

I waited for him to respond, then an unmistakable odor filled the car.

Urine.

Jesus Christ, the guy had pissed himself. Now I really wanted to get out of there.

"Okay," I said, trying to ignore the stench, "here's the deal. I know you guys are building an apartment and other stuff over at the old boarding school here in town. I want—"

"Please, just let me out of here, and we'll do whatever you want. I promise you."

"All you have to do is tell me some things," I said. "I want information about Jerome Iron Shell."

"Who?"

"The medicine man from Rosebud."

He shook his head vigorously. "I don't know who that is."

"Yes, you do. The holy man who was killed. Murdered."

He glanced at me again in the rearview mirror for a second before moving his eyes away. "Look, we've done everything we've been asked. We don't want any trouble, all right? We just want to move ahead with the project. I've got nothing but respect for you people!"

*You people.* This pissed me off, and I was tempted to give him a lesson in respect. But the clock was ticking for this little encounter.

"Russell, the quicker you quit bullshitting me, the faster you'll get out of here with all of your teeth left in your goddamn mouth." I tapped him again with the gun. "I know about the emails—the ones where you told your person on the Rosebud Reservation to take care of the medicine man."

Shock registered on his face, and I could see him attempting to formulate a response. "Please believe me, I had nothing to do with that. Skip Evans is running the project, and he can tell you—"

"Enough with the bullshit! You said, 'Take care of the medicine man . . . get rid of him.' What did you mean by that? Did you order an attack on him?"

I could see the panicked expression on his face. "You have to understand, I was scared, I didn't know what I was saying, I didn't mean it—"

Jesus Christ. This asshole had ordered a hit on Jerome.

"Okay," I said, "You're going to tell me—right now—who you're working with on the reservation. The person who was going to 'get rid of him.' Who did it?"

"What? I don't know, really. This is just, ah, very—"

I'd had enough of this guy and his lying. I put the gun down, took out my retractable police baton, and extended it. He looked back at me in the mirror, a panicked expression on his face.

"Warned you," I said.

Before he had a chance to respond, I placed the baton on his neck, then crossed my arms and started choking him. By crossing my arms and tightening, I was limiting the blood flow to his brain as well as cutting off his air with the baton. I applied a medium pressure, as I didn't want to kill the guy.

He started thrashing, his arms flailing uselessly as he tried to get a hold on me. He squirmed frantically, and his right arm knocked off my ball cap. This pissed me off, so I increased the pressure. Within seconds, he stopped resisting as his air and blood supply began to dwindle.

Russell Rowfield had about three minutes left to live if I didn't release him. One more minute would cause him permanent brain damage, and two minutes beyond that would send him to whatever hell awaited the vultures of American society.

I started to free him, but then I stopped. I could just end it right here and now for Russell Rowfield. There'd be one less greedy wasicu in the city, one less selfish racist causing harm to anyone who stood in the way of his profits. No one would know it was me who'd done it—I'd been able to sneak in here without anyone seeing me, and a quick wipe of the car would eliminate any traces of my presence. And there'd be a certain justice in Rowfield's death. He'd likely worked to facilitate the murder of Jerome, and the death of that peaceful man enraged me. It was no different, really, than the vicious murders of women and children at the Wounded Knee massacre, or the brutal killings of the Cheyenne and Arapaho people at Sand Creek in the 1800s, the soldiers later parading in the city of Denver proudly displaying the mutilated genitalia of Native women on their horses. Taking him out would balance the scales a little bit.

And then an image of Jerome came to me. It looked like he was standing outside the SUV, not saying anything, but just watching. I knew this was just my mind playing tricks on me, but I wondered what Jerome would say. He'd never tell me what to do directly, but he'd probably narrate a long story, the meaning of which would come to me over time. I remembered him talking about the Red Road, the struggle for our people to live in balance with the Creator, as opposed to the Black Road, the path of too many wasicus, the path of disrespect for oneself and the community, the path of exploitation and destruction.

I pulled back my arms and the baton from Rowfield's neck, and he started coughing and gasping for air. He didn't know how close he'd come to making his journey. The smell of piss was even stronger now. His hands came off the steering wheel as he started to feel his neck.

"Hands back on the wheel, now."

He instantly moved them back in position. I let him catch his breath for a few seconds, put my cap back on, and then tapped him on the shoulder.

"All right, let's try again," I said. "Who's the person on the Rosebud Reservation that you sent to get rid of the medicine man?"

He was still panting, and I could see some tears running down his face. I knew I should feel some sympathy, but I couldn't go that far.

"I'm— I'm telling you, I really don't—"

I put the baton back on the front of his neck and started applying pressure again.

"STOP!" he yelled. "It's, uh, his name is, I think it's—"

I applied more force.

"Mitch Gagnon! That's the guy, please stop!"

Son of a bitch. Mitchell Gagnon.

I should have known.

left Rowfield in his SUV, head down. He wasn't physically injured, but I knew his ego had taken a big hit. No doubt he'd always seen himself as an alpha dog, feared and respected by all, but today he'd encountered someone willing to take him down. I knew that his first impulse would be to call the cops immediately, so I'd left him with some strong incentives to keep quiet, including a promise to visit him again if he involved the law. Even if he did call them, I knew there was little chance he could identify me, given that I'd mainly stayed out of his sightline and hadn't mentioned my name.

My encounter with Rowfield had gone off as I'd planned, but the information I'd forced out of him had me reeling. I knew Mitch Gagnon was a shady bastard, but I hadn't expected this. He'd always struck me as the type who'd lie and cheat to get ahead, but not someone who'd get violent. Too much of a chickenshit to get his hands dirty. Perhaps he'd hired someone to hurt Jerome— that was more his speed. It was even possible that he'd been in contact with the Pine Ridge gang and recruited them, although this seemed unlikely. Still, I realized that I couldn't rule anything out now when it came to Mitch.

I couldn't wait to tell Marie what I'd learned about her tribal council opponent. I got home two hours later, happy to see Marie's car parked in front. I opened the door and walked in. Ava came trotting over to see me, tail wagging.

"Thank god," she said, embracing me. "I kept imagining that something had gone wrong. Nothing did, right?"

"No, it all went according to plan. You will not believe what I found out. But first, is there anything to eat?"

"Yes, of course! I'll make us a wild rice bowl. But tell me everything."

While we ate, I did just that, leaving nothing out. She was dumbfounded to learn that Mitch Gagnon had been working with the developers and had been ordered to take out Jerome.

"I can't believe it," she said. "My god, this just confirms everything we've known about him. And it kind of makes sense. He used to be the tribal treasurer, so he was part of all of the economic development that happens around here. But it boggles my mind to think he'd hurt a holy man."

"I've been thinking the same thing. But Rowfield didn't deny it." I got up and refilled my water glass.

"And does this mean that those Pine Ridge gangbangers aren't involved? I know you and Pudge thought they were the ones."

"I did think that, and I still can't rule them out. But maybe they're just trying to steal Pudge's business."

She sighed. "Which means they might still be after you." She started picking up the dishes. "The question now is, what do we do with this? I mean, you can't go over and beat the crap out of Mitch. He'd have you arrested and jailed. Probably me, too. He's already itching to get rid of us."

I'd been grappling with that myself. It was one thing for me to kick the bejeezus out of some drug dealer or gangbanger, but one of the top elected officials of our tribe was off-limits. Mitch would take official action against us, and no one would ever take my word against his. No, I needed rock-solid proof that he'd been the person who harmed Jerome.

"I guess I need to meet with Rose and tell her about this," I said. "She can start checking Mitch out. Maybe she can, I don't know, get his DNA or whatever. See if he has an alibi."

"Agreed. I don't think our police have DNA profiling, but the FBI does. If they're even working on Jerome's case. Not to mention, the election's coming up soon. The people deserve to know about Mitch. You should call Rose right away."

"I'll do it today."

She sat down next to me. "What's the name of your friend again, the computer hacker?"

"You mean Val?"

"Yes. Can she maybe look into Mitch? I mean, check out his records or whatever. It sounds like she's good at that."

"She's amazing at that stuff. I'll call her." Then I remembered. "Thing is, she likes to talk in person—she's kind of worried about someone hacking her phone."

Marie shrugged. "That seems a little paranoid, but whatever. Hey, why don't you invite her up here? I'd like to meet this mystery woman you've been bragging about."

Bragging? Pretty sure that never happened. Was Marie a little jealous?

"Invite her here? Why?"

"I could make dinner. Give us a chance to talk. We can do it at my parents' house if you'd like. Let's bring Nathan and Shawna, too."

I was surprised, as Marie preferred to stay away from her childhood home, given the memories there. But there was no denying that her parents' house was much nicer than my little shack. Unlike the FEMA trailers and Sioux 400 modular homes that dotted the rez, Marie's house had been custom-built, in line with big-city standards. I recalled that it had an actual dining room, spacious kitchen, intact windows, and ceilings that were much higher and less claustrophobic than the standard Native residence.

I texted Val and told her I had news, and that we should meet. She responded a few hours later, and I extended the invitation for dinner, which she promptly accepted. I texted again and asked—at Marie's request—if Val had any dietary restrictions or preferences. She quickly answered, telling me that she wasn't picky and that she'd bring some wine. I guess it had never come up that I didn't drink, but I didn't mind if Val and Marie had some.

The next day, I called Chief Rose at the police station. I was on hold for five minutes, but she eventually picked up.

"Rose Charging Cloud."

"Hey, this is Virgil. Virgil Wounded Horse."

A pause. "Jesus Christ. What do you want?"

"Uh, you told me that I should, um, let you know if I heard anything. So, I'm doing that."

Another pause. "This isn't about some stupid fight between you and another asshole, is it?"

I wasn't sure how to respond. "Uh. No. I think you'll want to hear this."

A sigh. "Okay. Do *not* come to the police station. Shit, don't drive by here or even look in our direction. I'll meet you out at Wisdom Corner in two hours, okay?" She didn't wait for me to answer. "If there are any goddamn drunks or junkies there, chase 'em away."

Two hours later, I was at Wisdom Corner in St. Francis. Apparently, Rose was willing to go a fair distance to avoid being seen with me. There was no one sitting under the gazebo, so I cleared off a couple of empty bottles and a few pieces of trash off the bench, then settled in to wait. It was peaceful and quiet. I could hear birds and some kids shouting, far off in the distance. I knew that wouldn't last; the dopers and drunkards would start to congregate once the sun started setting.

I heard the whine of a small engine as Rose's Mini Cooper appeared at the end of the street. She pulled into the parking lot and came over to the gazebo.

"This better be good."

No greeting or welcome. "Hi there, Rose."

An exasperated grunt. "*Hello*. Good afternoon. Anpetu waste. For fuck's sake, get on with it."

Rose was no Native Emily Post, that was for sure. "All right. Do you want to sit down and talk?"

Another exasperated utterance, then she sat down and crossed her legs. "Fine. Now what do you have for me?"

"Okay, it's about Jerome Iron Shell. I got some info about the real estate developers in Rapid City, the ones building stuff at the old boarding school. Looks like they were involved in the attack on him."

"Involved? Involved how?"

"They had someone here on the rez go after Jerome. Turns out Jerome was going to lead a big protest at the site, and they wanted to stop it."

She looked baffled. "What in god's name do you mean? Big protest? By who?"

"The Land Project. The Rapid City Indians who've been fighting this thing since the beginning. They were going to have Jerome lead a Spirit Dance around the building and get some publicity—try to stir people up."

"And they had Jerome murdered because of that? That's ridiculous."

"Not really. We've got emails from them, confirming it."

Her face knitted in consternation. "How would you get these supposed emails?"

"There's a hacker who busted in their system."

"Okay, can you show me these messages?"

"Uh, no. I don't have them, the hacker does."

Yet another sigh. "All right, who's this hacker?"

"I can't tell you. This person is like, uh, a confidential source. But I can ask them for the emails."

She pulled out her phone and started looking at it. "For crying out loud, you are wasting my goddamn time. Anyone can put together some fake email message. I don't have time for a wild goose chase."

I held up my hand. "It's legit. I verified it with the president of the real estate company."

"Verified it—how?"

I wondered how much to tell her. "I had a . . . meeting with this guy Rowfield last week. He's the big shot there. The boss. And he confirmed they had a person out here assault Jerome."

She looked skeptical. "This guy just confessed to you that he arranged for someone to murder Jerome Iron Shell? Please."

"Well, I had to use some pressure on him. A lot of pressure."

She closed her eyes. "My god. So you beat the shit out of some rich wasicu up in Rapid? There are probably state police heading to your place right now."

I smirked. "I don't think he called the cops on me. Even if he did, he doesn't know who I am."

Her expression was that of someone who'd been wronged a thousand times. "Okay, assuming I believe you, you said this rich guy had someone attack Jerome. Who was it?"

"Hold on to your hat," I said. "It's kind of shocking."

She rolled her eyes.

"It's Mitch Gagnon."

The bored look was gone from her face. "You're sure about this?"

"Yep. Positive."

"How sure?"

"One hundred percent. The rich guy confirmed it."

"If you're right, this is big. Huge. I never trusted Gagnon—always thought there was something off with him. Only reason I'm not kicking your ass right now." Then her eyes widened, and she pointed at me. "Wait a minute, isn't your girlfriend running against him for council? Is this some fucking scam you two are running?"

"No. No! Marie has nothing to do with this. Yes, she's his opponent in the election, but this is all true."

"Oh, man. You don't even know what a clusterfuck this could be," she said, suddenly deflated. "At the very least, I need to see those emails, even though they'd be completely inadmissible at trial. Can you do that?"

"Yeah, I'll ask," I said. "But can't the FBI test his DNA or something?"

"Sure, if we had probable cause to get a court order. Right now, we just have you beating the crap out of some white guy and inadmissible, unverified emails. We'd get laughed out of court."

I hadn't realized all of that. "Can you maybe hint to the FBI guys that they should investigate Mitch?"

She snorted. "What FBI guys? One of them showed up a week ago, took a report, and left. It's up to us to handle the investigation. Look, I'll think this over. If you hear anything more, let me know, ASAP." She pronounced it like "a sap." "But in the meantime, get me those emails."

She stood up and started walking to her little clown car. Then she stopped and turned around.

"Don't you fuck me on this."


THREE DAYS LATER, I drove to Marie's house, along with Nathan and Shawna. We'd considered bringing our pup Ava along with us, but didn't know how Val felt about dogs and so left Ava at my place. She gave us a little doggy sad face as we shut the door behind us.

Marie had been at the house all day, cleaning and cooking. I'd offered to help, but she'd shooed me away, telling me that my only requirement was to wear my best clothes, although that was a pretty limited category. My wardrobe mainly consisted of T-shirts, old jeans, and some fatigued and defeated flannel shirts. I'd done my best and found a red plaid shirt that I'd inherited from someone.

I rang the doorbell, but there was no answer. It was strange to be at Marie's house again; it was over a year since I'd last been inside. So much had changed since then for all of us. I've heard that time is relative, and maybe that was especially true on the rez. Buildings appeared to stay the same for decades, yet sometimes people seemed to transform and evolve at lightning speed. Perhaps this was due to the shorter lifespans on reservations—Marie had told me that the average lifespan for a man on our rez was just forty-seven years, compared to seventy-five just across the border in Todd County. I wondered if Natives burned faster and brighter, our lives arcing across a span that we couldn't see and could only dimly comprehend.

Marie opened the door, and we all went inside. The living room was immaculate. There were bunches of fresh flowers placed around the room, and a few candles were burning. A star quilt covered an armchair, and I recognized a few paintings by our local artist, Marty Two Bulls, hanging on the walls. The dining table was set with midnight-blue placemats, sparkling white dishes with a golden border, and tan linen napkins folded inside napkin rings. This was a far cry from my utilitarian dining system of cast-off silverware, paper towels, and chipped plates.

Marie smiled and motioned for us to sit down. She was wearing a turquoise ribbon skirt and a white blouse, her hair pulled back.

"You look great," I said.

"Yeah, freaking amazing," Shawna said.

Nathan looked a little scared. He rarely saw Marie dressed up, and he hadn't been to her house for a long time. "This place is, like, really nice," he said. "I kind of remember it from before."

"Thank you," she said. "It was pretty dusty in here, so I gave it a good cleaning. Got rid of some stuff."

"I would have come over and helped," I said. "Now I feel bad."

"No, this was something I needed to do on my own. It was time." She walked over to the kitchen. "You guys want something to drink?"

Before any of us could answer, the doorbell rang, chiming loudly. I jumped up and let Val in. She was wearing faded blue jeans, a silver belt with a large skull-shaped buckle, an olive-green fringed top, several Native necklaces, and beaded earrings. Her long black hair with purple streaks flowed down to her shoulders, the tattoos on her arms barely visible. I didn't see her nose ring, and I wondered if she'd taken it out in an attempt to appear more conventional.

"Hey, friend!" she exclaimed, and gave me a hug. "Great to see you. Thanks for the invite!"

I ushered her in and introduced her to Nathan and Shawna.

"Oh my god!" Shawna said. "I love your hair!"

"Thank you! I like yours. We're, like, purple hair sisters."

Marie cleared her throat and walked over to us.

"Hey Val, this is my girlfriend Marie," I said.

"I've heard a lot about you," Val said, smiling.

"All nice things, I hope," Marie said.

"Oh yeah, absolutely! I hear you're running for tribal council. That is so exciting. When is the election?"

"Six weeks. We're in the home stretch. But, please, come in and sit down." Marie motioned to the couch.

Val walked in and looked around the house. "Wow, this place is cool. So much art on the walls. Oh hey, I brought some stuff." She handed the bag to Marie and then sat down.

Marie opened it and took out a bottle of white wine and a six-pack of Shasta cola.

"Hey, how did you know?" I asked. "Shasta's my favorite."

"I'm a hacker, right? Even though I don't like that term."

"You are?" Shawna said. "Like, a real-life computer hacker?"

Val shrugged her shoulders. "I mean, sort of. I just use the tools of the capitalists against the system."

Shawna practically glowed. "Oh, I'm just, I mean—I want to hear more. I'd love to take, like, computer science in college. And other science courses."

Marie intervened. "We'll have time to talk in a bit. Let's get our guest something to drink. I'll see if I can find a wine opener."

"Uh, I think it's a screw top," Val said. "I got it at Walmart, sorry."

Marie smiled. "That makes it easy! Give me a moment."

She came back with two glasses of wine and three Shastas and set them in front of us. "Cheers, everyone," Marie said. "Val, we appreciate you making the drive from Rapid."

"No problem! Really great to meet you guys. And I don't get a lot of dinner invitations. Mainly dudes just ask me to come over and play video games with them."

Nathan piped in. "You play?"

"Not so much anymore. But I used to play a lot. How about you?"

"Yeah, I do! I mean, when I'm not studying or whatever."

I could tell Nathan already liked Val.

"Excuse me, everyone," Marie said. "I need to take some stuff out of the oven."

While we waited for the food, Val chatted with the kids about school, music, and video games. She had a natural talent for getting people to speak about their interests. Nathan talked about his favorite video games, and Shawna talked about music. Not surprisingly, Shawna and Val loved many of the same bands, none of whom I'd heard of.

"All right, everyone! Have a seat. Food's ready," Marie said.

"What can I do?" Val asked.

"Could you help me carry some plates?"

"Sure," Val said, and scurried off to the kitchen, leaving me alone with Nathan and Shawna for a moment.

"Hey guys, after dinner, we need to talk with Val about some stuff. Alone. Can you guys go to the living room and watch some TV?"

"Is this about what happened to Jerome?" Nathan asked.

I paused for a moment and decided to be straight with him. "Yeah, it is."

He looked at me accusingly. "Well, let me hear it! I can help, you know."

"No, dude, this is something you need to stay away from."

"Why? Are you still mad about the school thing? I stopped that, okay?"

This was good news. "I'm not mad. What's happening now is, uh, complicated." I looked at his face. He wanted so badly to be taken seriously, but I couldn't get him involved in this mess. "Look, here's what I'll say. If there's something that you can do to help out—safely—I'll bring you in. That cool?"

He nodded a little. I could tell he wasn't completely satisfied, but this was the best I could do.

Marie and Val returned, carrying plates and bowls of wild greens, maple sage vinaigrette, and three sisters bison stew, made with corn, beans, and squash. Marie had whipped up a Lakota feast.

"This looks fantastic," Val said as we began passing the food around the table.

"Shawna, that bowl there doesn't have any meat," Marie said.

"Thank you," Shawna said. "I appreciate it."

I saw that Marie had set out a Spirit Plate with small portions of the food to honor our ancestors and those who had passed on. I caught her eye and gave her a small nod.

We all dug into our food, which was outstanding. I especially liked the stew and ate two huge helpings. After we finished, Marie brought out fresh berries for dessert.

"Shawna, you said you wanted to study science," Val said. "What area?"

"I don't know yet—I mean, I'm thinking biology. Maybe bio-engineering."

"I don't even know what that is." Val laughed. "You must be really good in school."

Nathan nodded vigorously. "Hell yeah, she is. Like, the smartest kid in our whole grade."

Shawna looked down. "Nate, you're embarrassing me. You know that's not true."

"Yeah, whatever." He whispered, "It is."

"You guys are cute," Val said. "Are you both planning on college?"

Uh-oh. This topic was a minefield, but Val had no idea about that. Neither Shawna nor Nathan said anything.

Marie jumped in and said, "Shawna is considering applying to Dartmouth. Pretty far away from here, but a really great school. My sister went there, a long time ago."

"They do have some cool programs," Shawna said. "I could major in bio and minor in environmental science. And a lot of Natives go there. But I'm also thinking about South Dakota Mines in Rapid. Awesome tech school."

"Sure, I know it. Some good choices," Val said. "I've taught a few times at Oglala Lakota College. A class called Computer Basics—mainly teaching elders how to turn on a computer and use a browser. What about you, Nathan?"

"Uh, I might go to Sinte Gleska," he said. "I mean, unless I get a job or something."

Another land mine. I'd always wanted Nathan to attend college, but he'd made it clear recently that more school wasn't in his plans. I'd hoped that Shawna's enthusiasm for higher education would rub off on him, but that hadn't happened.

"Hey Nate, you wanna go watch TV?" Shawna said. "That okay, Marie?"

"Yes, of course," she said. "The remote is on the coffee table."

Nathan and Shawna went off by themselves, and Marie asked if anyone wanted coffee.

"I'd love some," I said. "I'll get the dishes."

Marie smiled at me, and I started clearing the table. A few minutes later, Marie set three cups of coffee down, then looked at me expectantly. It was time for the real conversation.

"All right," I said, looking at Val. "Kids are watching TV, so I can tell you what's up. There's some news, and I know you like to talk in person."

"Yeah, sorry to be weird about that," she said. "Occupational hazard. I get worried about someone hacking into my texts or DMs. I know just how easy it is. So, lay it on me."

"Okay," I said. "I went to the Willow Creek offices in Rapid City and checked them out. The guy you told me about, Russell Rowfield, the CEO—he's exactly what you'd expect. Rich guy, fancy car, big house. He shows up at the office every morning very early. So, I got there early myself and had a little chat with him."

"You did? Oh my god, that's incredible! What did he say?" Val's eyes were wide open—they looked like the coasters on my coffee table at home.

"At first, he denied it all. Said he didn't know anything. Tried to throw somebody else under the bus. But I used a little . . . encouragement to convince him to be honest."

"Yeah? What did he say?" Val looked straight at me.

"He didn't deny it—that he'd ordered someone to go after Jerome. Then I had to persuade him to tell me who that was."

"Yeah?" Val said, her eyes even wider. "Tell me, I'm dying to hear."

"Turns out the guy is from here, which is pretty disgusting. His name is Mitchell Gagnon. But he goes by Mitch. You know him?"

Val shook her head. "Never heard of him."

Marie jumped in. "It's pretty complicated. He's on our tribal council."

"You're kidding." Val looked astounded.

"It gets worse," Marie said. "He's my opponent in the council election. I'm actually running against him."

Val was speechless. "This . . . This is crazy. I don't even know what to say. And he's the one who killed Jerome?"

"Well," I said, "Mitch is no tough guy. I can't really see him going out there and smashing Jerome in the head. But he must be the one who set it up. That's where you come in."

"Me?" Val asked. "What can I do?"

"You're a hacker, right?" Marie said. "Can you, um, break into his messages at the tribal council and see what he's done? Is that possible?"

"Maybe," Val said. "It depends on what sort of security your tribe's got. Most tribal governments do not exactly have strong cybersecurity or access controls." She paused for a moment. "But you know, I really doubt he'd use his tribal government email to send anything sensitive. I'd need to know what other email client he uses."

"No clue," Marie said. "You know as much as we do at this point."

"Hey, I like a challenge!" Val said. "Let me do some digging and see what I can come up with. Does anyone else know about this?"

"Sort of," I said. "I had a meeting with our police chief the other day and asked if she could investigate Mitch. She said she couldn't do anything unless she had some proof—she said it's called, uh—"

"Probable cause," Val said. "I heard a lot about that from the people I used to work with."

"This is all so crazy," Marie said. "My head's been spinning."

"Me, too," Val said. "About this Mitch person, are you going to go, you know, talk to him, Virgil?"

"You mean rough him up?" I said. "I'd like to, but he's kind of untouchable at this point."

Marie took another drink from her coffee, grimacing as she swallowed. "It stinks, but he's kind of a big deal around here—you know, tribal councilman, board of directors, all that. We need to get some real proof. Val, are you willing to give it a shot?"

Val looked first at Marie, then me. "I'm in. Let's get this asshole."

"All right!" Marie said. "I like this team."

After we finished our coffee, we said our goodbyes to Val, and then the four of us piled into Marie's Subaru to get back to my house. I didn't mind leaving my truck at Marie's house overnight if it meant a more comfortable ride back for everyone.

"Val is so cool," Shawna said.

"I really like her," Marie said. "She's very kind and dedicated to our community. Where'd you meet her again, Virgil?"

"At the old boarding school in Rapid City. I had sort of passed out, and she came over to check on me."

"Leksi, why did you pass out?" Nathan asked.

I was touched by Nathan's words. He'd called me *leksi*, which means uncle in Lakota. He'd honored me by using that word, and I hoped this was a good sign for us.

"Toska," I said, pronouncing the word carefully, "some pain meds I took hit me pretty hard and I had to lie down. Val was really nice to me, and it turned out we both knew Jerome."

"Is she on socials?" Shawna asked. "I'd like to follow her, maybe ask her some questions about jobs and stuff."

"Don't know," I said. "But I'm sure she'd be happy to speak with you."

Marie turned down the county road near our house. It was a beautiful night outside, and it seemed like I could see the Wanagi Tacanku, our Spirit Trail, known as the Milky Way in English. I remembered my mom told me that every child is given a spirit when they are born, and that spirit returns to the Wanagi Tacanku when the person passes on. Memories of my mother flashed in my mind, and I remembered her face, her smile, her laugh. I made a mental note to show Nathan pictures of her when we got inside. I wanted him to know her face and make his grandmother part of his life, even though she'd been gone for a long time.

Marie turned down our street and into our driveway, and I looked down at my phone for messages. No one had messaged or called, which suited me just fine.

"Virgil, what—what is that?" Marie said and pointed at our house.

I looked up and didn't understand what I was seeing. White-orange flames and smoke were pouring out of the living room and bedroom windows.

Our house was on fire.

We all jumped out of the Subaru and stared at the house, trying to comprehend what we were seeing. The white-hot flames rose ten feet in the air, dancing and swaying, surrounded by dusky smoke circling the blaze. There was a bitter, acrid smell radiating from the inferno, and we heard the crackle and sizzle of wood burning, reminiscent of a campfire in the forest. I was transfixed, unable to move or think, as I watched my home turn to ashes.

"Oh my god!" Nathan yelled. "Ava's in there!"

Our beautiful and sweet little doggy was inside the firestorm.

He took off running, and I snapped out of my reverie.

"Nathan, wait!" I yelled, but it was too late.

He rushed to the front door, which was smoking and smoldering. He tried to open the door, but it was locked. He reared back, kicked the door open and ran inside.

I turned to Marie, who appeared to be in shock.

"Call 911!" I shouted, then sprinted to the house after Nathan.

I ran inside and looked around. The room was filled with dense gray smoke, the walls burning and fire ropes moving across the ceiling. The heat was overwhelming, and it was already difficult to breathe. I couldn't see Nathan, and I began to panic. My eyes were stinging, and I started to cough. I realized that I could only last a minute or two inside the house—the toxic smoke was already making me dizzy.

"Nathan, where are you?" I shouted as loudly as I could, then coughed again.

No response.

I peered around our living room and kitchen. He wasn't there, so he had to be in one of the two bedrooms. He was likely in the main bedroom, as that's where Ava loved to sleep when everyone was gone. One wall of the hallway was burning, but it looked like there was enough room for me to squeeze through.

I took a big breath of the smoky air and ran past the flames, holding my breath and keeping my eyes closed. I made it to the master bedroom door, which was slightly ajar. I pushed the door open with my foot and looked inside. The bedroom was blazing, a hellfire of yellow and orange flames and thick, choking smoke. I started to cough uncontrollably and began gasping for air, choking as the smoke and fumes overpowered me. My left shirtsleeve was on fire, I noticed. Strangely, I didn't feel any pain but realized that I should stamp out the flames. It was becoming difficult to concentrate, and I began to feel disoriented and confused.

I sank to my knees and tried to breathe, but that was becoming impossible. I tried to focus on finding Nathan, but my dizziness was increasing and I couldn't think clearly. My vision became blurry, and my head felt heavy. Images of my mother and father traveled through my mind, followed by memories of my sister Sybil. I wanted to speak to her and tell her how much I missed her. I wanted to tell her about Nathan and that she'd be proud of him. The room seemed to darken even though the flames continued to burn.

Then I looked up and saw Plenty Horses standing by the door. He pointed at me and started speaking, although it was difficult to understand him. I tried to tell him to leave me alone, but he wouldn't listen.

*Get up.*

*Get up and go to the closet.*

The closet.

There was a closet in my bedroom.

I remembered this.

Then I understood, and I swam through the currents of confusion in my brain and forced myself to stand up in the burning hallway. I peered through the smoke into the master bedroom. The walls were burning, as were the dresser, table, and desk. The room was almost completely ablaze, and I realized I was out of time.

I ran past the flames and threw open the closet door. Nathan was inside, bent over on the floor, shielding Ava with his body and protecting her from the flames. Both of them were motionless.

"Nathan, are you awake?" I said, then leaned over and shook him. "Get up!"

He opened his eyes and squinted at me.

"Come on," I said. "We have to get out of here!"

I helped him up and he began coughing. Ava had awakened as well. She was shaking in fear and began crying and yelping, her terrified sounds breaking my heart.

"Let's go," I shouted.

"Wait," he said. He stumbled, then scooped up little Ava and cradled her in his arms.

I turned to him. "You ready? Follow me!"

We rushed through the flames and smoke to the front door, then darted down the stairs to the lawn, gulping in oxygen as we ran. I collapsed on the ground, and Marie rushed over to me. The dizziness returned, and I dimly realized that Marie was beating on my arms and legs for some reason. I saw Nathan and Ava on the lawn, Shawna hovering over them. Ava was whimpering and crying, and I tried to tell Marie to give Ava a belly scratch.

I heard the sound of a siren in the distance as the world began to bruise and fray at the edges, my vision unraveling as everything became dark.

SOMETHING FELT WRONG WITH my face.

I opened my eyes and realized I had an oxygen mask on.

"How you doing there?" A paramedic hovered over me—a young Native guy wearing a cap. "You feel okay?"

I felt like shit. My head hurt, my chest was congested, my arm and leg throbbed, and I feared I was going to throw up. I began to take off the oxygen mask so I could speak, but the paramedic held up his hand.

"Why don't you keep that on for a bit?"

I shook my head and fumbled with the device.

"Let me help you." He slid the mask off. "I'll get you a cannula, okay? Fits on your nose. Be right back."

"Virgil, you need oxygen. You nearly died in there," Marie said. She was sitting next to me on the grass in front of our house. I rubbed my eyes and looked around. Fire trucks, an ambulance, and about fifteen people milling around.

The EMT returned with an oxygen canister and nasal cannula, which he placed on my nose, telling me to keep it on for the next few hours and that he'd be back to check out my burns.

Burns? Then I remembered. "Where's Nathan?"

"He's all right," Marie said. "They're taking him to the hospital to be observed. Shawna went with him."

I was still struggling to piece together everything that had happened. "Why, uh, what . . . is he burned?"

"No. I mean, a little bit. It's for smoke inhalation. He was wheezing, so they want to give him some medicine and make sure his throat doesn't swell up. I guess he took in more smoke than you."

"How about Ava?"

Marie smiled. "She's just scared. Nathan saved her, you know. She refused to leave his side, so Shawna took her along to the hospital. I'll go pick her up later. The poor little dog was trembling like I've never seen."

A wave of relief passed through me. Both Nathan and Ava had survived.

"You were burned too, you know. When you ran out, I had to put out fires on your leg and arm. But the paramedics said it didn't look too bad. They were more worried about your throat and lungs. They've got some pain meds for you when you're ready."

"I think I'm ready for them now." I was beginning to feel some pain on my upper arm. "How long was I passed out?"

"Maybe an hour. They talked about taking you to the hospital, but I guess bed space is short over there."

"Fine with me. You know I hate hospitals."

She smiled. "Yeah, I know. But if you start having trouble breathing, we need to go over there right away. I'm serious about that." She looked over her shoulder. "I'll go get those pain pills for you now."

I nodded. "It's funny," I said. "I've been craving a smoke for the last year. Guess I got my wish."

"You must be okay if you're telling dad jokes now."

I glanced at the remains of my home. "How bad is it? The house."

"Probably a total loss. They don't know yet, but it doesn't look good."

I didn't want to think about this right now. "Hey, do those guys have any water? I really need some."

"Sure, be right back with some water and the meds."

I looked around and observed that there were two fire trucks parked on the street. One was spraying water on what used to be my home, and the other one was off to the side, sending giant streams of water on the brush and land around my place. The dual trucks were a result of the strange policies of the Bureau of Indian Affairs fire department. For some reason, the BIA would only handle field and brush fires, not structures, while the Rosebud Sioux Tribe volunteer fire department was the unit that dealt with house fires. I'd heard that there had been a great deal of complaints about this situation, but that was the least of my worries at the moment.

Marie came back with a bottle of water and some pills. "Hey, look who showed up."

Rose Charging Cloud trailed behind Marie. "How you doing, big guy? See you got some oxygen going."

"I'm okay, all things considered." I took a big gulp of water, which tasted wonderful, maybe the best drink I'd ever had in my life. Then I swallowed the pain pills.

She nodded. "Good to hear. I heard the call come in over the radio, but I didn't know this was your address. Ty Bad Hand clued me in, so I thought I'd stop by."

"Appreciate it," I said. "My boy Nathan is at the hospital. Guess they want to watch him, but it sounds like he'll make it."

"So I heard. Really glad about that." She turned and looked at the damage, then whistled. "Damn, that's a bad one. I heard you ran inside?"

"Had to. Nathan had gone in to save our dog."

Rose whistled again. "That I didn't hear. Your boy sounds like a good one. I love dogs—anyone who'd risk their life for a pup is okay in my book." She looked at Marie and me. "Can I ask you two about the fire, or would you rather wait until later?"

"I'm fine," Marie said. "How about you, Virgil?"

"No time like the present. Go ahead."

Rose raised her eyebrows. "All righty, then. So, what happened here? You two have any idea?"

"You mean what caused it?" Marie said. "The fire?"

Rose nodded.

"No idea," Marie said. "I mean, we didn't leave any candles burning or anything like that."

"Uh-huh. You have any items like space heaters or propane grills inside?"

I didn't understand. "Uh, no. Who'd put a propane grill in a house?"

"You'd be surprised at the stupid stuff I see. Any flammable materials inside?"

"Of course not," I said.

"You guys have any electrical problems or malfunctioning appliances?"

I paused and tried to remember. "We've got an old blender that quit working."

Rose blinked. "Okay. You guys smoke? Cigs, anything else?"

"Not anymore," I said. "Gave it up a while back. But I never smoked in the house. Nathan hated it, said it smelled like old people."

"Ouch, that stings," Rose said. "You guys know of any ignition sources—anything you can think of?"

We were both quiet while we thought about her question. "Not that I can think of," Marie said.

"No one was inside when the fire started, right? Just the dog."

"That's right," Marie said. "We were having a dinner party at my place. My parents' house, out past the highway."

"Sure, fine. Did you guys lock up when you left?"

This I knew. "Yes, I always do. Without fail."

"Okay. Do you know when the fire started?"

Marie and I each spoke at the same time, but she stopped and motioned for me to speak. "We went to Marie's place at five, so it had to have been after that."

"You notice any strange odors before you left?"

I shook my head. "No, nothing."

"Okay. Any witnesses? Anybody see anything?"

"Don't think so," Marie replied. "I mean, nobody's said anything to us."

Rose nodded. "Virgil, you were inside the house during the fire. You notice any strange smells? Anything at all."

I had more water as I thought about that. "I do remember coughing and smelling something weird inside there. But maybe that was just stuff burning."

Rose raised her hand up. "Okay, thanks. I guess we're at square one. Doesn't sound like there are any obvious causes. Most fires around here are due to some problem with a propane system. Or some numbnuts cooking meth." She closed her eyes and shook her head. "Those people. The cranksters. Jesus."

She looked up and waited to see if we had anything to add to that.

"Terrible," Marie said. "I hate that stuff."

"Agreed. So, look, I know you two have been through a lot today. But, I have to raise the question of arson."

Arson. I hadn't even thought of that. "Wait, you think somebody did this on purpose?"

"I didn't say that. I don't know. But you're caught up in some stuff right now, Virgil."

Jesus Christ, the Pine Ridge gang. Of course. I'd been too addled after the fire to think clearly. "The gangbangers. Is that what you're thinking?"

She shrugged. "I have to look at all possibilities. Who knows, maybe this was just a gas stove going bad."

"We've got an electric range," Marie said.

"Sure, I understand. I'm just thinking out loud here."

I was still somewhat foggy from the smoke inhalation, but I recalled that the gangster called Shorty had threatened me just days ago.

"I think you could be right," I said to Rose. "Those fucking gangbangers. There's one who really hates me and talked some shit not long ago."

"Out in Pine Ridge?"

"Yeah, when I went there last week. It all lines up. What's next? Can you investigate them?"

She chuckled. "We don't really have the manpower to do arson investigations. Not to mention, the tribal penalties for arson are laughable here. An arson conviction gets a max of one year in tribal jail and a five-thousand-dollar fine. If this is really arson, the best bet is the feds. A federal conviction for arson gets five to twenty years in prison, double that if anyone is injured."

"So the FBI will take the case?" Marie asked.

Rose gave a pained smile. "I mean, it's possible, but I think you know that they decline most of the referrals I give them. But I promise you I'll send it to them."

My anger was starting to come back, along with some pain in my left arm and leg. "If the FBI won't do anything, maybe someone else can. Goddamn assholes." I tossed my empty water bottle on the ground.

Rose held up her index finger. "Wounded Horse, don't you get any ideas about vigilante shit. You stay out of this."

I glanced at Rose and Marie, who were both looking at me intensely.

"Yeah, sure. No revenge."

I smiled at them while the oxygen flowed into my lungs and through my blood, clearing out the toxic chemicals I'd inhaled. I breathed in deeply, attempting to regain the balance I'd lost.

The next few weeks were difficult for all of us as we came to grips with what had happened. Thankfully, no one had been badly injured. Nathan was in the hospital for only one night, and there didn't appear to be any lasting damage to his lungs. I had some minor burns, but I dealt with those with the help of the pain meds. Ava was fine, too; I wondered if she even remembered the events of that night. I envied animals' ability to move forward without holding grudges.

However, we were all damaged, mentally and emotionally. There'd been a deep sense of unreality in the first few days after the fire as we scrambled to regain some sense of normality. Nathan and I moved in with Marie at her parents' house. Marie was fantastic after the incident, buying clothing and other essentials for us, given that Nathan and I literally had only the clothes on our backs. She'd made us feel at home right away, but Nate remained traumatized by the fire. He'd been spending most of his time at Shawna's house, and I didn't object.

Although we were all depressed, the fire hit me the hardest, as it seemed like our hopes and plans for the future had been destroyed along with our possessions. Marie was busy with campaign activities, so I had some time by myself to think about things. In the evenings when Marie was home, we'd watch television—science fiction dramas, fantasy films, anything to take us away from our reality. It was hard not to feel hopeless, and that our lives would never be the same. Of course Tommy, Rocky, Pudge, Charley, and others had called and offered assistance and words of support, and I'd been grateful to hear from them. But the sudden upheaval caused by the fire left me disjointed and disheartened, detached from the routines and schedules of regular life, and feeling like a ghost in my own community.

The hardest part was realizing that we'd lost nearly everything. Our clothing, furniture, bedding, appliances, pots and pans, books, and—worst of all—our photographs and special items. Even Ava's favorite dog toy was gone, the one that she slept with. I'd always tried to not invest too much emotion in material goods, but it was difficult to realize that our precious photos and documents were gone. Snaps of Nathan playing basketball as a little kid, pictures of my mother holding me as a baby, photos of Sybil graduating from high school.

And of course we'd lost our house, the only home Nathan had ever known, the place where we'd existed as a family. Our little house had been modest, but it held a universe of memories for me. I'd been raised in that space, having moved there with my mother right after my father passed on to the spirit world. As the days progressed, I attempted to elude the sadness I was feeling, but the miasma of the loss shadowed me, becoming an almost physical presence.

To shake off this malaise, I decided to go out and visit the ruins of the house. I knew it would be upsetting, but perhaps visiting the site would allow me to move forward. Strangely, I felt nervous as I drove there, although I didn't know why. Perhaps I was afraid to face the finality of how our lives had changed, or perhaps I just didn't want to relive the horrors of that day.

It was quiet when I arrived. I parked in my usual spot and walked over to the remnants of our lives. Part of the house was intact—

the foundation, some of the beams and joists, a few walls. Inside, there was a tremendous amount of ashes, charred wood, and other debris and detritus. I thought I recognized some skeletons of our furniture, the charred and ghostly remains of our beds, chairs, and couches. Of course there'd be no compensation for those items, as we'd never had any renter's insurance for the tribally owned house, but I wasn't concerned with that. What I wished we'd had was some type of emotional insurance, a policy that could magically restore your mental and spiritual self to its former state.

I considered poking around in the ashes to see if anything had somehow survived the blaze, but I didn't have the heart for that, not to mention that there were likely several dozen nasty chemicals floating around in there.

I stood at the site for a while, alone with my memories. I remembered my mother cooking and laughing while her beloved country music played; Nathan assembling some toy on the floor of the living room, the entire room a mess but his smile as wide as the prairie; my times with Marie, listening as she spoke of her daily triumphs and disappointments. Our lives in that little structure were over, a fact that was hard to accept.

I moved around to the back of the wreckage, where the bedrooms had been and where I'd stored my few belongings. I realized that our cultural and ceremonial items were also gone—the eagle feathers given to me and Nathan by Jerome, my medicine bag, a canunpa that had belonged to my grandfather. These objects may not have been worth any money, but they had meant everything to me. Their loss left me feeling unmoored and unprotected.

I looked one last time at the charred structure, then walked back to my truck. I doubted I'd come back. The ruins of the place would remain, as the tribe had no funds for debris removal. The bones of our former dwelling would gradually be eclipsed by nature, the wood and metal and ashes transforming into something new, something that hadn't existed before.

As I drove away, I felt the sadness begin to lift. Our lives had changed irreversibly, and it was time to inhabit that new space. But to do so, I needed to right the wrongs that had been done to us. Whoever set this fire had destroyed more than our possessions; they'd stolen our balance and harmony. It was time to reclaim what had been taken.

THE NEXT DAY I called Rose Charging Cloud and asked her about the arson case. She didn't want to speak on the phone and asked if I could meet in Valentine, Nebraska, later that day. I readily agreed; Valentine was just twenty miles from the reservation, and I welcomed the chance for a change of scenery.

When the time came, I arrived early and wandered down Main Street, Valentine's business district. I looked at novels in the Plains Trading Company bookstore, then browsed in a little boutique for a few minutes. I kept walking and was surprised to see that the Stagedoor Bar was still open. The town had been trying for years to close the place, given that it occasionally featured exotic dancers.

At seven p.m. I strolled down one more block to the barbeque restaurant that Rose had specified. She was already there, seated outside on a picnic table and wiping her hands and face with a Wet-Nap.

"Hey there," she said. "Thanks for driving down. I had a meeting earlier and thought I'd get a quick bite of this BBQ before I head back."

"No problem. Happy to get out of town. How's the barbeque?"

"Not bad, not bad at all. Pretty decent beef brisket." She tossed her paper plate and napkins in the trash can. "I got hooked on BBQ when I lived in Texas way back when. They really know how to do it down there. I ate some ribs once at a gas station in the Texas hill country, thought I'd died and gone to heaven."

I'd only had real barbeque a few times, but I made a mental note to try the new Valentine restaurant when I was back on my feet financially.

"Anyway," she continued, "let's get to it. You want to talk about the fire at your place, right?"

"Yeah. You said that you'd send the case over to the FBI. Any news?"

Her lips pressed together and made a flat line. "Sort of. I did refer it to them, but they declined it. Didn't give any reasons. That's pretty much what I thought would happen."

This was expected, but still disappointing. "So that's it? No way to get them to change their minds?"

"Not really. I suppose if we made an arrest, we could try again. But that seems unlikely. Unless you have something new for me."

I didn't. I'd worked through multiple scenarios in my head about what caused the fire, and there was only one that made sense. The 705 gang. I'd made enemies in the past, sure, but those dimwits were especially motivated right now to strike at me.

"Nothing new. But I'm pretty sure the Pine Ridge gang did it. They vandalized my friend Pudge's car, so it's not hard to believe they torched my place."

She tapped her nose. "Yeah, it makes sense; I've been thinking along the same lines. I got something to say about that, but let me switch gears first. Another case."

She looked around to see if anyone was within earshot of us. "So, you got anything for me about Jerome Iron Shell? You dropped a bombshell not long ago."

It seemed like she was afraid to even say Mitch Gagnon's name out loud. No wonder she'd wanted to meet in Nebraska.

"No, I asked my hacker friend for the emails you wanted. I haven't heard back."

"Ah, okay. I've been doing some digging on our friend."

This was interesting. "You find anything out?"

"Nothing yet. Look, follow up with your hacker pal, okay? I'm getting signals that the FBI might take over Jerome's case, so I need some leads before they step in."

"Will do," I said. "So, what about the fire? The arson, I guess. If the FBI won't do nothing, maybe—"

"Hold on." She held out her hands as if in supplication. "I feel bad for you, Wounded Horse. You and your boy, losing your house that way. It's terrible. But there's not much I can do. Except . . ."

She stopped speaking and put her head down, her hand on her chin. After a moment, she looked up. "Okay. You remember the Pine Ridge police chief? I mentioned him when you got arrested out there."

"Uh, sort of."

"Clyde Conquering Bear. Thing is, Clyde and I had a little thing going, a long time ago. In Texas, actually. He's still pretty fond of me."

I didn't understand why she was telling me about her love life.

"He's the one who kept you safe in Pine Ridge after I asked him."

I still wasn't following this, but I nodded like I understood.

"Like I said, I agree with you it's possible those Pine Ridge idiots might have lit up your place. Sounds like the sort of crap they'd pull. So I called up Clyde a few days ago and asked for another favor."

She reached into her pocket and pulled out a sheet of paper.

"He made a few calls and got what I asked for. But you didn't get this from me, all right? In fact, we never had this conversation."

"Sure, absolutely."

I opened the paper and looked at it. A street address and a telephone number.

"What's this?" I asked.

"It's the address of the hooch house on Pine Ridge. The place where the 705 gang sells their booze. Bear and the other guys. And that's the number you call to set up a buy. You park in front of the house, call them, they come out with a bottle. You get it?"

I got it, all right. It was time for another trip to Pine Ridge to visit the 705. The last time I was there, I'd screwed up by falling asleep and nearly been killed.

I wouldn't make that mistake again.

barely focused on the road on the drive back from Valentine as I mulled over the information Rose had given me. It was surprising, to say the least. Given our past history, there was no reason to expect a favor from her, but she'd handed me a way to strike back at the assholes in Pine Ridge. A chance to get some Indian justice.

The people asking me to beat someone up for them always said that they deserved justice, but I still didn't know the real meaning of that word. Was it justice that we Native people had our lands stolen from us without any compensation? Not to mention the broken treaties and promises, the children abducted and taken to the boarding schools, the laws that made our spirituality illegal. Professor Cortings told me that, a few decades ago, the US government had made an official apology to Native people for all of the wrongs done to us, but without a promise to make things right. Perhaps this was the point: We'd never receive any remedies or reparations and would remain second-class citizens forever. That was our American justice.

But Jerome once told me that Native justice was a form of love and kindness—helping someone in need or showing mercy. Sadly, I didn't see much of that in the world, here on the rez or beyond. The best I could do was to keep my family safe. Someone had taken a match to our home, and it was sheer luck that we weren't inside. If I didn't do something, they'd come again. It was time to put an end to this.

That was the only justice I could see right now.

But I'd have to do it right this time. My mistake had been going out to Pine Ridge alone. If I was going to confront the 705 on their turf, I'd need some backup. Someone I could trust.

I grabbed my cell phone and hit the button.

"Hey homeboy, how you doing?" Tommy said.

"You got a few minutes?"

I told him what was happening with Rose and the hooch house. He didn't hesitate when I asked if he was willing to join me, but he said we'd need more people if we were going to throw down with the 705 boys. According to him, there'd been bad blood between the Rosebud and Pine Ridge gangs for a while, and some local guys might be willing to join us.

This was prime Tommy. Some people didn't take him seriously, but he knew everyone on the reservation and all the feuds, alliances, and beefs. He was friendly with all and moved easily among groups. And he wasn't afraid to mix it up when he had to. I once saw him fight a drunk rancher who was abusing a woman in the casino parking lot. Of course, once he'd saved her, she started screaming at Tommy and calling him names. He just laughed it off and went on his way.

The next days passed quickly. I spent as much time at home as I could, trying not to think about what was coming. Marie and I had discussed the situation, and she understood my position. She didn't condone violence, but the 705 gang weren't likely to engage in a restorative justice conversation. Nathan remained depressed, still shaken by what had happened. Shawna had been tremendously supportive of him, and they were inseparable, apparently past whatever problems they'd been having.

I woke up at six a.m. one morning and found Nathan at the dining room table at Marie's house, eating some oatmeal and berries.

"Morning, leksi," he said.

"You're up early."

He smiled apologetically. "I couldn't sleep. I keep having these really bad dreams."

I understood that. My dream life lately had consisted of images from the house fire combined with nightmarish scenarios in which I was fighting unknown assailants.

"Yeah, me too. It's a strange time. Trying to get used to living here with Marie. Sometimes I wake up and don't know where I am."

"That happened to me, too! Really bizarre, bro."

*Bro.* Not sure what to make of that, but I let it go. "You got school later?" I asked.

He looked at me strangely. "Leksi, it's Sunday."

So it was. The days had become jumbled for me as I worked through everything. "Oh, right. I'm a little out of it."

"I kind of noticed," he said. "I mean, it's totally understandable. I can, like, barely focus in school. I keep thinking about the people who tried to kill us. Shawna's been telling me about forgiveness and stuff, but how am I supposed to do that?"

I didn't know what to say to him. What had happened was unforgivable, and I didn't want to give him some horseshit that he'd see through immediately.

"Look, I understand what Shawna's saying. She doesn't want you to lose focus on what's important. You know, school, family, friends. But I can't tell you not to be angry. Because I am. I'm freaking incredibly angry at the people who did it."

He had a strange look on his face. "So, I feel kind of weird telling you this, but I can hear you talking to Marie. In the house. Your voices come through the air vent. It's strange, it sounds like ghosts. But I can definitely make out what you guys are saying."

I felt exposed and embarrassed, learning that Nathan had heard our private conversations. I guess it made sense. We had him in Marie's old room, which was right next to the master bedroom, where she and I slept. We'd talk in there when we wanted privacy.

"So, uh, you can hear us? Everything?"

He looked guilty, like he'd been spying. "I mean, a little. I usually have my ear buds in, so it's not, like, all the time."

This was not really comforting. I'd speak to Marie later about this and see what she could do about the situation.

"Not your fault," I said. "This is all new, and we're figuring things out. I appreciate you telling me."

"Yeah, about that," he said. "I guess I did hear you guys talking about the fire. And that you think some dudes from Pine Ridge did it. And that you want to go out there and kick their asses."

Shit. The one thing I'd tried to keep from him.

"Yeah, that's true, but it's complicated." I stopped and thought about how to put it. "I got involved because that gang was threatening my friend Pudge. We kind of got into it. Now it looks like they're striking back. I'm really sorry. I didn't know that all this would happen."

"So, what are you gonna do?" He paused. "Like, hurt them really bad?"

This was the question I'd been avoiding in my own head. I didn't have a definite endgame, beyond threatening the gang with severe harm if they bothered any of us again. But I couldn't lie to Nathan.

"I don't want to get in a fight with them, okay? My plan is to bring some people from our rez and scare them. But there is a chance it could get physical. I hope not."

"Leksi, those Pine Ridge guys are crazy! I'm worried about you."

His eyes began to tear up, and I saw that he was struggling to control his emotions.

"Toska, I'm going to be fine, okay? I promise you."

He didn't say anything, just looked at me, his eyelids trembling.

FOUR DAYS LATER, I heard from Tommy on my cell phone.

"Aight, my man," he said. "You still up for this? I got two of the Native Posse to join us. They itchin' to brawl with the 705."

Gang members from Rosebud. This sounded like an extremely bad idea, but I didn't have many options.

"I don't know, Tommy. Who are they?"

"Boots and Joe. I told 'em about the 705 coming to Rosebud and givin' Pudge grief. They said boo-shit on that. I think they get their hooch from him. And one of them's his cousin, maybe."

"All right, if you're sure."

"Yeah, they cool. I vouch," he said. "Hey, is Pudge gonna come along?"

"Good thought," I said. "I'll call him."

"Hold on, dude." I heard him taking a drink of something— probably one of his supercaffeinated energy drinks. "So listen, I got some deets on the 705 boys and the hooch house. Word is that a couple of them stay there, but the whole crew go there at night to party."

"You know which ones live there? Any names?"

"The big homie, for sure."

"Who?" I didn't understand.

"The shot caller. You know, the boss."

"Could be the guy called Bear."

"That the one you tangled with?"

"Yep. He's the one I want."

I heard him take another drink, then belch. "What if he ain't there?"

"I don't know. Maybe fuck up whoever's at the place."

He snorted. "There's the old Virg! I like it."

I thought about what Tommy had said about the hooch house—that the whole gang would party it up in the evenings.

"What do you think?" I asked. "Head over there late at night when they're drunk and stupid, or during the day?"

"Hit 'em in the day, for sure! They be all hungover and shit. Feel me?"

"Yeah, makes sense. Probably not as many people around."

"That's what I'm sayin'. You wanna go out there this weekend?"

"Let's do it," I said. "No reason to wait."

"An old-fashioned rumble! We gonna throw down. Dang, I like it."

I LEFT EARLY ON Saturday morning for Tommy's place, where we'd all agreed to meet. The plan was to drive out to Pine Ridge and arrive around noon, when the 705 guys would likely still be sleeping or nursing hangovers. We'd park near the hooch house and scope it out first, then call the number and ask for a delivery. When the door opened, we'd bum-rush our way inside and confront them. We hadn't discussed anything beyond that.

I parked my truck in front and went inside, not bothering to knock. Pudge was already there, sitting on the dirty blue couch that Tommy found in the garbage at the Sunrise Apartments a few years back. We'd gotten it to his place by balancing it on the roof of my old Ford Pinto, holding it down through the windows.

"Hey there, homes!" Tommy was wearing jeans with a hole in the knee and a T-shirt that read SAGE AGAINST THE MACHINE. "Coffee if you want. Got some Ding Dongs and Donettes, too."

I nodded to Pudge and shook his hand. He looked nervous, maybe a little scared. Even though he wasn't a fighter, I'd asked him to come along so he could get some closure with the Pine Ridge guys. Not to mention, Pudge was a very big guy. If you didn't know how gentle he was, you'd be intimidated by his sheer size.

"What the hell's a Donette?" I asked.

"Mini doughnut, man! Got 'em at the dollar store. What, you all fancy now that you stayin' at Marie's crib?"

They looked pretty dried out, but I grabbed one and some weak coffee and sat down.

"We waitin' on Boots and Joe," Tommy said. "They'll be here."

I had my doubts, but I focused on the coffee and snack. While we waited, we talked about the hooch house and our strategies. The goal was to intimidate the 705 guys so that they'd stay away from our rez and remain on their own turf. I didn't mention it to Tommy and Pudge, but I also planned to find out if they had any role in Jerome's murder. And of course I'd find out which asshole had burned down my house. I had a special punishment planned for him involving my brass knuckles and stun gun. When I was done, he'd never be able to light a match again.

Forty-five minutes later, Boots and Joe showed up.

"NP in the house!" Tommy said and hugged both of the guys. "Virg, this here is Joe, and this one is Boots. I think you guys know Pudge."

"Pudge!" Joe said. "Yo, cuz!"

Pudge stood up and greeted him. It wasn't surprising they were related, as everyone on the rez was separated by only a few degrees. When Natives said "We are all related," they really meant it.

I went over and shook their hands. They looked to be in their early twenties, both wearing bandannas around their necks and cutoff T-shirts, their arms and hands heavily tatted. I spotted the letters NP on both of them. Native Posse. Weirdly, the one called Boots also had a large tattoo of the old actor Bela Lugosi on his upper arm. Maybe the guy had a Dracula fetish. There was a faint smell of weed surrounding them, and I hoped they weren't high. Maybe that was just their residual odor.

"You two down to rumble?" Tommy said, looking at Boots and Joe.

"Shit, yeah," Boots said. "I hate them 705 punks. Fuck them."

"Ain't no one mess with my man," Joe added, nodding at Pudge. "We bring some Sicangu thunder on them mofos."

I liked their enthusiasm but wondered about their fighting skills. Hopefully, it wouldn't come to that. Boots and Joe helped themselves to Tommy's forlorn pastries, and we told them about the plan while they ate. I asked the Native Posse guys if they had any more info about the 705 gang, but they didn't offer anything other than to repeat that they were punks and bitches.

After they devoured the rest of the food, we loaded into my truck, Tommy and Pudge joining me in the cab, the Native Posse guys riding in the bed. Once we got rolling on Highway 18, I leaned over to Tommy and asked about Boots and Joe.

"Dude, are those guys stoned? They reek of weed."

He shook his head. "Naw, they good. Probably did smoke a little peji, but that's like a cup of coffee to you or me. You know, just gettin' their heart started."

"If you say so. Just want to be sure they can handle themselves."

"Homes, you ain't got to worry. Them two don't take no shit." He nudged me with his elbow. "I tried to get a couple more Native Posse guys to come, but they didn't show. You know, Indian time."

Indian time was the common stereotype that Native people operated on their own clocks and so were always late to jobs, school, or any other obligation. I'd hated the expression until Jerome explained it to me. He'd said that Lakota people didn't view time the same way as Europeans. Rather than using hours or minutes, we divided the day into four different periods—dawn, noon, sunset, and midnight—and we arranged our lives according to the rhythms of those phases. Living that way, he'd said, meant that you were always on time and always ready. The traditional phrase was "Nake nula waun," which means "I am prepared for anything." Lakota warriors often sang that before going into battle—a recognition of being ready for all outcomes, including death. As I drove, I repeated the phrase to myself, the words ringing in my head.

Two hours later, we arrived in the town of Pine Ridge. I stopped at a gas station on the edge of town to give everyone a chance to stretch their legs. Tommy sprinted for the men's room, and Pudge went inside to get a bottle of water. When everyone reconvened, we stood beside my truck for a minute.

"Everyone good?" I asked.

"Let's do it," Tommy said. "Hoka!"

"All right, I'll park around the corner from the house. Tommy, you stay with the truck and call for a bottle of booze. The rest of us will stand by the front door. When they come out with the hooch, I'll push my way in. You guys follow me inside and cover me. Make sure they don't grab no weapons, okay?"

Pudge cleared his throat. "Virgil, I ain't going in there empty-handed. Not after last time." He pulled a small handgun out of his pocket.

"Sheeit, Pudge!" Tommy said. "You ain't playin'."

I was surprised, as I'd never known Pudge to own a gun. I'd thought about bringing my Glock but had settled on my stun gun and knucks so I wouldn't be tempted to shoot anyone. Hopefully, this wouldn't turn out to be a mistake.

"Anybody else packing?" I needed to get a sense of our firepower.

Nobody said anything.

"All right," I said. "Look, we just want to scare these guys, right? No sense in anyone going to jail. If shit gets serious, let me handle it." I looked over at Pudge, and he gave a slight nod.

We got back into the truck and arrived at the hooch house just minutes later. I parked across the street from the place so we couldn't be seen from inside. The house was one of the manufactured homes that were common on reservations in South Dakota. It had once been painted bright blue, but time and weather had faded the color by several shades. There was a patch of dirt and weeds in front, with a few empty liquor bottles and scraps of trash scattered around. The house next door was boarded up, which meant it had been used as a meth lab and was no longer fit for people to live in. An old Chevy sedan was parked next to a rusty Ford Ranger truck in front, but the neighborhood looked deserted.

"You see anyone?" Pudge said. The curtains were drawn on the front window, so it was impossible to look inside.

"Seems empty," I said. "Guess there's one way to find out."

I got out of the truck, followed by Tommy and Pudge. Boots and Joe climbed out of the back and joined us on the sidewalk.

"Go ahead and make the call," I said to Tommy.

He punched in the numbers on his phone, and we all waited. Earlier, I'd tried to coach him, but he told me that he'd called plenty of bootleggers, and he knew exactly what to say.

"Yo," he said into the phone. "I'm looking to get a few skips, man."

There was a pause. "Maybe four?"

Another pause. "Yeah, that's cool." He gave us the thumbs-up sign with his free hand. "I'm out in front. Thanks, homie."

He ended the call and turned back to us. "They in there, for sure. Trying to sell water bottles at double price, too. No wonder they can't keep no customers."

"Is he coming out here?" I asked.

"Yeah, he said to give him five minutes, and he'd meet me at my car."

"Do you know which guy it was?" I asked. "The one you were talking to."

"Naw, he didn't give no name."

"Okay, let's do this. Tommy, you stay here for now, in case they look outside."

He nodded and leaned back against the truck.

I motioned to the others. "Let's go and wait by the side of the house. When the guy comes out, I'll grab him and drag him back inside. Then you come in, Tommy, and the fun can start."

Tommy flashed me a devil's horns sign with his hand. "Sounds good, chief."

Pudge, Boots, Joe, and I moved from the truck to the side of the house, about five feet from the front door. When the guy came outside, I'd be able to subdue him and allow the other guys to enter the house. We'd have the element of surprise, as I suspected the gangbangers were probably hungover or asleep. My only worry was the possibility that the gang had spotted us on the street—if so, we might be in for it.

The four of us crouched by the side of the house and waited; Tommy remained by the truck. Several minutes passed, and I began to worry. Perhaps they had somehow recognized me and were getting ready to come at us. If so, we'd have to fight them right out in the street, which would be hazardous.

Five more minutes passed. Tommy motioned to me from the truck, lifting his hands to indicate confusion.

"You think he's coming?" whispered Pudge.

"I don't know." I was getting increasingly nervous. If the boot-legger didn't come out soon, I was going to call the whole thing off and we could get the hell out of there.

"Maybe we should—"

As I was speaking, the door began to open.

We all stood up straight. I motioned with my hand for them to wait.

A young guy—maybe nineteen or twenty—emerged from the door, four plastic bottles pressed up against his chest. He looked around, then spotted Tommy across the street. The kid motioned with his head at Tommy, then took a couple of steps forward.

I let him take two more steps, then moved behind him and curled my arm around his neck.

"Drop the bottles."

His head jerked, and the hooch went crashing to the ground. I tightened the pressure before he could get his bearings.

"We're going back inside," I said, and tried to move him backward, but he began flailing and trying to pry me off his neck.

Boots and Joe quickly moved in and grabbed his arms. "Chill out, motherfucker," Boots said, as the guy continued to squirm.

Tommy came running over and opened the door.

"Come on, dipshit," I said, and we pushed the guy back inside, Pudge trailing behind us.

Once we were in the house, I released my hold on the guy's neck, but Joe and Boots kept their grip on his arms, preventing him from making any moves. Tommy shut the door, and I quickly scanned the space.

A tiny living room, with a large television in the corner. Empty Pizza Hut boxes and Subway wrappers on a small table. Scores of Bud and Natural Ice beer cans and a few vodka bottles. Ashtrays overflowing with cigarette butts, lighters, and a few tiny pipes. A broken bookshelf. Plastic lawn chairs. Dirty clothing on the floor and also, inexplicably, an old tire. The smell came next, a mixture of stale beer, filthy socks, and secondhand smoke.

Across the room, an old sofa with someone lying on it.

Bear.

The guy I'd been looking for.

He sat up and looked around, trying to get his bearings as he awakened, pushing his long black hair out of his face and behind his ears. He was wearing oversize gym shorts and a wrinkled T-shirt that didn't fit. His eyes widened when he saw the water bottle guy, who was being restrained by Boots and Joe.

"What the fuck is this?" he said.

"Why don't you just stay right there?" I said.

Bear gazed at me, and I watched the fog suddenly clear from his hungover brain. He glanced around the room and saw my guys.

"Oh shit, it's this motherfucking G with his little crew."

"That's right, asshole," I said. "Thought you could get rid of me? Burn my house down?"

He stood up, wobbling a little as he rose. "Get your fucking asses out of here!"

"Yeah, I don't think so."

He pulled back his arm and threw a weak punch that missed me by two feet, then lost his balance, stumbled, and leaned forward, his head down.

For a split second I stopped and thought about Nathan, rushing into our burning house to save our little dog, risking his life in the process. All our photos and possessions gone, the sadness and depression we'd been dealing with. My family's lives forever altered, all because this sorry asshole wanted to sell booze on our rez.

His arms were down, and his head was unprotected, wide open. I took a step closer, turned my hips, and transferred my weight to my front leg to get maximum power. I dipped my head as I threw an uppercut aimed straight at him. The punch went straight up, not across, and landed directly on his chin, a knockout blow. The force of the blow reverberated throughout my entire body as the hit connected.

His head snapped back about six inches, and his eyes dilated and lost focus. His skin tone went from copper to gray in the space of a second, and he collapsed on the floor. He was unconscious for a bit, then began rolling around, attempting to rise. If this had been a boxing match, the ref would have stopped the fight. Not to mention, if I'd wanted to kill him, it would be easy, given that he was completely incapacitated.

I looked over at water bottle guy, who had quit struggling and stared at me with a look of terror.

"You want some of this?" I said to him, holding up my fist.

He shook his head rapidly, a rat caught in a trap.

"Then shut up and don't cause no trouble."

Bear was still rolling around on the floor, trying to stand. Water bottle guy didn't say anything, but his eyes focused on something behind me, off to the side. I turned and looked around.

Standing in the hallway was the guy called Shorty. The one whose face I'd slashed open. And he had a handgun pointed straight at my heart.

"Shit, I feel like I'm dreamin'," he said, keeping the gun aimed at me. "Scabs, go ahead and sit down. I got this."

Scabs. That was what they called the guy with the hooch. I didn't even want to think about how he'd garnered that nickname.

I glanced over my shoulder and saw that Boots, Joe, and Pudge were standing stock-still. The gangbanger called Scabs moved away from them and sat down on the sofa. Bear had managed to sit up, although he still looked out of it.

"Damn," Shorty said. "You just came right here, makin' it easy. Must have a goddamn death wish. Put your hands up, homes."

I partially complied, moving my hands out to my sides, but not up in the air. Then I took a look at the gun, which was still pointed at my chest. It looked like a little Smith & Wesson M&P9 semiautomatic, but I couldn't tell for sure. At this range, any handgun was dangerous. I kept my eyes on his face to see what he was going to do.

"You know why I'm here," I said.

"What, get your ass capped?"

"You assholes burned down my house."

"What the fuck you talking about?"

I saw that he was trembling, shaky. From what I'd heard, these 705 bangers weren't hard guys. Maybe he'd never confronted anyone with a gun before. I looked over at Pudge and shook my head a little—hopefully he understood that I was telling him to keep his gun in his pocket. If Pudge pulled out his piece, Shorty would start shooting. Boots and Joe were watching me as well, taking my lead.

"You heard me," I said. "You guys fucked up Pudge's car, and you set my crib on fire. And you assholes threatened to hurt Pudge's family, too."

Shorty looked down at Bear, who'd apparently revived. Bear wagged his head and shrugged.

"You just talking shit. Yeah, we done this guy's car," Shorty said, motioning at Pudge. "So fucking what? Homeboy deserved it. We got beef with him and you, that's it. Ain't none of that other stuff true."

"Bullshit," I said. "You expect me to believe that?"

"I don't give a crap what you believe, G. I didn't light no fires or whatever else you say. Me and you, we settle our beef right here. You fucked up my face! Now you gonna pay."

He grasped the pistol with both hands to steady himself and kept it aimed at my chest.

"You want to shoot me?" I said.

He didn't say anything, but his eyes were blazing.

"Go ahead, but be a man and admit what you did. You lit up my house," I said. "Don't be a chickenshit."

"Fuck you!" He took a step forward and raised the pistol. The gun was just inches from my head.

I stood still, waiting to see what he would do, and tried not to breathe.

After an eternity, he stepped back and lowered the gun. I took a deep breath and looked over at Tommy. His eyes were wide, and his head was tilted at a strange angle, like he'd seen a spirit suddenly appear in the room.

"You ain't even worth one of my bullets," Shorty said, looking over at his fellow gang members and shaking his head.

It was quiet for a moment, and no one moved.

Bear got up from the floor and sat down on the couch. "All right, looks like everyone's done throwin' hands and talking shit. Maybe we call a truce and work this beef out. Y'all feel me?"

I glanced over at Pudge, and he nodded. Boots and Joe stayed silent, which I took as agreement.

Bear motioned with his hand at us. "You all makin' me nervous. Maybe cop a squat?"

After a moment I sat down, followed by the others. There weren't enough dirty lawn chairs, so Tommy sat cross-legged on the floor.

Bear rubbed his chin. "Dang, you can throw a punch, homie. I was seein' stars for a while. Thought I was talking to my iná, and shit, she died ten damn years ago."

"Sorry to hear that," I said.

"Yeah, she got sick real fast. Gone before I even say goodbye."

I wasn't surprised. The Holy Road section in the *Lakota Times* was filled with people who had died too soon. Seeing all of the notices for the babies was hard.

"My mom passed, too," I said.

He pursed his lips. "It's a bitch, ain't it? Guess it's my boys that's my family now. Even though they's a bunch a stank-ass mofos!"

Bear seemed oddly nostalgic, and I waited for him to say more.

After a few seconds, he held up his hand. "Yo, I want to say something, aight? We ain't set no fires, you hear me? That ain't us. Not gonna lie, we sent one of our li'l gangstas to fuck with this dude's car." He pointed with his lips at Pudge. "That wasn't no secret—we told baby G to tag the ride so y'all know it was us."

This was true—Pudge had told me that they spray-painted the gang's name on the car door. But did I believe him about the fire at my house? Maybe he was just trying to bullshit me.

"You expect me to believe that? After you fucked with this guy's ride."

Bear shook his head. "I told baby G just one tire. I guess homeboy got excited—he tells me he cut 'em all. But settin' fires ain't our thing. I don't know what went down, but we didn't do nothing."

I looked over at Shorty, who still had an angry red scar on his face. "Maybe this guy did it."

Bear looked at him. "Shorty, you ain't did nothing to this guy's house, did you?"

He shook his head sullenly. "Naw, you know I wanted to duke it out."

"True that," Bear said. "He was wantin' to throw down with you, man to man. But I say no, because our beef with the boot here."

He meant Pudge. "What's your beef with him?"

"He keeping all the sales! We just want to make a little coin. That's why I sent our boy over to his hoopty—get his attention, maybe he start talkin' again."

I was confused. For the last weeks, I'd been sure that it was the 705 who'd lit up my house. But they had no reason to lie to me now. After all, I was on their turf, and one of their guys was carrying a gun, which had been recently pointed at me.

"I got to ask you this," I said. "Did you guys do anything to our medicine man, Jerome Iron Shell?"

Bear held up his hand like a Boy Scout. "Hell no! None of my boys ever do that shit. Somebody fuck with a holy man out here, we put a smackdown on they ass."

I'd hated to think that these guys would hurt a medicine man, but it helped to hear him deny it. "All right," I said. "What now? You guys still holding a beef?"

"We talkin', it's cool," he said. "Look, I know we had some shit go down. But I'm thinkin' there ain't no reason we can't both do our thing. Your boy and my crew."

I looked over at Pudge, who shrugged. The other guys were silent, just watching and listening.

"What are you proposing?" I asked. "He don't want to join you guys. He stays independent."

"Yeah, I been runnin' all that in my head. I been thinkin'—maybe we run the hooch out on the west side of Rosebud. We do Parmelee and Norris, but stay out of Mission and Rosebud. Divide up the place, yeah? No more fightin', everybody cool."

"What about St. Francis?" Pudge asked.

Bear hesitated. "I was thinkin' that go to us."

Tommy cleared his throat and then spoke. "What if y'all take Spring Creek and Pudge keep St. Francis?"

Bear thought it over for a moment. "Aight, I guess that works."

"Pudge, what do you think?" I asked.

He shrugged. "I'm cool with all that. Just so long as I get to keep doing my own thing."

"Okay then," I said. "We're good now, yeah? No more beef?"

"Yup," Bear said. "We square. Shorty too."

And that settled it. We left Pine Ridge and headed back to Rosebud. On the drive back, Pudge told me he was relieved. Tommy was fine as well. The only people who seemed disappointed were Boots and Joe, who'd been expecting more action. Pudge promised to give them free hooch for a year, which seemed to chill them out. I dropped them off at Tommy's place and started off for home.

Alone with my thoughts, I thought about what had been resolved out in Pine Ridge. It seemed that the drama between me and the 705 gang was over. They'd told me they had nothing to do with the fire at my house or with Jerome's murder, and I believed them. But if they didn't burn my home, who did? There were so many people on the reservation who held a grudge for the poundings I'd inflicted on them and were waiting for their chance at revenge. Ghosts of my enemies drifted before me, all the people I'd beaten, their cries and wails echoing in my head. I'd tried to help the victims on the rez, those who needed someone on their side, but I never realized the price of my actions. I could bear the consequences, but Nathan and Marie deserved none of this.

The dim lights of the reservation smoldered as I drove down the deserted streets and alleys toward Marie's house, my own home now just a shell, a skeleton of ashes and dreams. A few minutes later, I pulled up in front of the house. A small car was parked in my usual spot. An orange Volkswagen Rabbit.

Val Tobacco's car.

I parked and climbed down from my truck. I could see Val and Marie through the large window in the living room—they were sitting at the dining room table, a laptop computer off to the side. I went inside and greeted them.

"Oh, thank god," Marie said. "I've been trying to call you. I was so worried." She stood up and embraced me tightly, and we lingered for a moment in each other's arms. Then I gave Val a hug and sat down.

"Sorry you couldn't reach me. No cell reception out there. So, what's going on?" I looked at Marie, then Val. "You okay, Val?"

"Yeah, I'm all right," Val said. "Sorry to surprise you, but there's some stuff I needed to tell you guys. Like, really urgent. I already gave Marie the scoop."

Marie raised her eyebrows. "There's a lot. But tell me, what happened out at Pine Ridge?"

I paused for a second and thought about what to say. "It was pretty crazy. Got tense for a bit. But we worked it out. Long story short, the Pine Ridge guys didn't burn down my place. They ain't no saints, but they didn't do nothing to me or Jerome. They're just trying to make some cash."

Marie nodded curtly. "Okay. You can tell me more later. But you need to hear what Val found out about Mitch Gagnon. She did some amazing work."

Val gave a thumbs-up. "Yeah, so I basically raced back home after you guys told me he was the one who killed Jerome. Or set it up, whatever. I mean, what a freaking scumbag. Who the hell hurts a holy man? Or sells out their own people, am I right?"

She stopped, apparently wanting us to agree with her.

"Yeah, he's a bad dude," I said. "No doubt."

"I'll say. Anyway, first I tried to break into his email, but no luck there. Then I tried to spoof him, but he didn't fall for it."

I wasn't sure what *spoof* meant, but I let her continue.

"He's pretty careful, which is a bummer. I did get a look at his public stuff: housing docs, old addresses, some social posts. Couple of pictures. No civil or criminal records, which was surprising, given he's a sketchy dude. But, politicians, right? They know how to get away with shit. Crafty mother—"

She stopped abruptly and held up her hand. "Oh jeez, Marie. I forgot you're, like, in an election. No offense, yeah?"

"None taken," Marie said. "Keep going. Virgil needs to hear the rest."

"Roger that. Okay, so I tried a bunch of other stuff but still couldn't get into Mitch's system. So I decided to try something different. It hit me that I should check out the Rosebud tribal council site—maybe luck out and see some of his files there."

She pulled the laptop closer and started typing on the keyboard, then turned to us and grinned. "Winner, winner, chicken dinner. Only took me an hour to get access to their system. Most of it is, like, incredibly boring—budget stuff, reports, notes from meetings. But then I found some crazy shit. Take a look at this."

She angled the computer to me. I tried to read the document she'd pulled up but didn't understand it. It seemed to be a legal document.

"What am I looking at here?" I asked.

Marie tapped the computer's screen. "It's a new tribal law, related to what he mentioned at the debate. Remember? He was talking about a proposal to crack down on drug dealers and criminals. I thought it was just campaign talk, but they met in executive session to discuss it. Val found the notes, and it's going to pass. No one on the tribal council is opposing it."

"Okay, so there's going to be some new crime law. We knew this might be coming, right?"

"Not exactly. The new law allows the tribal council to banish any suspected drug dealer, felon, or violent individual, even without a conviction. Their families, too. Permanent banishment from the reservation, and no way to appeal. You understand?"

"I think so. This is a violation of our rights. You can use that in your campaign, yeah? Expose him as a, uh, fascist or dictator."

She frowned and shook her head. "Virgil, no. You're not getting it."

"All right, so tell me."

Marie pointed to the computer, then touched me on the arm. "He's planning to banish you and me. We're going to be banned from Rosebud for life."

I was stunned. Marie reviewed what Val had uncovered and explained the legalities of the banishment law to me. Apparently, Mitch's earlier proposal to jail suspected criminals for five years had been struck down by the tribe's legal counsel because tribal courts only had authority to issue jail sentences of one year, maximum. Not to mention, his plan to put offenders' families in jail had been roundly opposed by nearly every council member.

But according to Marie, the ability to banish tribal members was well supported by law and precedent. Native tribes had the complete authority to decide who was allowed to live on their lands, and no court hearing was required. The new banishment law was scheduled for a vote at the next council meeting, which was just two weeks away.

"But we don't know if they're going to actually try to banish us, right?" I asked. "Assuming the law passes."

"It's going to pass," Marie said. "No question about that. Val found some emails. They are absolutely planning to start banishing people right away."

"Shit. That's bad news."

"I'll say," Marie said. "But it all fits together, right? I'm thinking that Mitch arranged the attack on Jerome and then got worried that you'd trace it back to him. Probably hired some idiots to set your house on fire, scare you off. That didn't work, so he came up with this plan to banish you. And me. If he banishes me, he wins the election by default."

"Wait," I said. "He could do that? It seems wrong."

"No rule against it. If I'm no longer living on the rez, I can't hold office. It's a twofer for Mitch—get rid of his election opponent as well as the guy who wants to solve Jerome's murder. Not to mention he gets to keep working on the boarding school project."

I'd been so focused on the Pine Ridge gang for the arson that I'd missed what was right in front of me. I'd presumed that Mitch was too cowardly to do anything himself, but the money he must be getting from the boarding school developers gave him a strong motive, without a doubt. He'd always been a greedy shitbag, and this looked to be his chance to hit the big time—so long as no one could tie him to Jerome's murder.

"I have to be honest," Marie said. "I've been thinking about withdrawing from the election. I don't know, it just seems like so much crap has rained down on us since I entered the race."

"Oh, no!" Val said. "We need you, Marie. A strong female voice. You can't quit!"

"I agree," I said. "We can't let Mitch scare us off."

Marie shrugged. "I'm just tired. Seems like we've been fighting so long."

I put my hand on Marie's arm. "Yeah, I get it. It's been a hard time. You know I'm behind you, whatever you decide."

Val's face darkened. "Marie, please don't do this. I hate that these guys can, like, bulldoze over everyone. Why do they get to decide what happens around here? I'm just saying that—"

A whipcrack rang through the air, along with the sound of breaking glass. Val cried out and sank to her knees. Marie and I looked at each other for a millisecond, unable to process what was happening. Then we snapped out of it and started talking at the same time.

"What the hell—"

"Val, are you all right?" Marie said. Val's hand was on her neck, blood dripping through her fingers.

"I think she's been shot!" I looked over at the living room window and saw a jagged hole about the size of a grapefruit just off center. Outside, a car was driving away, its taillights visible in the darkness. I squinted but couldn't make out the license plate or even the make and model. Val was on the floor, her hand still at her neck.

"Let me see, okay?" Marie got down next to her and gently moved Val's hand back. There was a nasty gash on the side of her neck, about two inches long, bleeding steadily. I quickly grabbed some paper towels from the table and handed them to Marie, who used them to carefully wipe the blood away. When she did, I was able to look more closely at the wound. I couldn't tell if it was caused by a bullet or flying shrapnel. Whatever the cause, we needed to act right away to stop the bleeding.

Marie stood up and looked around for her phone. "I'm calling 911."

"Is it bad?" Val asked.

"Let's get some pressure on it," I said. "Marie, grab me a towel."

"What the fuck happened?" Val asked. "Shit, that hurts."

"I think somebody shot at us," I said. "You feeling pain anywhere else?"

"Uh, just there."

Marie came back with some hand towels. I took one and pressed it against the wound. I heard her calling the paramedics, and I told Val to hold the towel in place.

"They'll be here in ten minutes," Marie said, then pointed at the floor. "Look at that. Be careful."

There were several shards of glass scattered around. I was surprised the entire window hadn't shattered, given the cheap glass that builders used on rez houses. I leaned down and picked up the biggest pieces, being careful to avoid the sharp edges.

Marie went back over to Val. "Let me take another look, okay?"

She removed the towel from Val's neck and blotted the wound with a clean one. "I think it's slowing down. The, uh, blood. You hanging in there, sweetie? How's the pain?"

"It hurts. So, what the hell? Were they trying to kill me?"

"Who knows?" I said. "I'm guessing they were coming after me. Or Marie."

"Who's 'they'?" Marie asked. "I mean, could it be—"

"Mitch," I said. "Or one of his fucking goons. Probably the same asshole who murdered Jerome."

Marie looked at me, the realization dawning on her face. "My god, do you think?"

"Who else? Bastard can't even wait to banish us. He wants to drive us out right now."

I checked on Val again and then went outside to investigate. I circled Marie's house, looking in her yard, around the sides of the building, and on the street. As I peered into dark corners, my anger sparked into a full-blown rage, a wildfire of fury in my gut. This attack had removed any doubt as to who'd been after us. I hadn't believed Mitch Gagnon capable of violence, but the bullet hole in Marie's window was proof.

I felt stupid for not taking action earlier. I should have confronted Mitch as soon as I learned that he was the rez traitor. I'd seen the emails where the developers told Mitch to take care of the medicine man, yet I'd continued to suspect the Pine Ridge gangbangers. I'd made the foolish mistake of believing that no white-collar person like Mitch would torch a house or arrange an attack.

But that wasn't my only mistake. As I circled Marie's house, I realized that Rowfield had almost certainly told his little group about our encounter in the parking garage—and no doubt Mitch guessed that it was me putting the fear of the Creator into Russell. Maybe the developers had ordered Mitch to scare me off the reservation, or perhaps he'd come up with that on his own. He'd tried using tribal laws to get us out, but he hadn't stopped there; he'd terrorized us with arson and gunfire. It was only through sheer luck that we'd all survived. I doubted that he'd had the balls to light my place on fire or take the shot tonight himself. But I'd find out soon enough.

I'd settle things with Mitch Gagnon on my own. Tonight this would end, one way or the other.

There was nothing more to see outside, so I went back into the house. Val was sitting quietly, still holding the towel against her neck, and Marie was in the kitchen, making a phone call. She held a finger up, telling me to wait, then hung up.

"I called the tribal police," Marie said. "Not sure if they're sending anyone out."

"Did you talk to Rose?"

"No, just the dispatcher. He didn't seem too concerned."

"That's fine," I said. "I'm going over there now."

"You mean, to see Mitch?"

"Yes." I looked straight at her. "I'm going to end this tonight. That rat bastard wants to shoot at us from the street—what a chickenshit. Hiding behind the skirts of his rich buddies up in Rapid City. Well, he can't hide no more."

She sighed. "I . . . I understand. I just don't know how it came to this. My god."

I nodded, then looked away. "Does he still live over by Turtle Creek?"

"Yes," she said. "As far as I know. He's been out there for years, all by himself."

"Any word from the paramedics?"

"They should get here soon. I'll take care of Val." She put her hand on my chest. "Go do what you have to."

I lingered for a moment, then turned away. I went out the back door, started up my motorcycle, and drove away.

kept my eyes on the road, trying to stay calm as I sped down the street. As I turned onto Highway 18, I thought I saw a vulture in the sky, which was strange. Vultures usually only fly during the day and rarely after sunset.

As a kid, I'd always been repulsed by the creatures, viewing them as dirty scavengers, harbingers of disease and death. But Jerome had corrected me one night. We were sitting on his porch drinking coffee when one landed nearby. I'd uttered a sound of disgust, and Jerome gently chastised me. "You don't like him? Lot of folks don't; I've seen people shoot at them. Makes me sad, because they don't understand. People think the only sacred bird is the eagle, but that's not true. The buzzard flies higher than any other and carries our prayers to the Creator. He does good work on the ground, too. Eats what other animals leave behind, don't waste nothing. He gets strong that way; no other birds mess with him."

I realized that vultures were not so different from Natives. We Indians had so much taken from us—our land, language, culture—yet we'd survived on the tiny plots of land we were allowed to possess. We'd resisted assimilation by holding on to the remnants of our culture and spirituality, the leftovers that we fought to keep. We'd taken what little was allotted to us and not only survived but flourished.

But there were some who'd turned their backs on other Natives—people like Mitch, a parasite feeding off the efforts of others. He'd worked to enrich himself by taking from the community, no matter the cost. Not just his attacks on Marie and me, but also his work to build the apartments at the boarding school, right over the graves of dozens of murdered Indian kids. I thought of Plenty Horses, and what he'd said in my vision, that I had a duty to protect our people from those who were at war with us. It had taken a while, but I'd realized that the war had come to me—and I was finally ready.

I arrived at Mitch's place thirty minutes later, pulling my bike over and stopping about a hundred yards away so I could check it out. His house was one of the larger ones on the reservation, standing on an eighty-acre lot. He'd taken part in a land exchange, a process by which, on our rez, landowners could trade the shares of land they had for another, more desirable plot. This was rarely done, though, as they then had to have a new house built from scratch, as well as paying for the installation of water and electrical lines. The total cost for one of these new homes often exceeded $50,000, which few people in this area could afford. I'd wondered how Mitch had been able to build his house on a tribal councilman's salary, but now I knew. The good news was that—because of his large lot—Mitch's house was far away from anybody else's, which meant that I didn't have to worry about any neighbors intruding on us tonight.

There were lights on inside the house, but I saw no movement. No cars were parked in front, so Mitch's vehicle was presumably in the garage. I found a comfortable spot and settled in to surveil the place. I couldn't see any outdoor cameras or security systems, but that was no surprise; few used these on our rez. Still, I decided to be extra cautious and make sure that Mitch was alone. The business we had to settle was between the two of us only.

I watched the house closely for the next fifteen minutes, but there was still no activity inside. It was difficult to resist the urge to get closer, but I stayed in place. Another twenty minutes passed, and then one window darkened, and another lit up. I cautiously moved up to a spot where I could peer inside the front picture window, although my line of sight was limited. Staying in the shadows, I spotted Mitch sitting down in what appeared to be his living room. I waited a few more minutes, but no one joined him. That was good enough for me. Mitch was a fairly big dude, but I was sure I'd be able to do what I came for. No doubt he had a gun somewhere in the house, but he'd never get a chance to grab it. I'd make sure of that.

Crouching low so I couldn't be seen, I moved slowly to the front door. Very carefully, I gripped the doorknob and tried to turn it, only to discover that it was locked. I knew what I had to do next, but then I paused.

I thought about Mitch Gagnon and all he'd done—his betrayal of the Native kids buried at the boarding school, the arson and shooting at our homes, the tribal law that would banish Rosebud citizens, the murder of Jerome Iron Shell. It struck me that Mitch and I had probably never spoken more than a few dozen words to each other over the years. In high school, he was one of the popular kids, involved in student council and clubs, too good to ever befriend me and my buddy Rob. I was a nobody to him, not even worthy of a bit of small talk.

But tonight, he'd listen to me.

I took a step back from the door. Aiming for the wood just to the side of the doorknob, I lifted my right leg slightly, took a deep breath, then stepped forward and kicked the door as hard as I could.

It flew open with a crash, and I rushed inside. Mitch was sitting on his couch in dark sweatpants and a blue T-shirt that read MITAKUYE OYASIN. *We are all related.*

"What the hell?" Mitch said, looking up in complete confusion.

His eyes widened, and he threw his hands up in the air, as if surrendering. "What—"

I quickly marched over to him before he had a chance to gather himself.

"Hi, Mitch," I said, and threw a roundhouse punch with all my weight, connecting with the side of his head. His head snapped back violently, and the force of the blow knocked him off the sofa. He crumpled on the floor, unconscious, his left arm folded under him, like a broken doll.

I looked around the place: a laptop computer on a small desk, an expensive-looking chair, hardwood floors, an original R. C. Gorman painting on the wall. A fancy McIntosh brand stereo system and speakers. Predictably, a high-definition television at the far end of the room. An ornate side table with a blue glass vase displayed prominently in the center. I picked it up and saw that it was actually an award from the tribe. His name and the words *With Sincere Appreciation for Your Service as Treasurer* were embossed in flowing cursive across the widest part. I chuckled and set it back down. From the looks of this place, Mitch hadn't been doing much service for anyone other than himself. It was clear he hadn't gotten all of this stuff on a councilman's salary.

I went to the bathroom, which was immaculately clean, and opened the medicine cabinet. I was looking for painkillers, any kind, as my right hand hurt like hell after the punch I'd landed. I spotted a bottle of extra-strength Tylenol, grabbed a few, and wandered over to the kitchen for some water. I opened his fancy refrigerator, which was stocked with a dozen glass bottles of Icelandic Glacial water. I'd never seen those before and had no idea where he got them—certainly not Turtle Creek, our reservation-owned supermarket. I popped one open and downed three Tylenols— two for the pain I was experiencing and one for the pain I had yet to earn. Mitch and I were just beginning.

I wandered back to the living room, where Mitch was still out cold, and opened his desk, not sure what I was looking for. Nothing in there but paper, envelopes, and a stapler. I supposed I'd been hoping to find some documents from the Rapid City people, but no matter. Mitch would tell me everything I wanted to know tonight.

I sat on the nice chair and massaged my hand for the next ten minutes, waiting for the pain pill to kick in. After a while, I checked on Mitch. He was still breathing, so I shook his shoulders and called his name. That didn't work, so I kicked him in the side.

"Ah," he said, his eyelids fluttering as he tried to rise. "What . . . how—" He turned to the side and threw up on the polished hardwood floor.

This meant he likely had a concussion. A few more punches, and he'd move up to traumatic brain injury. I needed to talk to him before he lost the ability to think clearly.

"Where'd you get this water?" I asked. The bottle of Icelandic Glacial was excellent—light and refreshing, with a silky texture and none of the chlorine taste you sometimes got in tap water.

He looked up at me and wiped the vomit off his face. Most of it, anyway. "Virgil? What are you doing here? Why did you—"

"Is it expensive? It's in glass bottles, not plastic. Must be pricey."

He began rubbing his head where I'd hit him. "What . . . what are you talking about?"

I held the water up. "I helped myself to one; hope that's okay. Took me a while to find your fridge, by the way. That dark gray thing, don't look like no fridge I ever seen."

He rubbed his eyes, and I could see him trying to make sense of what was happening. "Uh, it's a, a Sub-Zero, an old one." He wiped his face again and grimaced. "Why did you hit me?"

"Sub-Zero, huh? I think I heard about those in a movie. You must be the only dude on the rez with that. Maybe even in all South Dakota."

He got up off the floor, unsteadily, and sat down on his couch, then stared at the open front door. He looked confused and disoriented, and I hoped I hadn't scrambled his brain too soon.

"You still ain't told me about that water," I said. "Where do you buy it?"

He touched his face with a pained expression and sat down. "I get it sent in, okay? Take it all, I don't care. Are you, uh, robbing me? Is that what—"

I rose from the chair and tapped Mitch on the forehead. "No, I am not fucking robbing you! That's pretty damn ironic, given that you're stealing from our people. I mean, look at all the expensive stuff in here."

He frowned. "What do you mean? I'm not taking anything—"

I punched him again, this time in the solar plexus, so he wouldn't pass out again. The blow caused my hand to throb, and I sat back down. Mitch was doubled over, making choking sounds as he tried to get his wind back. When he recovered, I spoke again.

"Here's the deal, Mitch. I'm going to hit you ten more times, hard. Very hard. Five of those are for Jerome, who you murdered. One of them is for burning down my house. One is for shooting at Marie's house tonight. One is for working with the Rapid City jerks. And the last two are because you're an asshole." I stood up. "You ready?"

"Wait, wait!" he said. "You're talking crazy—none of that stuff is true."

I knew he'd lie; that was a foregone conclusion. The only question was how much of his horseshit I was willing to hear. My patience was limited due to the pain in my hand. If it didn't stop throbbing, I'd have to take a few more of those Tylenols. Maybe more than a few.

"Spare me, Mitch. Russell Rowfield told me himself that you're the guy he's working with here. I had to apply some pressure, but he gave up your name."

His brow furrowed, and he raised his hand. "That was *you?* You were the one who beat the crap out of Russ?"

I knew that Rowfield wouldn't be able to stay quiet, so it wasn't surprising that Mitch knew about it. But I'd assumed they'd have figured out it was me who'd laid down the beating on Mr. CEO.

"Yeah, and I'll do it again. Going after a medicine man—you guys are beyond evil. I mean, Jerome Iron Shell was like family to me. Did you really think I wouldn't avenge his death?"

Mitch's eyes widened, and he held out both hands as if to stop what was coming. "Are you drunk? Or on drugs? You're making no sense."

"Look, scumbag, I saw the email where Rowfield told you to *take care* of the medicine man. And you sure fucking did that. Or was it one of your goons who killed Jerome?"

A strange look came over his face. "You saw that email? I mean, how? Did Russ give it to you? But you got it wrong—"

"Never mind how I saw the emails. Point is, that Russell person told you to go after the medicine man, and you did it, you slimy bastard."

He started chuckling, which enraged me.

"What are you laughing at, you—"

"Oh my god," he said, shaking his head slightly. "Now I get it. You got the wrong guy! I don't know what Russ told you, but you must have misunderstood."

I jabbed my finger on his neck, just below his earlobe, on the pressure point where all of his nerves met. He winced and cried out.

"I understand that you and Rowfield are fucking murderers," I said. "I'll take care of him after I'm done with you."

"Stop! Jesus, stop. Just listen, all right? Let me tell you, okay? Let me speak."

"You got ten seconds, then we get started."

"Okay, okay! Yeah, Russ told me to go after the medicine man. Absolutely right! But not Jerome Iron Shell; my god, no. We had nothing to do with that. Russ wanted me to go after the bad medicine man, see? Not Jerome."

I didn't understand. "What are you talking about? Bad medicine man? What?"

"Yes," he said. "The guy who's been threatening us! He burned down the apartment complex in Rapid City, and he's been demanding money, threatening to hurt our families. It's been a nightmare . . ."

"Are you saying Jerome was threatening you—"

"No, not him! Listen, okay? The medicine man who's been terrorizing us is Leon Bellmore!"

Leon Bellmore? It took me a second to remember who that was. "The holy man from Cheyenne River? The one who runs sweats for white people?"

Mitch tapped the side of his head and then made a fist. "That's him. But he's no damn medicine man—that's just his cover story. He's a fucking con man and thief—came here a few years ago after getting out of prison. Probably thought we Sicangu are a bunch of hicks. He convinced everyone he was a medicine man, then he started with the threats."

"I've talked with him a few times. I mean, yeah, he seemed a little strange."

"You have no idea. The last six months have been horrible."

I wasn't sure I was buying this. "How so? What did he supposedly do?"

Mitch grunted. "Where do I start? He joined the boarding school protesters but then started threatening really bad publicity if they—the executive directors at Willow Creek—didn't pay him. Russ and his group didn't give a shit about that, but then Leon switched to arson. He burned down an apartment building that was under construction, said he'd torch more if we didn't pay up."

Arson. I began to have a bad feeling about this story.

Mitch went on. "But it wasn't just the apartments. He burned up one guy's garage at his house, which freaked everyone out. Then he started threatening to hurt their families. Kids. He'd been stalking them and sending photos of the executives' kids getting out of school. The entire group was terrified."

I was struggling to make sense of this and also figure out if Mitch was lying to me. So far, my horseshit meter hadn't gone off.

"So why didn't you go to the cops? Or did you?"

He shook his head. "No, the guys were too scared. And Leon was only asking for twenty-five thousand at first. Per month. That's chump change to the Willow Creek crew. There was a lot of discussion about going to the police, but then Russ was attacked. He thought it was Leon, but I guess it was you. Russ said he'd been assaulted by an Indian, so we thought it was him, or maybe somebody he'd sent. After that, there was no more talk of cops."

I paused for a second as I thought about what Mitch was saying. "All right, but tell me why you were working with the developers in the first place. I mean, they're knocking down our history. My own auntie is buried out there in an unmarked grave. These are not good guys."

He nodded twice. "Fair question. They came to me a few years back and invited me to join the project—said they'd create jobs for our people in Rapid City. So I joined their group, and I won't lie, they've paid me well. Really, really well. But I've been trying to get them to do the right thing. I argued—many times!—for renovation of the old school, but I lost that one. But they agreed to invest a million dollars on our rez. Of course, nobody talks about that."

"What about the graves? Building on top of them. Pretty fucking heartless."

He held up his hands. "I swear we didn't know about that at first. They found them once they started excavation and soil prep. I made them stop work right away and told them we needed to make this right, even though it put everything behind schedule. They didn't want to stop building, but I finally convinced them that the entire project could be at risk. I promise I'll get all the remains repatriated, even if it means tearing down that unit and starting over somewhere else. I know the whole thing with the graves is terrible, but I've been doing my best."

There was something missing in all of this, and I finally figured it out. "So, if Leon was this bad medicine man, why are you trying to have Marie and me banished from the rez?"

His eyes widened again. "You know about that, too? Yes, I absolutely sponsored the banishment ordinance, but I was trying to keep it quiet. That's why we discussed it in executive session."

"Answer the question!" I said. "Why banish me and Marie?"

He sighed. "Jesus, I'm trying to banish Leon, not you. He's got a felony record, so we might be able to use the law to get rid of him. That's why I was keeping it quiet, so he wouldn't have any warning."

I felt like an idiot. Mitch hadn't been trying to banish us. But it had been a reasonable assumption, given what had happened to Marie and me.

"But wait," I said. "If you didn't kill Jerome or burn down my house, then who did?"

"I did."

Mitch and I both looked toward the door. Standing there was Leon Bellmore, holding a gun pointed straight at me.

It took me a second to remember Leon. The few times I'd spoken to him, my attention had been elsewhere. Now I looked more closely and saw that he was a medium-sized guy with black hair, wearing jeans, an old brown flannel shirt, and battered Red Wing boots. Nothing memorable about him, except for the little snub-nosed revolver pointed at my chest. It looked like a Ruger SP101, a heavy workingman's gun, lethal at this distance.

"I got bored listening to you two jabber," he said, and motioned with the gun toward me. "I thought you'd split this idiot's head open right away. They say you're a tough guy, but you barely touched him."

"What do you want?" I asked. Mitch remained on the couch, looking petrified. I tried to signal him with my eyes, but he kept his gaze on Leon.

"Well, I wanted you to kill this moron, but it looks like that ain't gonna happen." Leon chuckled, then moved inside the house, away from the front door. "How you doing, Mitch?"

"I'm, uh, you know . . . not too good." Mitch was falling apart when I needed him to stay cool. If we worked together, we could take the guy and end this thing.

"Glad to hear it," Leon said. He aimed the gun at Mitch and fired, hitting him in the stomach. Mitch cried out and doubled over in pain.

"Damn," Leon said, then walked over to Mitch and shot him in the head, point-blank. Blood splattered over the living room wall, and Mitch's lifeless body fell to the floor. Then Leon shot him one more time in the chest.

"Jesus Christ, you killed him," I said, my ears ringing and buzzing.

"No, you did." Leon aimed the Ruger at me again. "Gonna be a murder-suicide."

"Oh no, you ain't hanging this on me."

"You don't got a choice. Everyone knows about the bad blood between you and Mitch. He was saying all that shit about your little girlfriend. You two argued, then you lost your temper and shot him, felt guilty, and killed yourself."

"You're crazy. Nobody will believe that."

He chuckled. "They'll believe it. You two battling was the best thing for me. That's why I shot out your girlfriend's window tonight. Knew you'd run out and throw down with Mitch. But you chickened out. I should have known."

My goal was to keep him talking so he'd let down his guard. If I could surprise him, I had a chance. "Okay, smart guy. Tell me why you killed Jerome. What the hell did he do to you?"

He scowled. "I didn't plan that, believe it or not. I went out to his place because he was mad at me. He didn't want me running no sweats or ceremonies here—said I was ripping people off. I say, who made you fuckin' King Lakota? We get into it, and I end up hitting him and he goes down. Hell, I didn't mean for it to happen. But can't really blame me—he started the whole damn thing."

"I don't see it that way."

"Don't give a damn what you think. The Jerome thing turned out fine for me. Now I got lots of folks coming to me for sweats. I like being a holy man; easiest work I ever done. I even snagged

Jerome's canunpa before I left his place. Smoke out of it every day. Pot, hash, anything."

So now I knew the whole story. Jerome Iron Shell, who'd spent his entire life helping others, had been brought down because he'd been trying to protect the people from this con man. And the final outrage was that he was using Jerome's sacred pipe to smoke weed. Truly sickening. But I still didn't understand what I'd done to incur Leon's wrath.

"Okay, whatever. But why'd you burn down my house? What did that have to do with Jerome?"

He waggled the gun a little. "Nothing with Jerome. You were getting too close to the Rapid City deal. That idiot Rowfield messaged me, all butt-hurt because he'd been beat up, thought I was behind it. I knew it had to be you that did it, and that was bad news for me. I got a good thing going over there and didn't want you fucking it up. So I started applying some pressure."

"And you thought I'd leave the rez when my house got torched? That was your goddamn master plan?"

He shrugged. "Worth a try. Most people would have left, but I guess you got some . . . attachment to this place."

Leon was batshit crazy, but this was the one noncrazy thing he'd said all night. As much as I bitched about the rez and the ridiculous stuff that happened here, I guess I was connected to this land. But there was no time to think about that now.

"Enough goddamn chatter," he said, and motioned with the gun. "Let's make this easy. You want a shot on the side of your head or under your chin?"

"Fuck you. You want to shoot me, you're gonna have to earn it."

"Have it your way," he said, and lifted the revolver.

I grabbed Mitch's glass award—WITH SINCERE APPRECIATION— and smashed it on the side table. The sudden movement distracted Leon, causing him to lose focus for a second, which gave me an opening. The broken trophy lay in pieces on the table and floor, so I grabbed the largest shard, cutting the palm of my hand in the process. The pain startled me, but I forced myself to ignore it.

Meanwhile, Leon had regained his composure, and he aimed his revolver straight at my face, no longer trying to set up a false suicide shot. The look on his face was pure hatred and disdain; I could see his contempt for all Rosebud citizens, no more than chumps and victims to him, dupes to be sucked dry before moving on.

I moved to Leon's right and tried to slash him with the glass shard. He jumped back, and I stepped forward, trying to force him against the wall. I tried to stab him again, this time aiming for his face. I missed but cut him on the right arm, just below his bicep. In doing so, I sliced my own hand on the glass, and I dropped the shard by reflex.

"You cocksucker!" he snarled, then fired the gun wildly, the noise deafening in the small room. The bullet hit the wall behind me, then he shot again, the round coming closer this time. I saw that my hand was bleeding, but not too badly. I shook off the pain, then squared off with Leon.

He'd taken his eyes off me for a moment, so I moved in closer. I feinted to the left, then shifted right and landed a solid hit on his solar plexus. He grunted in pain, and I made a move for his weapon, grabbing his hand and trying to pull the Ruger away. He fired again, just inches from me, the noise exploding in my head. For a second I couldn't focus or hear anything, and I lost my advantage. Before I could respond, he jammed the gun into my chest, the barrel pressing against my rib cage.

Then I heard the click of the trigger.

In the millisecond that followed, images of the reservation flashed through my mind. The Starlite Snack Shop, where I'd had ice cream with my sister and Nathan. The little house off Highway 83 where my aunt Audrey had lived, no heating inside, just a small woodburning stove. Jerome's porch, where we'd spent so many hours talking and drinking coffee. The hills where I'd walked with my father before he'd died. Rosebud Creek, where I'd first kissed Marie. These visions sped through my consciousness like a kaleidoscope as I waited for the bullet to pass through me.

But then I realized I was still alive.

I jumped back immediately, out of the line of fire. Leon lowered his gun, and I saw that he was out of ammunition and trying to reload. I hit him on his side as hard as I could, hoping to knock his weapon away. He grunted in pain but held on to the revolver. I stepped back and threw a hook, connecting solidly with his head. He staggered back, dazed, and I punched him in the gut with everything I had. He bent over, defenseless, holding his gun limply by his side.

I realized this was my moment to get the justice I'd been seeking so desperately. I'd spent too long chasing shadows and doubting myself. But standing before me was the true face of evil. *Wana iyehantu.* Now is the time.

I moved behind Leon and aimed for the back of his neck, just below the skull. Known as the rabbit punch, it was the most dangerous of all blows and strictly prohibited in boxing and martial arts, as it was usually fatal. I took a deep breath and raised my fist but stopped when I thought I heard someone—not Leon— speaking to me. I looked around the room, confused.

Leon saw me pause, then quickly stood up, grabbed my shoulders, and shoved me backward. As he did so, he swept his leg behind my ankle and pushed me, a classic single-leg takedown. I stumbled and went down hard, feeling embarrassed as I fell.

I landed on the floor next to the coffee table. The last thing I saw was Leon crouching over me. He gripped the handgun and slammed it down on my face, again and again. The world seemed to contract and narrow as my vision dimmed. Objects in the room lost their color and seemed to float away as I drifted into the darkness.

I opened my eyes and saw Mitch next to me, his arms at his sides and a serious expression on his face.

"Thought you were dead," I murmured.

"I want to say a few things, but I don't have much time."

This was strange. "Yeah, go ahead. Be my guest."

"Look, I'm sorry. The tribal council election with Marie. I know I caused her some grief. But it was just politics, okay? It wasn't personal."

"So why did you?" I asked. "You said a lot of nasty stuff at the debate. She didn't deserve none of that."

"True. I crossed a line. Tell her I didn't mean it."

"Why don't you say something to her?"

He smiled a little. "Not really possible. Just tell her that I always tried my best for the oyate, okay? And that I'm sorry and wish her well. She's a good one. The rez needs more like her."

I was unexpectedly moved by his apology. For so long, I'd thought of him as just another callous politician or worse, but his words seemed sincere.

"All right, Mitch, you got it."

"Thank you," he said. "And listen, I'm sorry for all of this craziness. I never meant for you to get involved."

"That's okay—"

"There's something I want you to have," he said. "You know, if you make it out of here. It's a box, buried under the bench in my backyard. Take it and use it well."

"What is it?" I asked.

"Virgil, I need to go."

I realized then that I must be dreaming, because Tasunka

Ota—Plenty Horses—suddenly appeared next to Mitch and took his arm, then spoke to me. "How you doing, star boy?"

"What does that mean?"

"I think you know," he said. "You remember what I told you, right?"

"Yeah, that it's good to die for your community."

"No, you muttonhead, I told you to be righteous. You need me to spell it out? Get your ass up, now. I got to take this guy out of here," he said, pointing at Mitch.

I tried to respond, but he was gone. Then I opened my eyes and looked around. Mitch's body was still there on the floor. Broken glass—the remnants of Mitch's trophy—was scattered around me. Leon was standing by the couch, reloading his Ruger.

He saw I was awake and frowned. "Shit, thought you'd be out for a while and give me a chance to put a bullet in your head nice and easy. Just hold on."

I tried to stand but was still too weak. I sat up and tried to summon the energy to fight again. But then I noticed flashing lights outside the house. Leon had his back to the door and didn't see them.

"All right, asshole," he said, aiming the revolver at me. "Finally loaded this fucker. Time to—"

"Drop your weapon!"

It was Rose Charging Cloud. She'd entered through the open front door and had her gun drawn and pointed at Leon.

"Drop the weapon now!" she repeated.

Leon glanced over at her but kept the gun pointed at me. "Tribal cop, huh? Take one more step, and I'll blow this guy's head off."

Rose looked at me, then Leon. "Drop your weapon or I'll shoot!"

"I don't think you will," Leon said. "Back up, or I'll kill him. You want his blood on your hands?"

Rose stared at him for a second, which felt like a thousand years, then moved back but kept her weapon trained on Leon.

"Lower your gun," Leon said. "Then we can talk." His Ruger remained pointed at my chest.

Rose shook her head. "Not going to happen. Why don't you sit down and let's end this thing?" She glanced over and saw Mitch's body. I could see the surprise register on her face.

"Looks like we got a standoff, yeah?" Leon said.

"I've got backup coming." Her voice wavered as she spoke. "Any minute."

He chuckled. "I hope so. Few more of you idiots here increases my odds."

"Leon, it's over," I said, holding my hand up. "You killed Mitch; Jerome, too. You made your point, so let's get out of here."

"It's over when I say it is!" he said. "Way I see it, killing another couple of Rosebudders is good for everyone."

He had his eyes on Rose, so I covertly grabbed a piece of broken trophy glass from the floor, the word *Mitchell* still readable on it.

Leon turned toward Rose, his gun now pointed at her. "Fuck you, tribal cop."

I reached out and slashed his leg with the glass. He screamed and looked down, his attention momentarily diverted. Rose fired twice, the shots hitting him in the chest. He dropped without a word.

Rose ran over to Leon's body, seized his weapon, then crouched down next to me.

"My god, what happened here?" she said.

I started to speak, but the distant and remote stillness of the reservation overwhelmed me as I pondered the deaths of Jerome and Mitch and all the other souls of our nation, trying to survive and endure and withstand, and I felt the pain of all Native people in that moment. I didn't know how to explain to her that there had been a battle, yes, but it was a war that had been going on for centuries with no end in sight, and there would be more casualties, too many, as we continued to raise our children and love our families and bury our dead, hoping, as we came to the end of our days on the land we loved—the People of the Rosebud, the Burned Thigh Nation, the Sicangu Oyate, the chosen ones— that the Creator would be merciful and just.

And in the end, I gave up trying to explain and just listened to the sound of the Wiyóȟpeyata, the west wind of endings and new beginnings. Rose sat down next to me, and we stayed there together, waiting, waiting, waiting.

# EPILOGUE

I PARKED MY TRUCK IN the lot in front of the new Wisdom Corner Park, which was being dedicated today. Over the last six months, the Willow Creek developers had made good on their promise to donate funds to the reservation. The first project had been the complete renovation of the Wisdom Corner site. Using money from the developers, the land had been obtained by the tribe, the old gazebo torn down, and the entire area cleaned up. Then a large park had been designed and constructed, including a giant slide, rope bridge, spinners, baby swings for the kids, and a special area for teens to congregate. A dozen picnic tables were scattered throughout the park, as well as several covered gazebos for the elders. A group of them were already there, sitting and talking with each other.

The dedication ceremony would start soon. I'd arrived early so that I could speak with Marie before it became too crowded. She was bringing trays of bison tacos and bowls of Lakota squash salad, two of the new Indigenous dishes she'd been developing. After Mitch's death, she'd withdrawn from the tribal election, telling me that her heart wasn't in it. Since then she'd been working to create a new type of Native cuisine that was both nutritious and affordable, food that reservation families could eat on a regular basis. Her dream was to open her own food truck and make it a permanent fixture on the reservation, but she was starting with a small catering business.

My stomach rumbled, and I realized that I hadn't eaten anything for breakfast. I patted my jacket for cigarettes and then remembered—for the thousandth time—that I'd quit. I'd hoped that the longing for tobacco might fade away, but I'd come to understand that this ghostly desire for a smoke was here to stay. I'd accepted that, as difficult as it was. I'd also come to accept my role on the reservation. The events of the last year had changed me in ways I hadn't expected, and I'd realized that I needed to continue to help people here, whatever form that took. Jerome had taught me to think of justice in a different way, not as reprisal and retribution but as a form of healing and forgiveness. He'd spent his life serving our community, and I'd follow his example. In the end, that was the justice I'd been seeking.

I spotted Marie at the west end of the park and wandered over there.

"Can I grab a taco?" I asked. "If you have enough for everyone."

"Help yourself," she said, smiling. "I made plenty."

I snagged one of the bison tacos and ate it in three bites. "These are fantastic. Don't let Nathan near them; he'll eat the whole tray."

She chuckled. "He already had four. He's over there with Shawna on the swings."

I was happy to hear that. Their relationship seemed to be stronger than ever, and Nathan had informed me that he planned to follow Shawna to college, wherever she landed. She was considering applying to Dartmouth, MIT, and South Dakota Mines, among other colleges, to study biology and public health. Nathan had stopped his grade-school protection racket and now intended to major in criminal justice at a community college, a goal that I fully supported.

"They brought Ava, too. She's in doggy heaven, getting all

the pets from the little kids." She looked over my shoulder. "Oh, there's Tommy."

"My man!" Tommy said, strolling over to us. "Hey, Marie. Glad you all come out. Big dang day."

"You're not working?" I asked. He'd been promoted to kitchen manager at the casino restaurant and remained enrolled at the tribal college. I doubted he'd ever graduate, as he only took one course a semester, which was about the right pace for him.

"Naw, asked for the day off. You know I love Marie's grub. Can't wait for her to get that food truck goin'!"

"Someday," I said. "We need more places to eat around here. No offense to Rations."

"None taken, dude. That reminds me, Pudge told me to save him a taco."

The biggest surprise of the last six months had been Pudge's entry into tribal politics. After Mitch's death and Marie's departure from the election, Pudge had stepped up and declared himself a candidate for the tribal council, having retired from his bootlegging business. No one held his previous occupation against him, and he'd won in a landslide.

My cell phone buzzed for an incoming text message. It was from Val, explaining that she couldn't make it to the dedication ceremony and sending her apologies. She was working full-time on the boarding school repatriation project. The developers had suspended all work on the new building while the children's graves were identified, and now the process of returning them to the reservations was underway. Val had made it her mission to identify every lost child buried there, and she'd been able to locate my auntie Josephine. Her remains had been returned to our reservation, and I'd had her buried at the Trinity cemetery near other family members in a solemn ceremony.

"Looks like they're getting started," Marie said.

We wandered over to the makeshift podium, where our tribal president and other officials were standing, waiting for their chance to speak to the people. A drum group played, a group of students from the elementary school sang, and an elder spoke in Lakota. Then the tribal president took the microphone.

"Welcome everyone, on this amazing day. We're here to celebrate the opening of Wisdom Corner Park, a space for children, families, and elders. A space where we can relax and play, tell stories, be with our loved ones, and enjoy all that the Creator has given us. It is truly a great day for the Sicangu people."

The audience applauded, and I joined in.

"There are so many people and organizations to thank. First and foremost, Willow Creek Development graciously provided the funding to build this park, and I cannot thank them enough. And of course our own Mitch Gagnon, who will live forever in our hearts."

More applause. Marie nudged me and rolled her eyes. Only a few people knew the full truth about the relationship between Mitch and the developers. The story that had been released to the public was that Mitch had died trying to protect our people from Leon, a felon who was trying to steal money from the tribe. Of course the reality was much more complicated, but I'd made my peace with Mitch, who I now saw as a decent but flawed person. Marie, however, still held a grudge against him for all the lies he'd spread about her during the election.

The tribal president continued with more words about Mitch and the good he'd done for our nation.

Marie poked me again. "Do you want to get out of here?" she whispered.

I nodded, and we started making our way back to the food tables. Once we were back at the edge of the park, Marie looked around to check that no one was in earshot. "Sorry I dragged us out of there, but I just couldn't take any more of that Mitch worship. I mean, I don't want to speak ill of the dead, but he was part of the crew that tried to build an apartment complex right over the graves of murdered kids. He was—"

"Yeah, but he claimed they didn't know about that. And he did try to stop them."

She sighed. "So he said. I guess we'll never really know."

Marie and I had talked about this repeatedly during the last several months, and we were never going to agree. She believed that Mitch was not the white knight he'd portrayed himself as during our final confrontation. I was more generous in my assessment, although I supposed it didn't really matter anymore.

"Hey, you mind if I take off?" I asked. "Got some stuff to take care of."

"Of course not," she said, and gave me a warm kiss.

There was something I needed to do, something I'd been putting off. But this was the right time. I headed out to the parking lot, where I saw Rose Charging Cloud standing by her little car, talking on her phone. Rose had become even more popular in our community after it was revealed that she'd shot Leon Bellmore. Of course, only she and I knew what had actually happened in that room.

She spotted me and motioned for me to come over. I came closer, and she held up a finger, indicating I should wait. After a moment, she finished her conversation and turned to me.

"Sorry about that. My niece is pregnant, and I'm making a baby star quilt for her."

"Hey, congrats."

She rolled her eyes. "Yeah, thanks. She's naming the child Roadtrip, can you believe it?"

"I don't understand," I said. "Is it a family name?"

She snorted. "No, the baby was conceived on a vacation they took to Omaha. Poor kid, he'll get roasted in school."

I shook my head. "Pretty crazy."

She looked over toward the park. "You leaving so soon? Sounds like it's still going on."

"I heard enough," I said. "Lots of talk about Mitch. All of his accomplishments and good deeds."

She smirked. "I figured. They asked me to say some words about him, but I declined."

I wondered if Rose shared Marie's opinion of Mitch, but I didn't ask. Instead, I just gave her a thumbs-up.

"Listen," she said, "I've been wondering—are you still working for Charley Leader Charge?"

"He hasn't had any papers for me to serve in a while."

"That's too bad. What are you going to do for a job?"

"Not sure yet, but I'll find something."

"So, I had a crazy thought last week. Just hear me out, okay?" She paused for a second. "Have you ever thought about joining the Rosebud PD?"

"The police department? You mean, become a tribal cop? You're joking, right?"

A wry smile played at her lips. "Not at all. You're pretty good with your fists and quick on your feet. With a little training, maybe you could actually become useful. Maybe."

This was the last thing I'd ever expected to hear from Rose, and I wasn't sure what to say. "That's an, uh, interesting idea. But even if I wanted to try that, I can't imagine the tribal council would allow it, given my history."

"It might take some fancy footwork, but I could push it through." She glanced at her phone. "Look, just think about it.

And don't get in any more trouble! Maybe we can have a little peace and quiet around here, if we're lucky."

She smiled and strode away, the sound of her footsteps like a drumbeat.

I got into my truck and started driving east, passing the Rosebud Buffalo Range on my way. The bison herd had been moved to an enormous grassland site purchased by the tribe, where they were part of a large-scale conservation effort for the animals, the land, and the community. The range was now a model for bison restoration efforts across the country, and the herd appeared to be thriving.

Thirty minutes later, I arrived at my destination. Mitch Gagnon's house was empty now, as family members had cleared the place and burned all of his clothing, per Lakota custom. This was done to allow the deceased to move to the spirit world and also allow the family to release their grief. Now the little house was abandoned, forlorn and desolate. I hadn't been there since the confrontation with Leon, and it felt strange to be back.

I went around the house to the garden in the backyard. There was a little wooden bench at the edge of the patch. I paused for a second, then went back to my truck and grabbed a shovel.

The ground was fairly soft, so it didn't take me long to dig under there. About two feet down, I hit something hard and dug around the object. Before long, I was able to pull it out. It was a big yellow toolbox, weathered and muddy, but still sealed. I opened it up and found several vinyl bank deposit pouches, the type that people used to store old checks and documents. I unzipped the first one and pulled out a stack of hundred-dollar bills, banded together and covered in plastic wrap. I opened the rest of the pouches and found even more bundles. All told, there appeared to be tens of thousands of dollars, maybe more. I quickly repacked the money in the toolbox, moved it to my truck, then filled up the hole in the garden.

I felt like I was in a dream as I drove away from Mitch's house. I hadn't really believed that there would be anything in the yard, and I'd felt embarrassed even going out there. It was pretty strange that Mitch had buried a box of money in his backyard, but a lot of people on the rez hid their valuables in odd places. But why did he have so much cash in the first place? Perhaps the developers had paid Mitch off the books, but I'd never know. Not to mention, I was still processing the fact that I'd learned about the money from a spirit. But there was no time to reflect on the vision I'd had at Mitch's house. I had to get that toolbox somewhere safe, and more importantly, I needed to decide what to do with all of that cash, which was more money than I'd ever had in my life.

I drove aimlessly around the reservation for the next hour, dazed and reeling. Images of Mitch flared in my mind, and I was unable to think clearly. More than anything, I felt confused and also vaguely guilty. Confused about the right thing to do, and guilty about possessing a dead man's money. I didn't know where to go or what to do.

But without thinking, I started driving to the place where I'd felt so much peace. The place where I'd always been welcome.

I slowed down as I crested the ridge by Jerome's house. His grandson Rocky stayed there now, living quietly and maintaining the keeping of the soul ceremony. I didn't want to bother him, so I parked outside the house and sat by myself, just thinking and remembering.

I turned off my phone and rolled down the windows, allowing memories of Jerome to surround me. I thought about the things he'd taught me, the lessons I'd learned, the stories he'd told. His serene wisdom and his strength. His dedication to the people.

The answer came to me then. I'd give the money—all of it—to

Marie to use for her Indigenous food business. She could spread the gospel of Native foods and feed the hungry people on our land. She'd try to refuse the gift, but I'd insist. And maybe in time she'd forgive Mitch as I had.

I heard a noise and saw Rocky open his screen door and come outside.

"Virgil? Is that you?"

"Yeah, it's me," I said.

"Well, come on in."

He brewed some strong coffee, and we sat there on the porch talking about Jerome for hours. And then we were quiet, staring off in the distance to the very edge of the reservation.

# AUTHOR'S NOTE

This novel is a work of fiction, but it is informed by current and historical events. To serve the dramatic narrative, I've freely invented places, events, locales, and incidents, as well as fictional characters, who bear no resemblance to any actual persons, living or dead. As in my earlier novel *Winter Counts*, I've tried to be faithful to my sense of life on the Rosebud Reservation, but the reservation depicted in these pages exists only in my imagination. However, I encourage readers interested in these issues to explore some of the scholarly and historical books on these topics.

As in *Winter Counts*, a central issue of *Wisdom Corner* is the problem of fair and efficient criminal justice administration on Native American reservations. I've written and spoken extensively about the federal Major Crimes Act, which in my opinion needs to be significantly amended—if not completely repealed—in order to further Native sovereignty and better protect Indigenous peoples. On a positive note, there has been a good deal of general and academic commentary on the Major Crimes Act recently, and I'm grateful if *Winter Counts* helped to contribute to that discussion in any way. Readers may wish to consult my *New York Times* essay on the topic, as well as some of the law review articles analyzing the law.

Another issue in *Wisdom Corner* is that of the Native boarding schools and how the children there were compelled to abandon their Indigenous traditions, languages, and spirituality as they were forcibly assimilated into American culture and values. These schools were generally run like military camps, and the children were too often neglected and abused. It is a sad fact that many thousands of Native children died at these institutions and were buried on the school grounds, far away from their homelands. My own grandmother was a student at three of these schools, including the infamous Carlisle Indian Industrial School in Pennsylvania. There are a number of books on this dark chapter in our history, including *Education for Extinction: American Indians and the Boarding School Experience, 1875–1928* by David Wallace Adams, and *Boarding School Seasons: American Indian Families, 1900–1940* by Brenda J. Child. There was indeed a Native boarding school in Rapid City, and the reader is directed to *The Rapid City Indian School, 1898–1933* by Scott Riney for an excellent historical overview of that particular school. In addition, a number of recent news stories detail the subsequent controversy regarding that institution.

An underlying topic in the novel is the fact that the US government entered into hundreds of treaties and agreements with Native nations, and virtually every one of these was violated or broken by federal and state governments. A classic work on this issue is *Behind the Trail of Broken Treaties*, by Vine Deloria Jr.; another highly recommended book is Walter R. Echo-Hawk's *In the Courts of the Conqueror: The 10 Worst Indian Law Cases Ever Decided*. Echo-Hawk's book also touches upon the criminalization of Native American spirituality, a deliberate and systematic policy of the US government that spanned over a century.

On a lighter note, I was delighted to learn about the Carlisle Indian School football team and how that group of Native athletes was able to revolutionize the game under the direction of Coach

Pop Warner. *The Real All Americans* by Sally Jenkins is a fantastic account of this largely forgotten piece of American sports history.

I'll close by noting that there are now a number of excellent new histories of the United States that center the Native experience, most notably Ned Blackhawk's *The Rediscovery of America: Native Peoples and the Unmaking of U.S. History*. Readers interested in learning more about the history of Indigenous peoples are advised to read that volume, as well as *The Heartbeat of Wounded Knee: Native America from 1890 to the Present* by David Treuer.

# ACKNOWLEDGMENTS

This novel is dedicated to James Cordry, my cousin, who was one of the last members of our family living on the Rosebud Indian Reservation. Jim spent the bulk of his career as the trust officer and financial agent for the reservation, helping Sicangu citizens with their land, estate, and other monetary issues. He also greatly assisted with this book, patiently answering my questions, providing information, and giving me much-needed context on many of the issues and themes contained herein. It is fair to say that this novel would not exist in its current form if not for him.

Tragically, James passed on to the spirit world just as this book was in final edits. He knew that I was planning to dedicate it to him and told me he was honored, which helps with the sadness of his passing. I was privileged to have Jim in my life, a sentiment that I know is shared by many on the reservation. I hope this novel does justice to Jim's passion and love for the Rosebud Reservation and its people.

I am truly fortunate to have been supported by a number of tremendous organizations and individuals in the writing of this book. I wish to thank my literary agent, Michelle Brower, for supporting this novel and being an amazing person and publishing partner. I owe a large debt to Helen Atsma, my fantastic editor at Ecco, for patiently working with me and providing insightful comments and suggestions as this book progressed. My sincere thanks to her and the entire Ecco and HarperCollins team, including Sonya Cheuse, Miriam Parker, Meghan Deans, Vivian Lopez Rowe, and Rachel Sargent. My thanks also to Miranda Ottewell, who once again gave excellent suggestions in the copyediting process.

I am deeply grateful for the opportunity to return to the MacDowell artists' residency, where I wrote the first several chapters of this novel. It was like coming home to be back in Garland Studio, immersed once again in Virgil's world. I also completed significant work on the book at Ucross, Ragdale, and Vermont Studio Center. I thank each of these tremendous residency programs for the support they've provided to me and other artists. I was also lucky enough to serve as a fellow at the Sewanee Writers' Conference, where I received wonderful feedback on early chapters from Jess Walter, Adrianne Harun, and the fantastic writers in our workshop.

I'm also grateful to Brown University, which gave me the opportunity to serve as Indigenous Artist in Residence on their beautiful campus and complete work on this novel. Creative West also supported this project, and I thank them as well for their assistance.

A number of individuals were kind enough to take time to answer my questions during my research for this book. Steve DeNoyer, the chief administrator of law enforcement services for the Rosebud Sioux Tribe Police Department, graciously allowed me to interview him, as well as take part in a ride-along with Officer Jody Charging Horse of the Rosebud police department. Harold Compton provided me with invaluable information during my visits to the reservation. My gratitude to all of them.

My friend Tony Magliero brought the Carlisle football team to my attention, and Sonny Skyhawk introduced me to Plenty Horses and the history surrounding his trial. Ben Whitmer gave me solid advice on guns and weapons. Many thanks to these gentlemen.

My gratitude also to X, my favorite punk rock band, who allowed me to use a line from a song from their latest album *Smoke & Fiction* as the epigraph for this novel. I had the good fortune to speak with John Doe after a solo show in Denver and asked about the possibility of using one of their lyrics. He passed me on to Exene Cervenka, who wrote that line, and she graciously consented. X has been one of the most important bands to me over the years, and it's an honor to have their words open this tome.

I also wish to acknowledge that portions of this book first appeared in short stories that I've published over the last several years. Many thanks to the editors and publishers of these anthologies: "Hooch," published in *The Perfect Crime* anthology (HarperCollins), edited by Maxim Jakubowski and Vaseem Khan; "Turning Heart," published in *This Time for Sure* (Down & Out), edited by Hank Phillippi Ryan, and reprinted in *The Best American Mystery and Suspense 2022* anthology (Mariner), edited by Jess Walter and Steph Cha; and "Skin," published in the *Midnight Hour* anthology (Crooked Lane), edited by Abby L. Vandiver. One important line in this book first appeared in "Carlisle Longings," an essay about my grandmother's time at the Carlisle Indian Industrial School in the journal *Shenandoah*.

Let me turn to my family. My sons, David and Sasha, continue to be the joy in my life, and both of them provided inspiration (but only the good parts!) for the character of Nathan. My partner, Erika T. Wurth, gave me incredible assistance with plot issues in the novel as well as general editorial notes. I thank Erika for everything, literary and beyond.

I also wish to acknowledge the elders and citizens of the Sicangu Lakota Nation. I have a deep connection to the land of the Rosebud Reservation, and the joyfulness and wisdom of the